Day of the Phoenix

The Sequel to 'A Ticket to Tewkesbury'

Neal James

PNEUMA SPRINGS PUBLISHING UK

First Published in 2014 by:
Pneuma Springs Publishing

Day of the Phoenix
Copyright © 2014   Neal James
ISBN13: 9781782283560

Neal James has asserted his right under the Copyright, Designs and Patents Act, 1988, to be identified as Author of this Work

British Library Cataloguing in Publication Data. A catalogue record for this book is available from the British Library.

Pneuma Springs Publishing
A Subsidiary of Pneuma Springs Ltd.
7 Groveherst Road, Dartford Kent, DA1 5JD.
E: admin@pneumasprings.co.uk
W: www.pneumasprings.co.uk

This is a work of fiction. Names, characters, places and incidents are either products of the author's imagination or are used fictitiously. Any resemblance to actual events or locales or persons, living or dead, save those clearly in the public domain, is purely coincidental.

Dedication

In memory of Eileen Persse

4th May 1956 – 22nd May 2013

'From one editor to another'

Rob Eldridge

Acknowledgements

My appreciation goes to a number of people who have made significant contributions to the progress of 'Day of the Phoenix' since its inception in 2010.

Robert Eldridge – my editor. Without Rob's enthusiastic commitment to the maintenance of standards in English grammar, I would not be in the position of having published six volumes of literary fiction. He is a tireless adherent to the correct expression of the written word, and I am also privileged to call him a friend.

Markus Stenzer – technical consultant. A long-time acquaintance from Bavaria, Markus has kindly advised upon the sections of the book relating to German translation, and also historical and cultural references.

Cath Anthoney – my reader. Cath's pragmatic, no-nonsense approach is an invaluable resource to which I am fortunate to have access. As reader of the final draft, the reassurance that the story was on the right track was the final piece in the jigsaw.

My wife, Lynn. For patience and understanding throughout the formative stages, and for the continuous supply of alternatives when the ones I used were 'lumpy'.

Pneuma Springs – for the constant support and flow of innovative ideas, my heartfelt thanks.

Prologue

The occupants of number 1, St Mary's Lane had become a fixture in the village, but Julie and Doug Martin had never been able to make any acquaintance with them which extended beyond the nodding of heads in passing. The date is mid-2002, and at a social gathering of a number of friends at the end of the little road, a stranger who had not been seen there before rolled up in a Bentley. He was tall, fair haired and carried himself with the self-assured manner of someone accustomed to being obeyed without too many questions being asked. He entered the cottage at the end of the row without knocking, and Doug frowned from his front garden vantage point at this show of familiarity.

Those inside, however, showed no such concern for the man's manner, and all greeted him with the warmth of a long-lost relative. It had been almost ten years since the purging of the Organisation from British political circles, and the blows delivered by George Watkinson had been all but fatal to the cause. The intervening time had been one of slow and painstaking progress, with meetings held in circumstances of the utmost secrecy, but now there was a hint of light at the end of a very long tunnel.

Steve Marshall, for it was he who had laid the foundations of today's gathering, had kept his role within MI5, managing throughout the years to keep his political activities out of the all-seeing gaze of Watkinson. It had been, at times, an extremely difficult road to travel, but since the general election in 2001 the present government had been coming under increasing pressure in relation to its foreign policy. With an unpopular conflict in the Middle East now looking increasingly likely, it would probably be a good time to strike. Those around him were all still fairly young for the onerous mantles which they were about to assume, but he had been in their position himself at one time and was certain that they would cope.

Looking around at their expectant gazes, and to paraphrase one particular political cliché from some years earlier, he felt the hand of history resting upon his shoulder as he read from a prepared set of notes. Funds left in a secret bank account by Gerald Montgomery had been more than sufficient to finance the phoenix of a new organisation rising from the ashes of the old, and this time there would be no room for any sentiment. The aims were clear, and anyone standing in the way would simply be mown down as the steamroller of progress made its inexorable way forwards.

His speech received a rousing reception. Outside in the peace of a summer evening, and in his garden, Doug Martin wondered idly at the party atmosphere emanating from the cottage at the end of the row. There had been a series of arrivals from early in the morning, but neither he nor Julie had recognised the occupant of the Bentley. As he passed their garden at the end of the evening, and with the broadest of smiles upon his face, Steve Marshall bade them both good night and drove off into the gathering darkness.

1

It had been over twelve months since the meeting at the cottage on St Mary's Lane in Tewkesbury, and more than a year of careful and highly secretive reconstruction. Carrying that out under the watchful gaze of all within the confines of Thames House had not been the easiest task which Steve Marshall had ever undertaken. Then there was George Watkinson. The head of MI5 had been led to believe that his own personal safety had been ensured with the killing of Gerald Montgomery on the platform of Nottingham's Midland Station, and Marshall's stock within the secret service had risen several notches on that fateful day.

Montgomery had had to go. Not the most stable of participants in the resurgence of the fascist group, it was by no means certain that under interrogation he would have kept his mouth shut. In the event the choice was clear, and the bullet took care of the rest.

Now it was time to move on once more. Those chosen few at the meeting in Gloucestershire last year were about to step up to the mark. Upon their shoulders now rested the entire future of the Organisation's aims for Britain, and the ambitions of Steve Marshall personally.

Of those who had given their lives for the cause, Montgomery had been the megalomaniac. Useful at the outset with his financial clout, he was nevertheless a liability when it came down to the rhetoric. Too many eyes were being cast in his direction at a critical time in the plan. With Timson it had been status, and the chance to sit at the top table of something special, as opposed to being at the beck and call of transient politicians. Mason was the idealist; close and careful with his words, he would have been a true asset. Even he had lost it at the end, however. No, only Steve Marshall had the complete overview; only he was capable of steering the country towards its true future.

Staring out across the Thames into the city on a cold and grey November afternoon, he was interrupted from his musings by the shrill tone of the telephone. It was a private line, and not linked to the outside world in the same way as most of the others inside Thames House. There were only a few such connections, and Watkinson was the owner of one of the others. Marshall looked at the mobile number on the display and frowned. It was not one which he recognised, and a feeling of unease settled across his normally calm exterior. He could ignore it of course, but that would go against all of his instincts. He let it ring out a little longer before pressing the 'connect' key. He sat in silence. They both sat in silence. Nothing at the other end of the call gave the faintest clue as to location. The voice which broke the spell bore a grating edge and, initially, Steve did not recognise it.

"Steve?" There was the rasp of an old man in the tone and timbre.

"Who is this?" Marshall scowled at the familiarity of a voice which he could not place.

"Steve. That you? I'm deep in it, and I need your help." A deep, guttural cough followed.

"Who are you, and how did you get this number?"

"Chris. Chris Morse. Remember me?"

Christopher Morse. The mole at the centre of so much of what Watkinson believed to be going wrong inside the agency, Morse had come close to bringing the entire thing down. Watkinson's banishing him had been a stroke of pure luck; telling him to report in only to Marshall himself had been highly fortuitous. That had enabled Steve to leave the man to his own devices and simply forget all about what he had done. Until now. Now he resurfaces; now he needs help. Morse was completely unaware of Marshall's status as a double agent, and this could be very dangerous; it would require handling of the utmost care.

"Where are you?" His finger hovered over the button which would place an automatic trace on the call. He thought better of the action and let his hand fall.

"Oh no." The laugh was that of someone aged beyond his years. "Been there - seen it all, and done some of it as well. You won't catch me out again that easily. Too many bad memories."

"All right. What do you want?"

"Help. I thought you were supposed to keep in touch. That's what Watkinson said, wasn't it? I've been hung out to dry."

"Okay, Chris. What have you done?" Marshall did not like the way that the conversation was going.

"The police are after me. I need somewhere to hide until it all dies down." Morse's voice, shaky at the start, was now breaking up.

"Calm down, Chris. What exactly has happened?"

"It was an accident. I didn't mean to kill her…"

"What? You fool! How do you expect me to protect you if you've killed someone?"

There was an ominous silence at the other end of the line, and for a brief moment Marshall thought that Morse was gone. He was wrong.

"Listen, Steve, and listen carefully. I've got nothing to lose now. The stuff I could tell the Sunday papers would blow a hole right through Whitehall, and you know it."

Marshall shuddered. Morse was right – he knew enough to compromise what remained of the Organisation's structure, even by exposing what had now ceased to operate. The ripples would still flow outwards far enough to expose what had been set in motion over twelve months earlier. His silence would have to be ensured, one way or another.

"All right." Marshall sighed. "What do you want to do?"

"I'll meet you, but on my terms and at a place of my choosing."

"Okay. Where and when?"

"The Blind Beggar – thirty minutes."

"The Blind Beggar? You expect me to pick you up in Whitechapel? Have you taken leave of your senses?"

"It's that or the papers. Make your mind up, Steve. I'm running out of time." Morse coughed again, and Marshall wondered at the wording of that last statement. If his health was failing, that in itself might push him towards the unthinkable. He gave in.

"Okay. Look, I'll be there as soon as I can. Just don't do anything that either of us might regret."

It took Marshall the better part of half an hour to get from Millbank to Whitechapel tube station. His training at MI5 had taught him to be prepared for any eventuality and, stopping off at his car, he had opened the boot. A change of clothing, to give him a rough appearance, should be enough to ensure that the sharp eyes of any one of a number of East End informants would not be alerted to his presence in their midst. The tap room at the Beggar was practically empty as he walked through the door. Morse was sitting in the far corner, nursing a half pint. Marshall nodded to the barman.

"Two pints, mate." His change of accent, skilfully perfected down the years, was enough to fool the man.

"You took your time." Morse downed the rest of his drink.

"Try getting across town at the drop of a hat; and how do you think I'd fit in, dressed as I was?" The reproof nettled Marshall.

"Hmph! Well, you better get me out of here before the boys in blue find out where I am."

Over the course of the following half hour, and with an eye ever watchful for strangers, Morse related to Marshall the way in which life, for him, had taken a nosedive since his departure from the employment of MI5. With no regular form of income, and despite an implied assurance from Watkinson that a use would be found for him, he had been forced to live off his wits on the dangerous streets of the capital.

He had quickly slid into the murkier side of London society. Drink and drugs had taken their toll, and he had visibly aged a dozen or more years. It became clear to Marshall that, were he to find some way of utilising the man, Chris would need a sustained period of rehabilitation beforehand. Then, and only then, would he be fit to use as a means of re-establishing the platform that had so nearly borne fruit ten years earlier.

"Chris, we need to get you cleaned up. I might then have a job for you, but you're going to have to stick to the rehab programme. I won't be able to help if you can't stay off the booze and drugs."

Marshall had given considerable thought to the strategy which had failed them in the past. Perhaps it had lacked subtlety; maybe a more considered approach would be needed to get past the naturally cautious British psyche. The British Democratic Party could provide a vehicle for just such a purpose, and its aims were not too dissimilar from those which he, and those before him, had tried to instil by coercion. He may have underestimated the power of the ballot box after all.

2

The small, but highly vociferous, British Democratic Party had emerged in 1982. Under its then leader, Paul McIntosh, it had pursued a fascist, and specifically anti-Semitic, attitude as its flagship policy. That had changed in 1999 with the succession of Robert Grafton to the leadership. As with all militant organisations, the BDP had been on the MI5 radar for a number of years, and it was not unusual for Steve Marshall to be perusing the dossier which the intelligence agency had compiled. He therefore had no cause to conceal its presence upon his desk the following day when the figure of George Watkinson appeared at his door.

"Morning, Steve. Problem with our right-wing friends?" Watkinson reached into his top pocket and put on his spectacles. He approached from the side and looked over Marshall's shoulder.

"Nothing recent." Steve turned the file towards his boss. "Just keeping up to date as far as we can. You never know what these people are up to. Might try getting someone on the inside."

"Think you can? They're pretty cute about picking up on that kind of thing." He returned the glasses to his pocket.

"Remember Chris Morse?" This was a gamble, but one which he was reasonably certain that Watkinson would not see through.

"Didn't we put him out to grass a while back?" Watkinson's face betrayed nothing.

"Yes. You banished him after the affair with the Nazi papers, and told him to report in to me." He closed the file nonchalantly.

"You think you can rely on him now?"

"He called me the other day. I'd forgotten all about him until then. Apparently he has a problem with our friends in blue, and would appreciate a little help to extricate himself from an awkward situation."

"How awkward?" Watkinson was never too keen on the idea of involvement in what he regarded as strictly police matters unless there was a very good reason for it.

This was the point where Marshall had to tread very carefully. He and Watkinson had worked together for quite some time, but the head of MI5 could still catch him off guard on the odd occasion. A false step at this particular moment could derail what Steve was starting to think could be an open door into the kind of politics which would suit the re-emerging Organisation. The truth seemed, in this instance, to be the best tactic.

"He says he's killed someone."

Throughout his years as head of the agency, George Watkinson had tried, with varying degrees of success, to adopt a reasonably straight bat to all matters of national security. By no means the archetypal 'M' of the Ian Fleming novels, he was nevertheless all too aware of the boundaries which had existed between the ideas of good and evil since the years of the Cold War. He stopped at the door to Marshall's office and turned back to face his number two.

"Murder? That's going to be a very tricky situation to deal with. You know what I think about getting involved with the Met on their own turf."

"He didn't say 'murder'; he just told me that he thought he'd killed someone – a woman I believe. It could have been accidental."

Watkinson puffed out his cheeks, closed the door, returned to the desk and took the chair opposite Marshall. Over the course of the next half hour, Steve revealed the details of the entire conversation at the Blind Beggar, and at the end of the story believed he had his boss convinced, as far as he could ascertain, of the benefits of using the ex-operative in a scheme to infiltrate the BDP.

"It'll be risky, but all of that risk will be Morse's. I haven't worked out the details yet, but if we can get someone on the inside, think of the benefits of knowing what they're going to do before it gets out of hand."

Marshall stared into the eyes of his boss, hands clasped under his chin, a wry smile inching its way up the sides of his face. Watkinson, leaning back in his chair, shook his head slowly, but there was a sparkle in his eyes.

"Where are you thinking of sending Morse to dry out?"

"The Bartlesham Clinic. I'll get him in there under a false identity. We're going to have to provide him with a new one in any case. That'll keep the police off his back, and the BDP won't be able to track him back to us once it's done."

"I knew from your first day here that there was something about you that would come to the surface in good time." Watkinson narrowed his eyes. "I'd like to be in on the briefing when you've put some detailed plans together. Keep me posted."

He rose, took a good, long look at his deputy, and left the room. Steve Marshall let out a sigh of relief. Round one to him, but George was far too canny to have the wool pulled over his eyes as easily as the last half hour may have suggested. There would have to be weeks and months of planning prior to any attempt being made to insert Christopher Morse into the ranks of the BDP, and the man himself would need to undergo a strict regime of rehabilitation before it could even be considered. Nevertheless, once he was in place, the direction of the infiltration would be one which the head of MI5 would not expect.

There did, however, remain the matter of the files which the security services had succeeded in recovering way back in 1992. It was vital for the Organisation's success that they be destroyed but Watkinson had hidden them away, and any attempt on Steve's part to begin a search would be certain to raise suspicion. He would bide his time, and that was something that was definitely on his side. He looked down at the file once more, and flipped through the pages. The dossier was comprehensive, and not only tracked the origins of the party, but also the emergence of a number of its leaders since 1982. There had been a spate of internal conflicts during the intervening period, and it was only in the first years of the twenty-first century that a semblance of stability had settled around the BDP under its current head, Robert Grafton. Now would be an ideal time to move the Organisation forward once more, and the text message to his mobile could not have come at a better time.

'3pm. Serpentine.'

Marshall smiled to himself at the irony of the choice. Hyde Park had been at the centre of Alan Mason's activities when it did seem, for a short while at least, that MI5 could be on the run. The copper's death was a significant blow; with his connections in the Met he had been a valuable resource.

'Yes.' His reply was suitably terse.

Morse had been given a very short time to consider his options, and had clearly come around to Steve's point of view. Now would be the start of his reintroduction into the world of espionage, but this time he would be kept on a very tight leash. Marshall pressed a button on his phone.

"Yes, Steve." Watkinson's voice was its usual flat quality.

"Off out for a while, sir. Picking up Morse and taking him to Bartlesham. Not sure when I'll be back."

"Okay, keep me posted."

The journey across the city gave Marshall time to think. It would take around six months to get Chris Morse into any fit state for MI5 to use his skills, and word on the grapevine had come to him of a TV exposé involving the BDP in a Derbyshire town. The timing was almost perfect, and initial surveillance feedback indicated that the production team would be setting up their first stage in less than a month. It always paid to have sources within the media.

George Watkinson, meanwhile, was scheduled to meet a young man who had impressed him the previous year. Plunged into a situation which he did not understand, Barry Newman had nevertheless come to the aid of an agent of a NATO ally, and had helped prevent a situation of considerable gravity from turning into a disaster. Now inducted into the corridors of MI5, having been poached from New Scotland Yard, he had all the makings of a promising member of the department.

The head of the security service flipped through the pages of Newman's file. Single, of no political persuasion, and an unblemished police record, he would be the ideal candidate were the need to arise for someone to operate covertly within the department. He nodded slowly to himself and closed the folder. The intercom on his desk buzzed.

"Yes, Shirley?"

"Mr Newman is here to see you, sir."

"Very well. Ask him to take a seat; I'll just be a moment."

Watkinson took that time to study the young man as he waited. He found the CCTV system, now widely installed after the theft of the Nazi dossier by Graham Poundall, a highly useful tool in assessing the demeanour of those waiting to see him.

3

Barry Newman sat in the office outside the door of the head of MI5. After six months of intensive training this was his first day on the job, and although he had met George Watkinson before, it had not been in a professional capacity. His career path had changed after a chance encounter with a beautiful French woman over a year ago. In his mid-twenties, he had graduated to the Metropolitan Police via the tried and tested route of the Hendon training school, and transfer to CID had come early after exemplary performances in uniform. It was on an away trip up north with his favourite football team that events took a completely unexpected turn.

It had been a four hundred mile round trip to St James' Park, Newcastle, and a whole day out to see them lose five-nil. It wouldn't have been too bad if the opposition were something special, and now filthy weather all the way back home if, that is, he could get out of this infernal traffic jam caused by a set of road works.

Barry was in a really bad mood. Not only had his team just been trashed, but his girlfriend had chosen the previous evening to tell him that they were finished. They had been seeing each other for about three years and he thought the relationship was fine, but clearly he had been wrong. At twenty-six, and in a steady job with the possibility of promotion, change was not something that he was particularly looking for. However, it hit him like a thunderbolt when one of his rear passenger doors opened, a body dived inside, and shut it after them. Stories about carjackers were commonplace, and he was cursing himself for not taking the precaution of securing the car before leaving the north east. For a moment there was no sound, but then a female voice hissed.

"Hide me. I must get away from here!"

"What? Who are you?"

"They are after me and I must escape. Is there anywhere in this car I can hide?"

He told her to pull down one of the back seats, climb into the boot area, and reset it behind her. The fabric cover would provide concealment from any prying eyes, and they were not too long in arriving. Two men appeared out of the darkness and, in the now driving rain, were peering into a selection of vehicles including his own. Fortunately, at that moment, the lights controlling the queue of traffic changed and he was away from the place. All this had happened so quickly that Barry had no time to consider what to do other than vacate the scene as fast as possible, but now that the initial events had passed he took the opportunity to pull in at the next lay-by to confront his new passenger.

The rain had eased as he got out of the car and, having walked slowly round to the rear, he raised the tailgate. There, in the corner of the luggage compartment, curled up in a ball and shivering in the cold and wet, was a young woman in her twenties. The light bulb caused her to shade her eyes as he reached his hand in to help her out of the hiding place. Handing over the blanket which he had always kept in the car, he told her to wrap it around her and get in the front passenger seat. She was of medium height, slim, and had brownish hair. Her clothes were soaking wet and she would need to change out of them as soon as possible. He pulled off the road at the next junction, having seen a sign for a designer outlet site with late opening hours. Returning to the car some thirty minutes later, she was kitted out in new dry clothing and shoes, together with a cheap overcoat, all at his expense.

Now was the time to find out exactly what was going on. Her name, she said, was Danielle Moureau and she had been kidnapped during a day trip to Calais. Her father, Phillipe Moureau, was a wealthy French industrialist and her captors had issued a ransom note threatening to kill her if their demands were not met. She showed him a photograph in the locket which was around her neck – it was of a man in his late forties or early fifties. She had no idea where she was except for the fact that she was somewhere in Britain, and asked Barry if he could return her safely home, saying that her father would be extremely grateful. They lived in a large house in the Bois de Boulogne area of Paris and she said she needed to contact him urgently, but when questioned further would not give the reason. Barry frowned and agreed to take her to the nearest telephone – he was starting to get a bad feeling and was half tempted to drive away right now. She was in and out of the booth in five minutes, thus rendering his dilemma irrelevant. Her expression was calmer, but she said that she would need to get as far away as possible from the place where he picked her up.

"I am sure that if we can get as far as Calais, the rest of the trip to Paris will be easy. My father will be so grateful for the help you have been. You are very brave."

Her soft French accent had him entranced, and all initial fears started to dispel as the story she told became more plausible – if it was a fabrication she was certainly an accomplished liar, and looking at her now he found that difficult to believe. Barry decided to go along with the explanation of events and her ideas for getting home. Resolving to call work tomorrow morning and take some of the leave which his sergeant had been nagging him about for the past three months, he reasoned it would give them time to plan the journey across the Channel via Dover towards the end of that week. The problem was that she had no papers, and so would need to be concealed amongst the luggage in his car. His own passport was up to date, and he was fairly sure that they would pass through the document checks at the port without any trouble.

It was on the Thursday when he had gone out, telling her that he would be back in a couple of hours, that Newman was intercepted. It all happened so fast that he was taken by surprise. Coming out of the Crown and Anchor where he had stopped for lunch, he was approached by a couple of men posing as friends. They made all the usual noises of people who hadn't met for a while, and he felt a sharp pain as a needle entered his arm. A sense of dizziness enveloped him and he slumped into the arms of one of them. Passers-by would just assume that he had been drinking too much and that these friends would be taking him home. As he was ushered into the back of a waiting car, Barry lost consciousness. He opened his eyes sometime later and took in a small, but clean and well-furnished, room containing a uniformed police officer who immediately radioed that he was awake. He was served with a cup of tea, and shortly afterwards two plain clothes men entered the room, introducing themselves as a Mr Foster and a Mr Grant of Special Branch. Foster spoke first.

"Mr Newman, you've given us quite an interesting time since Newcastle, and at one point we thought that we'd completely lost you. There's no need for concern, but I'm afraid that you've been led up the garden path by Miss Moureau which, incidentally, isn't her real name."

Barry looked at them both with a furrowed expression, and Grant picked up on it as he continued the conversation, placing a photograph of Phillipe Moureau before him.

"Her name is Maria Charkov and her 'father' is Dimitri Ostrovsky. You've been the unwitting victim of a plan to return her to her handler in France.

She's a spy in possession of certain information stolen from one of our nuclear research establishments in the north. It's vital that we not only recover what she's taken, but also that the cell from which she operates is eliminated before further damage can be caused." He paused. "I can see that you need some convincing of the situation, and we were prepared for this eventuality."

Stepping outside the room, he summoned a uniformed officer.

"Constable, would you ask Detective Inspector Marks to join us, please?"

The PC returned with a man whom Newman recognised immediately. DS Marks (as he was then) and Barry's father had been friends for many years, and he started to relax at the sight of a familiar face. When Tom Newman died, Dennis Marks became one of the guiding lights in young Barry's life, and he duly followed his 'uncle' into the force.

Marks shook hands with the two Special Branch officers and confirmed the facts which they had related. He also pointed out that, like himself, Barry would be required to sign the Official Secrets Act before they could proceed any further. The appropriate documents were produced and, after the formalities were completed, the briefing (for that was what it was) continued. Marks remained whilst Foster took up the story.

"We believe that you've been requested to take the lady home, and can ensure that your passage through whatever port has been selected will go unhindered and yet remain convincing. Be in no doubt that when Miss Charkov reaches her destination there'll be no further use for you. They'll kill you and ensure that no trace of your body is ever found. However, we need you to carry through your plans in order that we can eliminate the threat at the other end."

Barry took a few moments to absorb what had been said and turned to look at Marks, who nodded. It was clear that he had no real option other than to proceed as planned whilst remaining as casual as possible in Danielle/Maria's presence. They provided him with details relating to his point of departure from Dover, and what to expect in Calais. He was then to follow precisely the instructions given to him by the woman as to the route to Paris. The real problems would be at the end of the journey, but Barry was to hold his nerve and act as surprised as if he knew nothing at all of the true facts.

Disembarking at Calais at the end of the ferry crossing, they were waved through the port by the local gendarmerie and headed off down the E15 towards Lens on the two or three hour journey to Paris. They had been travelling for about an hour when the police car sirens alerted Barry to a potential problem. The distinctively marked vehicle moved alongside, and an officer indicated that they should pull over immediately. Newman had no choice, and a glance at Danielle revealed what he believed to be a genuine look of concern on her face. The police officer got out of the car which had pulled up some twenty yards behind them, and was removing a notebook from his pocket when a speeding black Citroen roared past them, swerving wildly from side to side across all lanes of the auto route. The gendarme immediately got back in the squad car and charged off in pursuit amidst a cloud of smoke and burning rubber, leaving them in the lay-by where they had stopped. Disappearing back into the general traffic, Barry wondered if the forces of law and order had just given them a lifeline to Paris, and that somewhere further down a slip road the local police were being clued in to what was happening. They were certainly not bothered again.

After making one further stop at a service area they continued on the rest of the trip to Paris, arriving at the outskirts of the city at around nine o'clock. Danielle took over the navigating at this point, and some fifteen minutes later they turned up the driveway of an imposing house set in its own grounds in the Bois de Boulogne. Barry wondered how the security forces were going to effect entry to the premises without being seen, but since he hadn't spotted them during the entire journey (with the possible exception of the Citroen) he didn't give the matter too much thought – he had to focus his attention on appearing to be what Danielle believed him to be, a knight in shining armour.

They were met at the door by a butler whom Danielle called François, and he escorted them to an imposing drawing room. Behind an ornate desk towards the window, a silver haired man in his fifties was rising from his seat to meet them. He and the woman exchanged the traditional greeting of a kiss, and Danielle introduced him to Barry as her father, Philippe Moureau. They were ushered towards three leather chairs at the other end of the room and the butler was called and instructed to serve tea. When he returned, it was in the company of another man whom Moureau greeted and introduced as George Watkinson. Barry's feelings of unease now started to return as they had done at the telephone booth near Newcastle - a lifetime ago.

A sudden commotion outside the room banished all such thoughts from his mind as he went back to the statement made by Foster and Grant that 'the real problems' would unfold at the end of the journey, and that time was now. Whatever had happened was very loud and over very quickly, with Barry expecting to see the two Special Branch officers burst through the door backed by whatever law enforcement agencies had been following them on their journey. He was dismayed instead to see them both restrained and in some disarray, accompanied by four burly individuals wearing dark combat clothing. He turned back to Moureau to see him holding a small pistol and it was pointed in his direction.

"Yes, I suppose you are a little surprised, Mr Newman, but this is not the time for regrets."

He pulled the trigger and Barry winced at the expectation of pain and, ultimately, death. Instead, a small orange flame appeared at the end of the barrel, which was then extended to the man introduced as Watkinson.

"Let me light your cigar for you, George. You never do carry matches, do you?"

The whole scene began to turn into some surreal dream as Barry looked around him for someone to make sense out of the last week of his life. The two prisoners were now brought forward into the room and stood before the assembled group. A number of other uniformed men had appeared at the door and were now making their way towards them. It was Watkinson who spoke next.

"Now that our little game has played itself out, it's time to explain to you, Mr Newman, what exactly has been happening. I'm George Watkinson, the head of MI5. The two men before you whom you know as Foster and Grant are, in fact, agents of a foreign power bent on the elimination of key members of NATO staff. They had managed to infiltrate the British security services, but became noticed by us at an early stage. We've been aware of their activities for a while but were not completely sure of their ultimate objective until last week when they did, in fact, kidnap Danielle. Their intention was to lure her father away from this place and kill them both after extracting whatever information they could. Thanks to you, and a little deception on our part, they were allowed to believe that they were approaching their final objective."

Moureau now joined in the conversation.

"You see, Mr Newman, with your help we have been able to identify and eliminate a dangerous spy cell. Unchecked, its activities would have had serious consequences throughout Europe and the Middle East. Danielle really is my daughter, and also an agent working within an area of NATO which must, by its very nature, remain covert."

Watkinson shook the hand of the still bemused young policeman, and smiled.

"The man known to you as DI Marks was on our team from the outset, and makes himself available to us as and when he's needed. This was something of an elaborate trap, and the incident with the Citroen on the E15 almost derailed the whole thing – we don't know the identity of the occupants of the car and they have yet to be traced. Who knows, you have actually signed the Official Secrets Act; we may be calling on you again some time."

Back in the present, Barry Newman smiled to himself at the events which had propelled his career in quite a different direction to that which he had envisaged only a relatively short time ago. The relationship with Danielle, promising as it seemed at the time, had never developed, and she was becoming something of a fading memory now. More intriguing was the possibility of working in the shadow of one of the most powerful men in the country. An involuntary shudder ran the length of his spine as the intercom on the desk burst into life.

"Shirley, would you bring Mr Newman in now, please?"

"Right away, Mr Watkinson."

She smiled and beckoned him to follow her. Barry took a deep breath and made his way to the door.

4

Steve Marshall had only seen Christopher Morse in the dim light of the Blind Beggar in Whitechapel, and though his attention had focussed on what the ex-operative had said, he was also keenly aware of his surroundings. Not only was he in an area of London where he felt less than comfortable, the Beggar was also one of the stamping grounds of the Krays back in the 1960s, and the place where George Cornell had met a violent end. The spectre of the twins had never really disappeared from the area, despite the fact that they were both now dead. Loyalty died hard in London's East End, and it always paid to keep one eye looking over your shoulder.

Consequently, this would be the first time that he had encountered the man in broad daylight for some time, and as he made his approach to The Serpentine from Exhibition Road he was not prepared for the spectre which was about to greet him. The shallow lake at the centre of one of Europe's busiest capitals was flat and grey in the early November afternoon light, and the chill in the air was the herald of a very hard frost to come during the night. With few pedestrians braving the increasing cold, he stopped at the side of the bench on Rotten Row where Morse was currently sitting, shivering visibly as a chill wind swept across the water from the other side of Hyde Park. He turned up his collar against the cold and sat down.

"Hello, Chris."

Morse started; he had clearly not heard Marshall's approach. Hunched in a corner seat at the Beggar, Chris had not revealed the complete extent of his decline into the world of drink and drugs, but now, as Marshall was exposed to the full effect of the ex-spy's year on the streets, he fought hard to suppress the gasp which the gaunt features almost forced out of him.

"Steve. Thank God you're here. I had to make a run for it yesterday after you'd gone. The local plods arrived about five minutes later, and the landlord at the Beggar shoved me out of the back door just before they would've found me."

Marshall took a deep breath and looked hard into Morse's face. From being a fit young man, the pounds had fallen away to leave a haggard, emaciated figure who had visibly aged a decade or more. His eyes were sunken into a pallid face, and his flesh bore the grey, waxy complexion which betrayed a prolonged use of narcotics. It was imperative that he be taken off the streets and into Bartlesham without delay.

"Come on." Morse pulled him up from the bench and almost carried him to the waiting car on Queensgate, close to the Albert Memorial. "We need to get you dried out and back to some kind of normality."

Morse's reply was indecipherable, and he fell inside the rear of the Audi. Marshall threw a blanket over him and gave the driver instructions for the trip.

Their journey took them away from the centre of the capital and down the A4 towards Hounslow. From there, the short distance along the M4 had the car across the London Orbital and into the Berkshire countryside which was the location of Bartlesham Hall. Lying within easy reach of Windsor Great Park and Runnymede, Bartlesham stands in its own grounds just off an anonymous country lane affording it a measure of privacy. It is one of England's most beautiful country houses, and was purchased from its former owner in the late 1980s.

Once past the lodge house to the right, and through a set of electronic gates, Marshall's car made its sedate way along a tree-lined drive which curved through the grounds and up the gentle slope leading to the front entrance. He had seen the place before, but the imposing Italianate, Victorian four-squared building took his breath away with its sheer size and style.

Morse had fallen into a deep sleep within minutes of boarding the vehicle, and it took some fairly rough shaking for Steve to arouse him from his slumber.

"Chris! Wake up. Come on, we're here!" A pair of barely focussing eyes rolled around as he was pulled from the car.

In truth, without Marshall's intervention Morse would have been knocking on death's door very soon, and he leaned heavily on the vehicle's roof as a case was produced from the boot. He licked his dry, cracked lips and swallowed hard.

"Got anything on you?" It was a desperate plea, and Marshall was not sure which of the addictive substances he meant. It was academic anyway.

"No, you fool! Just get a move on; we're here for your health, not your entertainment." Grabbing him under the arms, Steve and the driver frogmarched their passenger across the car park, up the entrance steps, and into the clinic's reception area. They were met by a senior nurse who had been expecting them.

"Mr Marshall?" She smiled, coldly.

Steve never heard the question. His eyes were drawn almost hypnotically to the magnificent entrance hall. With its gold and red marbled walls and white marble statues running the length of the room, it heralded the splendour of the inner quarters to come and he stood transfixed, still supporting the frail frame of Christopher Morse.

"Mr Marshall!" The reproving reminder snapped him out of his trance. "If you would follow me, Mr Ransome will see you right away."

"Yes, of course. Please lead the way." He felt like some schoolboy caught straying on a day out.

Bernard Ransome rose from behind his desk as Marshall and Morse entered the consulting room. He stood six feet three and cut a fine, sixteen stone figure as he stepped forward to meet them. A position in rugby union as a flanker had been cut short by a cruciate ligament injury during an England trial, and his medical training told him right then that he would never achieve his dream of stepping out onto the hallowed turf at Twickenham.

Left to concentrate upon a career in medicine, he had graduated from Oxford with a first and, after a brief placement within the NHS, had been headhunted by a Harley Street specialist. Further moves had taken him into the world of toxicology, and Bartlesham was the culmination of that progress - he was now a very wealthy man. The smile on his face was genuine, and the handshake sincere.

"Mr Marshall and…?" He glanced at Morse, eyebrows raised.

"We'll just say that he's my cousin, Tom Harriman, shall we?"

"That's fine by us." He turned to Morse. "Well, Mr Harriman, we need a few details so that the clinic can provide you with the best use of its resources. Shall we start with a list of the substances which you've been taking, and the length of time you've been under their control?"

Christopher Morse had, during the initial conversation, been staring out of the window into the fading light. He was clearly still under the influence of his latest fix. Marshall elbowed him sharply in the ribs.

"What? I'm… I'm sorry, I didn't hear what you said." His voice was slurred, and Ransome picked up very quickly on the dilated state of his pupils.

"Pay attention!" Marshall's voice cut sharply through the ensuing silence, but Ransome raised a calming hand.

"That's all right. We don't normally get much information out of our guests at an induction anyway, and toxicology reports will tell us all that we need to know. I could show you around the clinic's facilities, though, while your cousin is taken to his room."

Steve nodded in agreement, and whilst one of the nursing staff led Chris away with the case they had brought along, he and Ransome moved out of the consulting room and along the first of a number of corridors which led into the depths of the property.

"Bartlesham's come quite a long way over the past ten years." Ransome spoke with much arm waving as they passed by a series of separate facilities within the confines of the property. "We've developed a state of the art fitness area, which incorporates a gymnasium, an Olympic standard swimming pool, a sauna, and a steam room."

Marshall missed nothing during the half hour he spent with the clinic's owner, and picked up on the security fences which he had noticed on the approach to the place.

"Yes." Ransome nodded. "It's sturdy stuff, and keeps the paparazzi out of our hair. We have some very high profile guests from time to time, and the security staff are here more to prevent unwelcome intrusions than to watch over our clients."

"What if someone tried to make a break for it?" Marshall frowned; he could not afford to lose Morse once they had started down the path he had in mind.

"Mr Marshall, this isn't a prison and our guests are free to leave anytime they wish. However, they may find getting any further than the gate a little problematic, since there's no bus service along this road, and nights tend to be rather chilly around here at this time of year."

They had returned to the entrance hall, and Marshall took his leave of the head of Bartlesham as the driver outside was stubbing out the last in a succession of cigarettes which had punctuated his lengthy wait in the gathering gloom. He turned at the door.

"How long before you'll have any progress?"

"Good question." Ransome pursed his lips. "We'll wean him off the heroin if, as I suspect, that's what he's hooked on. Methadone's the substitute, but we'll take care that it isn't just swapping one addiction for another. I'd say he's in for a tough two or three months."

"I'll call you in the new year, then." Marshall turned, and was gone.

Back in the car, and on the way out of the grounds, he took a good look around at the security systems. Closed circuit cameras were everywhere, and the gate at the bottom of the drive slid smoothly and silently back as they passed through. The guard made a note on a clipboard as the Audi turned onto the country lane. Marshall shook his head – it would take a very determined paparazzo to even consider making an attempt on the fencing, and there was a series of sinister-looking cables along the top of its length. He sat back and smiled; things were slowly coming together, and all Chris needed to do now was exactly as he was told.

5

It was now February, and three months into Chris Morse's treatment at Bartlesham. Ransome's report had indicated a fair amount of progress following an initial difficult period and, after successfully being weaned off the heroin, work was now concentrating on reducing the dosages of methadone which had been needed to accomplish it. Physically, he was in better shape than for some time, and early summer should, according to the clinic, see him free from the addiction which would surely have killed him but for Marshall's intervention.

Steve closed the folder. This part of the plan seemed to be on course; now it was time to lay the foundations for the next stage in its development. He picked up the telephone and dialled a number he had not used for some considerable time. He wondered whether the individual at the other end would even recognise him after so long.

"Miles McAndrew. Can I help you?" The voice was that of a typically efficient secretary, and Marshall smiled at the familiar ring to it.

"Sandra?" He sat back and prepared to enjoy the game.

"Yes…" There was a pause as Sandra Miles struggled to put a face to the voice which she recognised. "Who is this, please?" She gave in.

"Steve…"

"… Marshall! Good grief, after all this time!" A smile erupted across her hitherto puzzled features. "How are you?"

"I'm very well. Is Peter in?"

"He'd better be for you! How long has it been…?"

"Too long, and I'm about to put that right."

After a few more moments of pleasantries, she put the call through to her husband's office and sat back to re-run some of the memories from before Marshall's move to the capital. They had all been close since their days at the

27

local grammar school, and there had not been a time when that relationship had ever faltered. Friends inevitably fell out and made up again, but they just seemed to stick like glue. If she was right about what Steve had in mind, there was going to be plenty of time to resurrect some of those days. Her train of thought was interrupted by Peter's sudden emergence from his office.

"The bugger's coming up here for a holiday! Wants to know if he can stay with us. I'll be damned, and after all this time as well!" He sat down on the chair at the side of her desk.

"When?" Sandra was already thinking of the logistical side of the matter. It was one of the things that had attracted him to her at the very start.

"Couple of weeks. Says he wants to take another look around the area, but you know Steve; there'll be another reason as well. Reckons he's coming up on the train – I can pick him up at Derby station."

"He can have Stuart's room now that he's at Keele. I'll move some of his stuff into the loft."

"That's that then. I'll ring him and give him the good news." With that, he was gone, back into the depths of his inner sanctum.

Steve's life had not always been one amid the bright lights of the nation's capital city. He had left his native Derbyshire some six years earlier and, as far as Peter and Sandra were concerned, worked in the civil service. His birth, in 1969, was one of those accidents of nature for a couple in their forties. Tom and Mavis Marshall had all but given up hope of having a family of their own, and complications during his birth had ensured that Steve was to be an only child. They doted on him, and their deaths, hers from cancer and his in a motorway pile-up, had hit him hard.

He shook the countryside dust from his feet, found a job down south, and left the area. This tragedy was not the only reason for his migration, and Sandra had plans to resurrect the other matter at the first available opportunity. That chance was now just clearing the horizon.

The train from St Pancras pulled in at the station on Derby's Midland Road right on time, and after the usual greetings had been exchanged, they were on their way out of the city. The town of Longlea lies a stone's throw from the Derbyshire/Nottinghamshire border, and was the home of the Mileses. Steve drew in a deep breath as he stepped from the car. The new house, on a recent development, stood on the very spot where his father had spent the final days of his working life at a local printing company. Their own home had been half a mile away in Aldersford, and just off the main road which, taken to its extreme, connected to the motorway network.

"Come on, no time for daydreaming." Sandra shook him from his reverie, and they made their way up the front path and into the house.

"Nice." Marshall was impressed with the interior.

"Hmm." Peter responded. "Sandra's skill, not mine. We were fortunate that the builders hadn't finished the inside. It was just a shell, and we more or less had the freedom to tell them how we wanted it."

The property was a four bedroom detached with integral garage. The room sizes were very generous for the time, and after the customary tour of inspection the three of them sat down to an evening meal.

"So, how's life down in the Smoke?" Peter smiled as he sat back with his glass of Shiraz.

"Pretty dull really." Steve smiled. "Footie's not as good, and the price of a beer is outrageous."

"Anyone on the horizon?" Sandra this time, testing the water as she had planned to do since the initial phone call.

"Nah. Done with that for the present. Got a career to think of."

"Beverley's still around, you know." This got her a kick under the table from her husband, but she carried on regardless. "Are you still sure that you did the right thing?"

Marshall took no offence at this prying into his private life. Beverley Drake had, after all, been the fourth member of their little group until... He sighed and stared out of the window. Peter picked up on the change in his manner.

"We shouldn't be bothering you after all this time..."

"No, it's ok. What *are* friends supposed to be to each other? It's as finished now as it was then. There's no going back on the matter. I'm over it; there's no problem."

That, for the time being, was the end of the story, and conversation moved on to the more weighty issues of football, pubs, and an evening out. Sandra smiled knowingly. She was a fish out of water where the two of them were concerned when they got onto such matters, and chose to go with the flow. Plans were made for the remainder of the time which Steve would spend with them, and he retired to his room a few hours later intending to get a good night's sleep.

He had not come up to Derbyshire merely to check in with a couple of old friends; there was also the matter of the BDP to take into consideration, and with Morse's stay at Bartlesham due to come to a close in the not too distant future, he would have to prepare the ground for the man's attempt at infiltrating its ranks. He had, however, been side-tracked by Sandra and the mention of Beverley Drake.

They had been an item six years earlier, and everyone was looking forward to the inevitable wedding plans. All was progressing quite nicely towards that goal until the evening of the Christmas party at the company where Beverley worked. Steve had been unable to accompany her, and angry words were exchanged at his change of plan at the last moment. They had parted the previous evening on acrimonious terms. When he found out that she had cheated on him with a work colleague, he hit the roof.

Sleep did not come easily to Marshall as he lay there thinking about the events of those two fateful days. She had realised the severity of her mistake, of course, but had reckoned without the speed that the news of her infidelity reached him.

"How can I ever trust you again?" His rebuke was calm, too calm, and it frightened her.

"I'm sorry. It was a moment of madness. I don't even like the guy." The floods of tears were genuine – she had no guile in such matters back then.

"And yet," Marshall snorted, "you sleep with him on the basis of one evening in his company. Am I just supposed to take that on the chin?"

The reprimand - it was not a conversation - had ebbed to and fro for more than an hour, and at the end of the evening Steve had put on his coat and left. She thought that she was never to see him again. If the deaths of his parents had hit him hard, this was to be the final nail in the coffin of his life in the Midlands. By the end of the following week, he had packed up his belongings and headed south. Sandra had started to tell him where it was in Nottingham that Beverley was living, but Marshall merely shook his head.

"She's on her own, Steve. There's been no-one else. Why not…"

"Sorry. It would be stupid to think of seeing her again. She was wrong then, and she's wrong now."

That final sentence stopped the conversation in its tracks, and Sandra gave in… for the moment. The morning, when it came, was a bright one, but Marshall was not back into his stride until well into the afternoon.

The first of Steve's two weeks with his friends passed with no further mention of Beverley Drake, and he had let the matter slip quietly from his mind. They passed evenings together and those portions of the days where Peter and Sandra could take time out of work. Steve occupied his time alone to reacquaint himself with some of the places where he had spent his childhood - a visit to his former home in Aldersford being one - and the memories came back as clear as a bright summer day. The following weekend brought the three of them back together, but Peter had made plans for the morning. Sandra smiled, and let them go out to play.

She had made her own arrangements to spend the day shopping, and Peter took the opportunity to drive Steve around some of their old haunts. They inevitably ended up at one of the pubs that the four of them used to frequent, and it was not entirely by chance that they walked into the Midland Hotel on the corner of Cromford Road and Station Street.

"Why here?" Miles frowned. "It wasn't our favourite; that was the Crown in Highridge."

"Good pint, though." Marshall sought to deflect the statement.

The Midland had become, of late, a meeting place of the local branch of the BDP, and would be close to the centre of a planned TV documentary exposé of the party's activities in the area. Covert surveillance had been organised from the back of a Transit van stationed in the car park of the Railway Tavern – its target was a shop on the opposite side of the road. As they sat in the window seat of the pub, some fifty yards from the Tavern, Marshall nodded to himself. This should be an easy assignment for Morse to carry out if he kept himself clean. It was important, though, not to arouse the suspicions of Miles and, satisfied that he had all the information which he needed at present, he allowed Peter to persuade him to finish the pint and move on to the Crown, two miles up the road. Unbeknown to either of them, Sandra, in the guise of spending a day out shopping, had made the trip into Nottingham, and was meeting up with their old friend, Beverley, in town. It was all smiles as they saw each other across the Old Market Square, and after a considerable portion of the day spent in the Victoria and Broadmarsh Centres, they finally came to rest in Starbucks on Clumber Street over a couple of lattes.

"All right." Beverley smiled and looked over the top of her glasses at the now pensive figure on the opposite side of the table. "What's this all about? It's been ages since we saw each other, and you call me out of the blue."

"Never could keep stuff from you, even at school, could I?" Sandra laughed nervously. The next few moments would need careful handling.

"Come on, then. Spill the beans; out with it." She leaned back in her chair.

"Okay." She took a deep breath. "Peter and I have a visitor staying with us this week, and we wondered…"

"Still trying to play cupid? I thought we put that to bed a few years back." Beverley was still smiling, and this was a good sign.

"Well, sort of. You see…"

"Okay, what's he like? Tall, blonde, hunk, rich…delete as applicable." She threw the comment out like a discarded hand at poker.

"He's tallish, light brown hair, definitely fit, blue eyes, and from down south." Sandra paused, scanning the face of her old friend for some kind of sign.

"You know," Beverley mused, "That sounds just like…" She stopped abruptly. The expression changed, and Sandra squirmed in her seat.

"It's Steve." She jumped in before her friend had the time to finish the sentence.

"What have you done? That was supposed to be over years ago." The voice carried a hard edge, and it was clear that a boundary was in danger of being crossed.

"Nothing. I'm out on my own with you, and neither Steve nor Peter know that we're together. Will you at least come and say hello?"

Beverley was stunned. Steve had dumped her - there was no other way of looking at it. She had been stupid and he had walked away. Part of her could not blame him, but he had been so unforgiving and his words still caused her heartache. There really had not been anyone serious during the time that they had been apart, and she had no idea what effect seeing her again would have upon him. He had a temper in those days; perhaps he still did.

"Do you think it's a good idea? I mean, what about you and Peter? Steve could be very hard back then. You know how difficult it was getting him to change his mind once it was made up."

"You'll never know if you don't try." Sandra pleaded. "Come on, what's there to lose?"

Beverley stared across the table at her friend. Sandra could be very persuasive at times, and all through school she had followed her lead; they hadn't always come up smelling of roses, but overall the track record had been good.

"Bev?"

"I'm thinking." She shook her head, glanced away and, for a moment Sandra feared the worst. Then she looked back at her friend and smiled. "It would be nice to see him again, and I suppose you never know…"

"Great! Come on, the tram's about due and I'm parked at the Phoenix Centre." She grabbed Beverley by her coat sleeve, and they were away along Exchange Walk, heading for the tram stop outside Wetherspoons on Old Market Square.

6

The arrival home of the two shoppers did not coincide with the presence of the two men, who had taken the opportunity provided by Sandra's absence to make the short trip to Highridge United for the afternoon kick-off against local rivals Woodville Athletic, in the FA Trophy. Consequently, it was almost half past five when they strode through the front door, still discussing the merits of a draw against a team from several leagues higher. Peter headed for the kitchen and his wife as Steve turned right into the lounge. He stopped dead in his tracks at the sight of the figure sitting on the sofa. Their eyes met for the first time in six years, and the initial silence was deafening. Beverley's heart pounded like a jackhammer, and her mouth dried instantaneously. She cleared her throat.

"Hello, Steve."

"Beverley… I had no idea…" He was at a loss – a rare occurrence these days.

Marshall felt himself trapped; if he left the room there would be nowhere to go other than to pack his bag and head out. If he stayed there would be the need for at least some sort of conversation, even if it were just for the sake of form. The decision was taken out of his hands by Sandra.

"Out of the way, then." She elbowed him into the room, her hands occupied with a tray. "Find yourself a seat, and for goodness sake say something."

The impish smile on her face told him that this was some kind of setup, and he edged towards an armchair at the side of the fire. Peter followed her in, and from the look on his face there had clearly been words between the two of them: Sandra had obviously won the exchange.

"So…" She said with the hint of mischief in her voice, "… isn't this nice? The four of us together again after all this time. Tea anyone?"

Sandra's planning had gone well beyond a brief snack with some old friends, and the ringing of the doorbell heralded the evening meal which she had arranged prior to making the ten mile trip to Nottingham. Peter had not been in on this part of the surprise, and she shepherded him into the kitchen to help prepare the dinner. Steve and Beverley were alone for the second time, and this one was not so brief. He broke the silence.

"I had no idea that…"

"Yes." Beverley interrupted. "I gathered that. She almost bulldozed me to the car once I realised what was happening." She took a deep breath. "It *is* good to see you again."

Despite all of his earlier talk and the years of being convinced that he had been right, Marshall began to melt before the face of the woman he had abandoned. She was still as beautiful, and her voice was starting to thaw the ice which had formed around all of the memories which he had tried so hard to suppress.

"You're looking very well." He was struggling for words – another rarity, and he felt now just the way he had felt on their first date.

"You too. Look, this is silly. It's not as if we don't know each other…"

"I know, I know. I'm sorry, it was just such a surprise seeing you again after…" He let the sentence tail off.

She smiled and he smiled back. He couldn't help it; she always had that effect on him and his resolve was weakening by the minute. He got up from the chair and moved to the side of her on the sofa. He had forgotten how brown her eyes were; deep, deep brown, and the effect was almost hypnotic. Automatically he reached for her hand, and almost immediately their fingers were intertwined. The effect was electric, and they kissed. It was no act of passion however, but a reconciliation of years of regret, a tender act born out of a longing so deeply buried. Peter chose that moment to appear at the door and they parted, both thinking, without truly believing, that they had not been seen. He coughed and feigned to look away.

"Dinner is served."

Conversation over dinner, and for the remainder of the evening, focussed on the years they had spent together at school, their time at respective universities, and returns home after varying degrees of success to meet up once more. Care was taken to avoid any reference to the issue which had separated Steve and Beverley, and when the hour came for her to take her leave, he was almost desperate to prolong their time together.

"I'll walk you to the bus." The free flow of wine during the evening prevented the car being used, and Beverley accepted his offer with another one of her smiles.

"We'll wash up." Peter interjected, shoving Sandra before him and back into the kitchen.

With the front door now firmly closed, he stood and leaned against the refrigerator, a look of mock concern on his face.

"You crafty bugger. I never thought you'd do something as underhand as that."

"Oh really?" Sandra smiled, turning from the sink. "Did you truly believe that they weren't meant for each other?"

Peter had to concur. Steve had taken the split very hard, but no amount of persuasion had appeared to work. Yes, she had been stupid, of course she was wrong, but the argument which had fuelled the incident had been brewing for a while – that much he could remember. The rest of it was lost in the mists of time.

The walk to the bus stop was not very far, and should have taken no longer than a few minutes, but Steve was loathe to let the evening pass away too quickly now that he and Beverley had taken the first step. Instead of heading for the main road along North Street, he prolonged their stroll by turning right onto Thompson and heading for the more circuitous route of Upper Dunstead Road. This would extend the trip by some half a mile, and she would miss the next connection to Nottingham. His tactic had not gone unnoticed – she took his hand; there was no resistance.

"Steve…" She broke the silence after what seemed an age. "… there's been no-one else since… you know."

"Sandra told me." He stopped and turned to face her.

They stood beneath the orange glow of a street light, and he marvelled once more at the beauty that he had forgotten. She pulled him close, and the kiss was longer this time in the relative privacy of the outdoors. She electrified him, and he started to curse the decision which had kept them apart for so long. She pulled away.

"My bus! I have to go."

They ran the hundred yards to the stop at the bottom of Peel Street, and as she got aboard she turned back to him.

"Call me. Sandra has the number – make it soon." With that she was gone, and he stood there, a sudden emptiness taking hold where only moments before there had been a sense of purpose.

A cold breeze shook him from the trance-like state, and he shivered; whether it was from the chill or the intensity of the last half hour, he couldn't say. Pulling his collar up around his neck he headed off for the short walk back to the Miles home.

"Well?" Sandra was on him in a flash as soon as he set foot inside the door.

"Well what?" He knew how she liked to play these games, and Peter stepped in to save him the doorstep interrogation.

"Let the man get in, Sandra. It's cold out there."

"He'll be warm enough after half an hour with Beverley, won't you, Steve?" That smirk again.

He was faced with little option, and related the events of the walk to the bus stop, admitting for the first time that he *may* have been a little precipitate in the decision he had made all those years ago.

"When are you seeing her again?" The woman was ruthless.

"I'll phone her tomorrow… maybe." Marshall mentally retreated from the position into which he had been manoeuvred, and Sandra sensed it.

"Give her an hour and ring tonight. Here…" She reached into her bag and opened an address book. "… that's the number; you can borrow my car next week."

Marshall made the call and, as he drifted off to sleep that night, had just the merest doubt at the wisdom of what he had done. The coming week would give him plenty to think about on a number of scores – a resumption of the relationship with Beverley could have a dramatic effect on the plans he had for Morse and the BDP in the area. That was something that could not be allowed to happen after all of the careful planning since the disastrous events of 1992.

7

The following week flew past for Steve and Beverley. With Sandra's car at their disposal, it gave them the freedom of the entire East Midlands as Marshall struggled to concentrate on the true purpose of his trip. Much as his revived feelings for the woman at his side came constantly to the forefront of his mind, he could not let that be a distraction. It did, however, provide him with something of an unexpected bonus.

His time spent with Peter had not been solely social, and with finely-tuned senses always on the alert for snatches of conversation, he had been able to build a picture of the political spectrum of the area. Local pubs and clubs provide a forum for debate in any region, and feelings on the subject of immigration and jobs were running high on the Derbyshire border.

"Foreigners! Come over here, take our jobs, scrounge off the state, and then stick their grubby hands out for more!"

The impassioned diatribe from a well-built toper at the Midland Hotel had made Marshall sit up and take notice one evening. It was directed at a group of three Poles who had taken up seats in a corner of the public bar; their entrance had gone unnoticed by the majority of those in the room, and the table had been chosen quite deliberately in order to keep a relatively low profile. A lack of response to the jibe merely served to ratchet up the tension; Marshall sat listening intently – he had no intention of becoming involved.

"Why don't they sod off back to their hole of a country, and leave the rest of the civilised world in peace?!" He turned now, leaning back against the bar and glaring directly at them.

There was a murmuring of what Steve interpreted as support, and he noticed for the first time the swastika tattoo on the speaker's neck.

"Come on, I'm going." Peter began to rise from his seat, but Marshall pulled him back.

"Stay where you are." He whispered. "I've seen this kind of thing before, and if we get up it'll send the wrong signal. Do you want to be the first in the line of fire?"

"What?" Miles was incredulous.

"Stand up and it might be seen as some sort of support for the guys in the corner."

Peter resumed his seat, and Marshall stared into his beer glass, listening intently once more. There had been no reaction from behind the bar whilst the insults were being issued, and clearly the landlord was in on whatever the belligerent customer had in mind.

"What's the matter..." the monologue continued, "... can't even speak da lingo?" he stepped away from the bar this time, the provocation now unequivocal.

The three Poles sat in silence – trapped in the corner farthest from the door. It was becoming evident that some form of violence was on the cards, but then, at the last moment, another customer from the far end of the room stepped forwards and came to face the stocky figure in the centre of the floor.

"Not now, Dave. There'll be a time, but not now." A hand on the shoulder was all that was required.

"Okay, Mike." He glared into the corner. "Just this once."

Marshall watched in astonishment as the bruiser backed off. The newcomer was shorter and of a much slighter build, but the retreat was immediate and the command unchallenged. The Poles, sensing that this was to be their only opportunity, vacated the corner which had held them prisoner and, with a glance towards the landlord, made their escape. The other two returned to the bar, where a further brief conversation was followed by a pat on the back of the larger man.

"Now can we leave? This place is starting to give me the creeps." Whispered pleas from Peter received a nod in reply, and they headed for the door.

Steve was none too disappointed at his friend's insistence on returning home. Whilst his memory was good enough under normal circumstances, the events of the past half hour would need to be committed to paper for future use. The guy, Mike, who stepped in was plainly someone of superior standing in the local right wing community, and Marshall was sure that, once back at base, further details relating to the man's identity could be extracted from the MI5 database.

"Hey! Have you been listening to me?" Beverley's nudge to his ribs brought him back to the present and out of the daydream of the previous week.

They were in the centre of Nottingham on Monday afternoon, and Marshall had seized upon her suggestion of the trip as a means of gaining some additional feeling for the political atmosphere of the region's major city.

"Sorry, just thinking about something I should have done before I came up here." He turned to find Beverley scowling at him, and that was an expression which took him back a few years.

The reproof was good-natured and the moment passed without further comment. Marshall nevertheless found the time, whilst she was at a cash point, to insert a memo into his mobile phone. His training at MI5 had given him the ability to engage in one conversation whilst simultaneously scanning others for information; this was to prove a highly effective tool during the week as a whole. The isolated incident at The Midland was more than borne out by a greater unease amongst the public at large.

Like all large cities, Nottingham had proven to be a magnet for citizens of the new EU member countries of the former Eastern Bloc. The face of the area was changing to meet the needs of these economic migrants, and rumblings of discontent bubbled just below the surface. Beverley and Steve had passed a few such groups as they made their way around town, and a number of heads turned at the unfamiliar language.

'Gippo! Wog! Polak!' These and similar comments were hissed at them. The threats were clear, and few rebuking glances came to the aid of those targeted.

Marshall frowned, and the returning figure of Beverley gave him the opportunity to test a theory which had been in his mind since they had met up again.

"Something wrong?" She picked up on the change in his manner.

"Sort of." He looked again in the direction of the source of the racial taunts. "Is there much baiting of foreigners up here?"

"The Poles? Oh, it comes and goes, but they only have themselves to blame." She replied, putting her purse into the handbag. The statement had been delivered in a surprisingly casual manner.

"How so?" He dipped his toe deeper.

"Economics, Steve. We're a small island with, what, sixty plus million of us? They've been coming over here in their thousands since the EU was expanded and no-one seems to be interested in putting the brakes on it.

They claim social security benefits and send the cash straight back home."

"That's the EU for you – free movement of labour and all that." He feigned innocence and shrugged his shoulders.

"True…" She stopped and grabbed his sleeve, "… but there's more than me would like to see this country get back to some good old-fashioned British values and standards. We fought for their freedom and they now come over here scrounging our benefits. Don't forget that your mum and dad as well as mine paid into the system they're taking advantage of. Have *you* ever tried claiming for anything?"

"Yeah, okay, but what's the answer?" This was the make or break question, and would tell him once and for all whether the idea he was considering had a foundation. She pulled him to one side, and her voice dropped several levels.

"Listen, you might not like the sound of this, but I'm so fed up with what's going on, I've joined a party that seems to have the right ideas."

He stood there, nonplussed. The surprise was genuine but she misunderstood, and took it merely as his being dense. Her eyes closed and she shook her head.

"Look, let's go somewhere a little more private." She took his hand and they moved from the corner of Exchange Walk and into Wetherspoons on South Parade.

Here, they found a quiet corner and ordered a meal. The pub had not yet filled up with the usual crowd of diners, so there was no-one to overhear what Beverley said next.

"So, what's this group that you've joined then?" His face was a picture of innocence.

"The BDP." She sighed at his fake expression of horror. "Yes, I know they had a reputation for strong-arm stuff in the past, but look at where they are now. People are starting to listen, and the things they're saying make sense. They made some inroads at the last round of local elections, and there's a couple of councils up in Lancashire where they took control."

"They're fascists." Steve decided to push a little further, still not entirely convinced of her feelings.

"Tell that to the folks of Burnley. Do you realise that they got three councillors in at the 2002 local elections?"

Steve shook his head and feigned a smile. "A protest vote – it happens all of the time." He shrugged, and she drew closer over the table.

"Okay, but what about the share of the vote? Oldham 35% and 30% in two wards; Burnley 31% and 28% in two others, and in Sunderland they hit 28% as well."

"I still can't believe that the British public can so easily have forgotten what happened sixty years ago in Germany. They'll never make any impact at national level." The devil's advocate in him was now at full steam.

"All right, but it's a start, and with another set of elections just around the corner, they're looking to use those results as a springboard."

"They're still thugs in suits." He snorted.

"They're British." She corrected him, nettled at his attitude. "Wake up and smell the coffee. It's not just the Poles, for God's sake. Look what happened in New York in September 2001; what makes you think that something like that isn't being planned for us?"

"Where did you get all of this information? I mean, it's not the kind of stuff that the ordinary person in the street would remember." He frowned, and for a moment, Beverley thought she may have let her mouth run away with her. There was no other option than to tell him the truth and damn the consequences.

"I didn't just join them. I'm the area secretary." She looked around, suddenly aware that her voice was not as quiet as it had been. Fortunately there were no other customers in their area of the room. "It's *our* country; we simply can't allow a bunch of foreigners to take over."

The next few moments were the turning point for her as she searched his face for some clue as to what his thoughts might be. The spell was broken by the arrival of the meal, and the subject was dropped.

For Marshall, it was the convincing statement. Now that he knew where her political affiliations lay, there was the distinct possibility that the two of them could take the Organisation to the top of the political tree. The remainder of the day, and indeed the week, passed in a more relaxed manner. The train journey home would be one filled with thought and planning.

8

The BDP had occupied its headquarters in Bexley since the party's formation in 1982. That it had managed to survive economically in the capital since then had been down to substantial donations received from a number of anonymous sources. Successes two years earlier at the 2002 local elections, although welcome, were not enough to guarantee a continuation of the financial backing, and a number of those presently standing in the shadows had made their feelings plain – step up the progress or no further funding would be available. A crisis meeting was currently in progress on this very matter.

"All right! Let's have some quiet! This is getting us nowhere!" Robert Grafton hammered the table with his shoe. Nikita Khrushchev had used the same tactic in October 1960 at a meeting of the UN in New York, but Grafton's action could not have been further removed – he was a desperate man.

The meeting had started badly, with recriminations flying all over the room as a variety of factions sought to lay the blame for the financial mess at each other's door. A temporary lull in the chaos allowed him to gather his thoughts.

"Listen to me! We're on the threshold of a breakthrough, and all you lot can do is chuck your toys out of the pram!"

"Okay then, what *are* you going to do? We can't stay here if we can't pay the rent, and the capital's where all the major political parties are based. Moving out isn't an option. At least around here we know we're amongst friends."

It was now May, and getting close to the date when Christopher Morse should be fit again for action. In readiness for that time, Marshall had been making tentative plans to prepare the ground for a takeover of the right wing party. They were, as Grafton had hinted, at a turning point; with a fresh set of local elections in the not too distant future this was a particularly bad time for investors to be talking of pulling the plug. At a very private meeting, a proposal had been put before the BDP leader which would provide new backing for a more concerted push on the ballot boxes. This information was now laid before the fractious members in attendance.

"This…" Grafton held up a paper to his audience, "… was paid into our bank account yesterday afternoon."

Silence fell like a stone, and all eyes tried to focus on the text of the message. He smiled. With their attention now on him and nowhere else, he read out its contents. Half a million pounds had been deposited and had cleared for the organisation's use.

"With this amount of cash, and more is promised, we can fight every single ward in the country. Then we move on to the general election – over six hundred seats, and we'll be able to contest all of them. This will be our big chance, but we have to put a stop to all of the infighting. If we can't show the British public a united face we're finished. Now, does that answer your question?"

There followed a murmur of grudging approval. Grafton seemed to have the ability to pull a rabbit out of the hat at the most critical time. He'd done it before on a number of occasions, and it did appear that the gods were smiling down on him. Three of the assembled crowd, however, made their way to the door and out into the street.

"Bugger's gone and done it again!" This from Mike Summers, the man Marshall had observed as the restraining influence at the Midland, back in Longlea.

His was not one of the more belligerent of the regional factions but, in his earlier days, he had headed a militant arm of the BDP, organising violent clashes with any ethnic minority group which happened to cross his path – the incident at the Derbyshire pub was just one such opportunity. He had also been the voice of dissent earlier in the meeting.

"What now, then?" The question came from Dafydd Jones – chairman of the Welsh BDP Assembly, and leader of the Porthcawl branch. "He's takin' the party too far to the centre. This isn't what I signed up for, and you know it!"

"Yes, I'm aware of what we all want, and Grafton's selling us down the river. I need time to think. Come on, let's find a pub where we can talk in private."

This was always the way with the militant arm of what Summers regarded as the traditional BDP – its formation in 1982 had given him, and those of similar opinions, cause for hope that a new dawn was just around the corner. He had hoped to use the organisation's current cash flow problems to oust Grafton from the leadership; that now seemed out of the question, and other methods would have to be found, and soon.

In another watering hole, some three weeks earlier, Robert Grafton had responded to a cryptic message delivered to his mobile. The source was unknown, but the substance was clear. The sender appeared to be acutely aware of the financial straits in which the BDP now found itself, and was offering something of a way out of the present difficulties. Sitting at the bar of the Bricklayers Arms in Luton, he had been kept waiting a full half hour beyond the appointed time, and was on the point of leaving.

"Robert Grafton?" The voice to his left had appeared suddenly, and its quiet tone betrayed nothing to any other casual customer. He turned.

"Yes? "He eyed the newcomer suspiciously. "You are?"

"That's not important right now, but just call me Steve. Shall we sit down somewhere a little less conspicuous?" He indicated a snug in the far corner of the room. "Two pints please, landlord." He called over his shoulder.

"Okay, what's this all about?" Grafton looked around before taking the seat indicated.

"Money, my friend. Considerable amounts of it, all of which your organisation desperately needs in order to fulfil its aims." Marshall smiled as the barman deposited the two glasses on the table. "Cheers."

"How much do you know?" Grafton could sense that he was in a corner, both physically and politically.

"More than enough to enable your organisation to step up several gears and give this country what it truly deserves." Marshall put down his glass, steepled his fingers, and stared across at his prey, chin resting on his thumbs.

"So where's this money coming from?" He was bitten, and Marshall knew it. The BDP had run out of funds – quite simply they could no longer afford to run any kind of political campaign.

"Oh, I have recourse to amounts that you could only dream of, and I'd say that you're in no position to be particular about the source."

The truth of that last statement was undeniable. Gerald Montgomery's death had released a vast amount of cash to the Organisation in 1992 and, as its current head, Marshall was in control of all disbursements.

Montgomery had taken over the engineering company which had been set up by his father, Frederick, after the end of the war, on the old man's death. Success had been spectacular and fast in the reconstruction years of the fifties, and the personal fortune which the man left had enabled continuance of his vision of the future. The Third Reich had been a wonderful dream for them all, soured by the megalomania into which the inner cabal had descended. As one of the senior army officers after the suicides which took the Nazi leadership away, he escaped to England along the route laid down by Martin Bormann, Hitler's private secretary. Bormann had seen the end coming, had fully understood the nature of what was in store for Germany in the aftermath of the holocaust, and had laid down plans to rejuvenate the better parts of the dream in another society.

The young Gerald had seized upon several opportunities to invest not just in the engineering company, but also in a portfolio of other enterprises in the 1970s when all about him were losing their way. Towards the end of that decade, the foreign funds into which he had ploughed surplus cash deposits had multiplied his initial capital many times. When the Dot-Com boom began in 1994 with the founding of Amazon, he was one of the first to recognise a gold-plated chance to increase his personal wealth far beyond the imaginings of his late father. With the peaking of the FTSE and the Dow Jones in December 1999 and January 2000, Montgomery jumped ship and cashed in all of his shares. By the time Boo.Com went bust in May 2000, he was in the clear.

This, then, was the source of the financial backing which Marshall was now offering to the beleaguered Robert Grafton. The silence between them had lasted for only a few moments, but Steve knew that he had the man well and truly on the hook. It was merely a matter of time. Grafton frowned; he was in a jam, and he did not relish the feeling.

"All right, let's say that I don't just walk away. I'd have to clear this with the party."

"Since when has the BDP taken democracy seriously?" Marshall laughed, but seeing the barman turn his head, stifled any further acts of humour. "Look. You know and I know that your party is on the brink of collapse.

Those results in the last round of local elections will be nothing more than a memory if you don't take what I'm offering."

"All right…" Grafton sighed; he was beaten. "What do we, that is I, have to do to benefit from this backing?"

"Nothing more than you are doing right now. The party's come a long way since 1982, and you've managed to tame the militants amongst your number. Look at the way that you and the committee have smartened yourselves up – you almost managed to unseat the Labour leader in Amber Valley, didn't you? What was the majority? Five after half a dozen recounts?"

Grafton smiled. That one really had been something of a surprise, and the sight of the man sitting on the stage at the count, head in hands and spectacles pushed back into his unkempt hair, had been a moment that he had savoured many times.

"Yeah, we almost tipped the council on its head that night, but we still only got two onto it."

"That'll change once you reorganise and start thinking big. I'll start with a donation of half a million, and we'll see where it goes from there, shall we?"

"Half a mil….?!"

"Quiet, you damn fool!" Marshall hissed. "That's exactly why you are where you are. The BDP's like a leaky bucket right now. You wouldn't believe how easy it was for me to dig up what I needed."

"Okay." Grafton was on the edge of his seat. "What next?"

"You call a meeting of the national committee and announce what I've said. No names mind - I need to keep my end of this under wraps, and if it gets out you'll find that the well's dried up. Show them a deposit slip from your bank, but make sure that no-one gets too close to it. Watch out for members leaving the meeting, and have them followed. They'll be the ones that you need to weed out, and I don't much care what methods you use, understand?"

Amid the clamour at the close of that meeting, Robert Grafton had indeed watched the three leaving quietly. He nodded to two of those on the raised platform, and the scene was set for the removal of the heads of the troublesome militant arm in one fell swoop. The Thames is a deep and secretive river, accustomed to holding onto anything deposited deeply enough into its murky arms. If anyone did manage to drag the three corpses out of the water, identification would be all but impossible by the time that the fish had taken their fill.

He shrugged; further information related to him during the clandestine encounter with this 'Steve' indicated a potential change in the political makeup of the British Parliament. With an election on the cards for 2005, the government had been the focus for a mounting tide of discontent, both within Westminster and the country as a whole. No mug, Grafton had been keeping an eye on events, but the depth of knowledge which his contact had revealed pointed in the direction of an opportunity which was not to be missed. Time would tell and, picking up his coat, he left the current meeting to ponder things further.

9

Christopher Morse came to a full stop and bent forwards, his lungs pumping fresh air down to aching legs. The sweat was pouring from him, and his running vest was drenched.

"Excellent! Excellent!" Maurice Coop strode over from the side of the running track with a stop watch in his hand. "Five minutes twenty, and you ran that last lap in sixty-seven."

Morse sat down on the track and looked up at the coach from between a curtain of rat tails which represented his hair. He was panting hard, and unable to pour forth any of the vituperation which he was feeling upon the man who had driven him so hard since his first steps inside Bartlesham. It is now the middle of July 2004, and close to the time which Ransome had set for the end of the former spy's drying out period. Progress, though patchy and unpredictable at first, had accelerated during the past two months – Morse was now in better shape than he had been for quite some time. The alcohol and drug dependency which had been dragging him towards an early death was now a thing of the past, and the mile which Coop had just timed was the pinnacle of his performance.

"Coop!" Morse finally coughed. "You nearly killed me there!"

"Nonsense!" He scoffed. "Would you *rather* be dead?"

"Isn't this what it's supposed to feel like?" He struggled to his feet, surprised that his legs were able to respond. The first time they tried this he had failed to reach the half-way point.

Steve Marshall had been standing some way off, Bernard Ransome at his side, observing the proceedings around the running track through a set of field glasses. He smiled and turned to the owner of the clinic.

"Is he ready?"

"Well…" Ransome exhaled a plume of smoke as he removed the briar from his lips, "… I shouldn't think that we could do any more. He's as fit as we can make him, and once we got him off the heroin and onto methadone it was fairly straightforward. Mind you, that step was a big one, and as long as you keep him away from temptation for the next three months or so, I would expect that his problems could be over. Has he got a job to keep his mind off the stuff?"

"Oh, I think that he's going to be far too busy to fall back into those kinds of traps."

"In that case he can leave today. Mr Coop's final ordeal for him was the test. That mile he just ran wasn't at all bad."

Morse had been through the mill during the period he had spent at Bartlesham. Coming off the heroin had left him with feelings of anxiety and depression which had been hard to control, even with the methadone substitute provided as part of the treatment. Nights of sleeplessness and sweating, and the nightmares which had been a part of his psychosis, left him a drained and unpredictable patient. Marshall was waiting, case in hand, as he emerged from the changing rooms.

"Are we done here? I don't think I could last another day under that animal Coop."

Close up, Marshall could see the old Christopher Morse, and yet there was a hardness to his demeanour which had been absent before he left MI5. His eyes now carried a steely look, and there was a set to his jaw which suggested he was no longer a man to be messed with. He would be one enormous asset for the plan which Steve had spent the intervening time perfecting.

"Yes. You're clean, and by the look of that last mile that Coop put you through, we could set up the job I have in mind next week."

"What if I said 'no'?" Morse met Marshall's stare, and for a moment it was two gunfighters eyeing each other up.

"What do you mean?" Marshall put down the case.

"Well, I'm clean, and thank you very much for that. I could simply walk away from this place, pick up the first car coming past, and you wouldn't see me for dust."

"Yeah; go ahead and see how far you'd get. Have you forgotten the trouble you caused us? You could have been on the wrong end of some pretty serious stuff back then. And what about this dead woman? Don't forget that you came to me on your hands and knees for help. Watkinson knows about that too, so yeah, go on, run away... if that's what you want to do."

Morse stood in silence for what seemed an age. He never knew what charges MI5 had lined up for him after the killing of Graham Poundall, and that Sword of Damocles was still hanging just above his head. The bravado had not worked – Marshall was too canny for that, and he ought to have known better. He capitulated.

"Okay, you got me." He smiled – it was a nervous one, and he had now shown his hand to the only man who could keep him out of trouble with the law. "Let's go."

The drive back from Buckinghamshire passed by largely in silence, punctuated by the odd instruction to the driver. The house where Morse's temporary stay had been arranged was in Kingston-upon-Thames, and the car pulled into Orchard Road towards the end of the afternoon. With a little extra security due to Morse's relative anonymity, the two of them sat down in the lounge and Marshall outlined the job he had lined up.

"We, the department, are going to infiltrate the British Democratic Party, and you are going to be the principal tool which we will use."

"The BDP?" Morse stiffened. "They're a pretty heavy lot from what I can make out."

"You've been out of circulation for a while; things have changed. They've managed to tame the militant arm, and Robert Grafton is going for a more, shall we say, subtle approach."

"Hmm, as house bricks they used to be. So, what have you got in mind?"

Marshall filled in the details of the meeting with Grafton, and the gathering at the BDP headquarters which he had managed to attend, quietly, in a back corner of the room. He had seen the signal that the leader had given to a pair of heavies, and had followed their progress to the pub where Mike Summers and his two cohorts had reconvened. There was no doubt in his mind that the seeds which he had planted in the man's mind as an incentive for the financial backing were about to bear fruit.

"I want you up in Derbyshire, and getting closely involved with the East Midlands branch where Summers was in control. You'll have to blend in quickly, and that'll mean learning the dialect so that no-one picks you out as a spy."

"I can do that - you know I can - but what about a job? I can't exist on nothing up there."

"Taken care of. Go and see this bloke." Marshall pulled a business card out of his wallet. "He's expecting you. I called him while I was waiting for you at the clinic."

"So, what am I doing?"

"You're a sales rep. Don't worry, it's a cover, and all the leads and information will be provided – there'll be no cold calling. Just do as he tells you and things will be fine."

"Is this guy in on the scheme?"

"No. He works for us, but knows nothing of what I want you to do, and it's vital that, from his point of view, you keep your nose clean. The rest of the plan will be carried out in your spare time, just as it would be if you really were a member of the party. There's also this." He gave Morse a folder. "It's your new identity. Learn it thoroughly, and fast. The guy I'm sending you to doesn't know who you really are. We're sticking with Tom Harriman as the name, but the background is very detailed."

"All right. Have you got a list of meeting places, or am I expected to figure *that* out for myself as well?"

"You find that out. Just make some appropriate noises, and try to fit in with whatever the locals do and say. I picked Summers out at a pub called the Midland in Longlea – that's close to the Nottinghamshire border. See if you can get in with their number; they're pretty anti-immigrant from what I recall."

"Tomorrow then?"

"Yes. Here's a train ticket from St Pancras to Nottingham Midland. The company on the card is based in Woodville, and we've already arranged somewhere for you to stay. I want reports on a regular basis, say every two or three days, but try to keep a low profile where I'm concerned."

"Is there any other background info?"

"No, you'll have to get that where you can, but I do have one bit of news. There was a sort of failed exposé that a TV documentary programme tried to run, and it centred on a corner shop in Longlea. They were keeping tabs on the local branch of the BDP and set up the business with some Asian family. The idea was to blow the local party open and show the residents what it was that they had in their midst."

"So, what went wrong?"

"It was a disaster. The BDP just sat and watched while the local community ran the family out of town. There was no party involvement, and CCTV footage just showed the neighbourhood kids stealing from the shop, and throwing stuff at the windows. Fertile ground for you to work in, eh?"

"Sounds like it. What about some funds to get me started?"

"Five hundred should be about right." Marshall pulled a wad of notes out of his inside pocket. "And you sign here for it." He dropped a paper before Morse. "My name's on this, and I don't want you going crazy – stay off the drugs, ok?"

"All right." Morse scowled. "Tightarse. What's the matter, don't you trust me?"

"Let me think… no. Get some sleep tonight. You have a very early start in the morning."

10

"So, how's our recalcitrant doing?" Watkinson was straight to the point with regard to MI5's use of the former operative, Christopher Morse.

Steve Marshall sat down and took the file he had prepared from the briefcase which he occasionally used. He slid it across the desk and gave his boss the customary few moments to peruse the contents.

"He's fit, and acutely aware of his somewhat exposed position. He's completely under our control, and has no alternative but to carry out the instructions that I've given him."

"Is he still capable of carrying out an assignment like this, bearing in mind what he's been through?"

"Yes. I saw him on his last day at the clinic; I was there for some hours, unobserved, and they've put him through a fair number of hoops. There's also a report from Bernard Ransome, the owner of the place, and it gives him a completely clean bill of health."

"The clinic don't..."

"No. They have absolutely no idea who he is, or who's paying the bill. All the invoices were settled in cash." Marshall smiled – it was always good to get one over on the boss.

"Good. Well, let's get down to the detail. Tell me precisely how you plan to get inside the BDP, and how we're going to stop them causing the kind of trouble that the National Front used to get involved in."

Marshall took his boss on a step-by-step journey through the entire scenario which he had set for Morse. Watkinson remained stone-faced throughout, and asked no more than a handful of questions. Those which were posed had ready answers produced immediately from a separate dossier that Steve had built up during the time Morse had spent at Bartlesham. The atmosphere during the meeting had changed from that which Marshall was accustomed to, and it made him uneasy. Watkinson was an extremely hard character to read when he so chose; Steve had never managed to get behind the man's façade if he decided to shut up shop, and that is precisely what appeared to have happened now. As he rose to leave and head for the door, he had the strangest feeling that George was watching his every move.

Steve Marshall's absence from Thames House for a few weeks had given George Watkinson time to think alone and undisturbed. Since the action against the Organisation in 1992 had come to what many had regarded as a close, there had been little to arouse the suspicion of the security services in general. However, on a more personal front, things had just seemed to have fallen too neatly into place. He had been over and over the events of that year many times, and something gnawed at the back of his mind. He had little doubt that Montgomery had been at the forefront of the plot, and that Marcus Timson had presented its acceptable face in the higher echelons of Whitehall. He was certain that the roots of fascism still lay dormant just beneath the surface, and that there lurked in the shadows another figure, as yet unidentified, ready and able to light the fire once more.

"Shirley." He pressed a button on his telephone.

"Yes, Mr Watkinson."

"Find Barry Newman and ask him to step into my office, please."

"Right away, sir."

This was going to need considerable care, and would be the first real test of Newman's capabilities. Digging around in an outsider's business was one thing – investigating the confidential affairs of another member of the department was something else altogether. The knock at the door brought the department's latest recruit into Watkinson's private office. He was in shirtsleeves rolled up to the elbow – a trait which had been remarked upon by several colleagues. Watkinson smiled to himself; the young man's willingness to get stuck in to anything which came along stood in stark contrast to one or two others in the service whose futures were by no means secure.

"Barry. Take a seat. I have a job which requires some of those skills of yours which we talked about a while back."

"Thank you, sir. What exactly do you want?" He leaned forward, eyes narrowed; he was becoming accustomed to Watkinson's sometimes cryptic manner of speaking.

"Well now, I have a piece of information which has come to me from a reliable source, and I need you to dig around to see where it leads." He slid a piece of paper across the desk.

"Is this all?" Newman turned the slip over and frowned. "Just a number?" It was ragged at the bottom edge, and had obviously been torn from a larger piece of paper.

"Yes. It arrived on my desk yesterday. It was in the pocket of a man pulled out of the Thames at Richmond Lock at low tide early in the morning."

"How do we know…?"

"Barry, we're privy to a lot of information which tends to bypass the normal channels, and this particular one has yet to see the light of day at New Scotland Yard." Watkinson's look over the top of his spectacles told Newman all that he needed.

"I see. So, what is it that you want?"

"Everything that you can dig up. I've no idea at the moment what's involved, but from what I already know about you, and the results which came from your induction, I wouldn't think it presents too much of a problem."

"No, sir. Timescale?"

"Immediate, if not sooner." He smiled and Newman rose to leave. "Make sure that you report back to no-one but me, please."

"Of course."

Back at his desk, Barry Newman stared at the paper given to him by Watkinson. The number was indeed the only thing upon it, but other tests may reveal further information not visible to the naked eye. Copying it first, he took it down to the labs on the floor below; back at his computer, he logged on and began his search.

Steve Marshall thought long and hard about the meeting which had just taken place, and spent the rest of the day going back over the events surrounding the chase for the files brought back from Germany by Roger Fretwell at the end of WWII. Whilst he was as sure as he could be that there had been nothing which could be traced back to him, it was always possible that Watkinson had managed, in the intervening period, to elicit information from a source which he had not anticipated. He had been pacing up and down his office, when the shrill tone of a mobile phone brought him back to the present.

Day of the Phoenix

"Steve, it's Beverley. Are you free this weekend?"

Beverley Drake. She had slipped his mind since he had arrived back in the capital, and he had quite forgotten their reconciliation up in Derbyshire. His trip up there had not anticipated her, or some of the things which she revealed to him – time to tread carefully.

"Oh, hello Beverley. Look, I'm sorry that I haven't been in touch. Things have been extremely busy down here recently." He tried to sound conciliatory.

"I know. Sandra told me about your work for the Department of Work and Pensions. It must be busy with the Autumn financial statements coming out soon. I wondered if you had some spare time; there are one or two things that I think you should know, and I don't feel like talking about them over the phone."

This caught him wrong-footed, and he struggled for an immediate reply. Stalling whilst attempting to side-track her, he lost the initiative and found himself cornered.

"Well, I suppose I could move things around a little. It's not as if there are other people to take into account. What time are you coming down here?" He knew right then that she would already have bought the ticket.

"Friday night. I'm arriving at St Pancras at around a quarter past eight. Make sure you're not late; have to rush now, 'bye!"

She was gone. Beverley Drake had let slip a more than casual allegiance to the BDP when they were in Nottingham, and he had wondered at the time whether to involve her in his future plans. That had been forgotten in the return south and Chris Morse's successful trip to Bartlesham. Perhaps this was now the chance to explore the possibility a little further. Watkinson's change of demeanour was beginning to persuade him to speed up the process of taking control of the BDP, and Beverley could well be an able ally.

Not wishing to cross paths again with his boss today, Steve rang his secretary, Shirley.

"Hello, Steve. What can I do for you?" Cheerful as always, she was worth her weight in gold.

"Hi, Shirley. Look, don't want to disturb the boss, but I have to go out for the rest of the day. Could you let him know, please?"

"Of course I will." She said. "See you tomorrow."

57

Marshall was not to know it right then, but Watkinson had already set in motion the wheels which would start to see the unravelling of his plans. He was nothing if not cautious, but now was not the time to allow the grass to grow beneath the department's feet. He too was acutely aware of an impending general election which Marshall had mentioned to Robert Grafton, but his sources told a story of deepening rifts for Labour, both within Parliament and at constituency level. Support for the government had been wavering for a while, but a series of unpopular policies were now beginning to undermine the authority which it had enjoyed since successive landslide victories in 1997 and 2001. He frowned – surely the British public would not fall for the kind of government which beset the Germans in the 1930s.

11

Christopher Morse paused at the gates to the light engineering firm which was to be his cover for the period of the attempt to infiltrate the local branch of the BDP. It was not much to look at, and the entire area was an industrial backwater in terminal decline. Nevertheless, it was within easy reach of the rented accommodation in Woodville and less than four miles from the link to the M1 motorway. Setting the alarm on the rented Focus, he strode across the small car park and entered the reception area where he was met by a woman in her late twenties.

"Can I help you?" She smiled – it was a plastic one, right off the training school shelf.

"I have an appointment with David Greenwood. My name's Tom Harriman, and he's expecting me."

David Greenwood was the owner and chairman of Chromex. In his late fifties, he had established the company in the mid-seventies when the rest of the UK manufacturing sector seemed to be in free-fall. It had grown from small beginnings in Woodville, and had been at the present site since 1984, when the textile company occupying it had gone into liquidation. The smile on his face belied a steel in his nature – he was a businessman first, and a covert MI5 resource second.

"Mr Harriman. Glad you could make it; weather's not been too kind of late. Let's go to my office." He turned to the receptionist. "Tea, Cheryl." There was no 'please'.

Greenwood's office was spartan, overlooking the car park and the A610 feeder road which led to the M1. By the constant vibration from below it was clear to Morse that the company was busy, and the drone of machinery was punctuated by a cacophony of voices as the work progressed. Greenwood picked up on the slight change in his manner.

"Aye, we're busy, and there's not many that can say that around here right now. Mr Marshall says you need a job for a few months while you do some work for him. That's fine by me, 'cos it's not Chromex that'll be paying your wages. I'll just fire you in around three months when you don't come up to scratch."

He smiled again, and Morse knew instinctively that this was not a man in whom he could place much in the way of trust. He smiled back.

"What are the duties?"

"You'll be on the road. This…" He shoved a folder across the table, "…is a list of the customers I want you to visit. They're all long-established, and shouldn't cause you any problems. Mr Marshall fill you in on what we do, did he?"

"Yes, and my dad was an engineer, so I sort of know my way around the trade."

"Good. You'll be using your own transport." He nodded across the car park. "No sense in giving you a company car, seeing as how you won't be hanging around long. Cover the customers, and fill out the appointment sheets in the folder. What you do outside of that is your own business. I haven't a clue why you're up here, and quite honestly I don't care. All right?"

The job looked simple enough and, right at the outset, Morse could see that there would be plenty of time for carrying out the assignment that Marshall had set for him. The first call was in Nottingham, on the other side of the River Trent, and along Poulton Drive. The meeting lasted about an hour, and he left the premises looking for a place to eat. Pulling on to the Victoria Embankment, Morse headed for the Trent Bridge Inn and a place to listen to local gossip. He didn't have long to wait.

Finishing off the ploughman's he had bought, Chris went to the bar for a fresh drink, and quickly latched onto a conversation between the barman and another customer.

"Swine went and fired us." The speaker was a thickset man in his late forties, with tattoos along both arms.

"What, all of you?" The barman was obviously familiar with the situation.

"Too right. Soon as we asked for better conditions, he's off down the job centre like a whippet and sets on a gang of immigrants!" He swallowed the remainder of his beer and pointed the empty glass at the tap for a refill.

"He can't do that, can he? What about the union?"

"Union? That bunch of…" He bit his tongue. "About as much use as a chocolate fireguard. Told us we should have come and talked to them first. Useless prats; all they *do* is talk. Time we stopped all these foreigners coming over here, nickin' our jobs."

The conversation progressed along these lines for a further quarter of an hour, until Morse caught the attention of the two parties involved. There was a momentary silence, and the customer turned to his left, bringing them eye to eye.

"Something you want, mate?" The look was not friendly.

"I was just interested in what you'd been saying." Chris shifted on the stool where he had taken up position. "My dad got on the wrong end of a similar situation, and it cost him his job. Drove mum mad, him being at home all day. Ended up topping himself."

This was enough to draw Morse further into the session, and by the time he left the pub details of the local branch of the BDP had been supplied to him by the barman, along with an offer to introduce him to the organiser. An address in Woodville, scribbled on a piece of paper, had him heading that way the following evening.

The house on Robin Hood Close is an anonymous three bedroom semi in a cul-de-sac. It was used as a staging point-cum-meeting place for the local BDP activists, and had remained free of the more rowdy elements of the party. The local residents were completely unaware of the level of fascism festering right beneath their noses. Morse knocked at the door to be greeted by Beverley Drake; he was, at that time, unaware of any link back to Steve Marshall.

"Yes? Can I help you?" She looked beyond him, her eyes scanning for evidence of possible media coverage.

"My name's Tom Harriman, and I was given this address by two guys in a Nottingham pub." He handed her the note.

"Brian Potter. I recognise his handwriting. Come on in." She closed the door and led him into a roomy lounge where several other people were gathered.

After brief introductions, Morse took a seat and listened carefully to what was being said. The conversation was of a different type to that at the Trent Bridge Inn, and the general level of the debate centred more around political than personal goals. It was clear that this group was highly efficient and committed to subtle background operations, rather than the open conflict which had dogged much of the organisation's early days. He was soon given clear evidence of the level of awareness in the group. Beverley took him to one side in the kitchen.

"We're not all bully-boys, you see. There's a lot more to this than simply going round throwing bottles at groups of immigrants."

"I can see that now, but what can we do… really?" He played the innocent card, baiting for more information.

"Watch and wait. There was a documentary on TV a while back, and they tried to expose what they thought was a militant BDP cell operating in Longlea. A corner shop had been set up with a Pakistani family running it, and the documentary team believed that we'd take action to run them out of town."

"So, what *did* you do?" Morse sat down at the table, sensing that this was to be longer than a mere chat.

"Nothing. We knew what was going on; it was so simple really. They had a camera team set up in a Transit van parked in the pub yard opposite the shop, and it ran day and night trying to catch us out." She shook her head and laughed. "We used to sit in the bar at the Midland Hotel and watch. Mike Summers was the group leader…" Her voice dropped slightly "… but he seems to have gone missing now."

"So, what happened then?"

"What really freaked the lot of them out was that it was the locals who were chucking the eggs and brick ends. It was the kids stealing from the shop. The family inside had taken to wearing their national dress when things stayed quiet for the first week or so, but when banners appeared in the shop saying 'I Love Pakistan', well, the yobs went to town. It wasn't long after that that they upped sticks and left."

Morse listened intently to the rest of the episode, and by the end of the evening was convinced that there was enough happening in the locality to enable him to ease his way into the party structure. Once back at his rented accommodation he set about compiling the first of his reports back to Steve Marshall, completely unaware that Beverley Drake was formulating some plans of her own.

12

With Morse now firmly established in the Midlands and reporting back on a regular basis, Marshall was feeling, on that score at least, relatively easy. The situation with Watkinson was quite another matter however, and the call from Beverley Drake, out of the blue, had caught him cold. It was now the Friday evening of her arrival and some three months after Morse's induction into the BDP. Despite David Greenwood's intention to dispense with his new sales rep's services, Marshall had persuaded him to hold off on the action; agreement had been reached for a further period. Chris, it would seem, was a better salesman than either of them had anticipated.

"Hello there." Steve spun around to see the smile which had melted him back in Derbyshire.

He had arrived at St Pancras in plenty of time to meet the train, and was mildly annoyed that she had caught him unawares for the second time – she had obviously taken an earlier one.

"Beverley. Good to see you again." He leaned forwards to kiss her, and was surprised when she, instead, reached for her case. It was a momentary lapse on her part, but for an instant Marshall was wrong-footed.

"I've booked in at the Novotel." She smiled and returned his embraces. "Shall we have something to eat?" Her voice had a business-like edge, and Steve looked deeply into her eyes.

"Suits me." His earlier misgivings began to fade somewhat, but he felt that there was a little more to Beverley's trip than she was presently letting on. He did not have long to wait.

Throughout their meal, she was full of the issues which had been raised at the Wetherspoons in Nottingham. It was becoming apparent that the ground had been prepared to approach him on a formal basis in his role as a civil servant.

"We, that is, the party, need people on the inside of Whitehall. We have to know what's going on within Westminster. I'm going out on a limb here – are you coming on board?"

There was a silence whilst Marshall took in what had been said to him. He had believed that he had been in control up in Derbyshire, but here she was wresting the situation away from him, and with a confidence which he had not seen before. The ace in his hand was the fact that she had no idea of his real intent – he decided to play along.

"So, what happened up there; it was all a sham?"

"Steve…" She smiled at his feigned surprise, "… I missed you, I really did, and my life had changed. It was so good to see you again, and I did wonder whether we could put it all behind us and start over…"

"So, why not?" Marshall continued the ruse - she was swallowing it.

"I didn't say that we couldn't. All those feelings have come back again, and this time I need to be sure that you won't walk away and leave me once more."

"So, you're just going to use me to find out if *you* still feel the same? Is that all I am now?" God, but he was good at this. Her reply was immediate; with the meal finished, she took his hand and they walked to the reception desk where she collected her key.

"Would I be doing this…" she whispered, "… if I wasn't serious about us?" They walked to the lifts, and ten minutes later were in each other's arms in the privacy of her room.

She aroused in him passions which had lain dormant for so long that he hardly knew that they still existed. A career in MI5 had taken up almost all of his spare time, and weekends were carbon copies of his normal working day. This was something quite different, and as they lay there afterwards he questioned once more his reasons for leaving her all those years ago. Beverley, however, was not one to be easily deflected from what was the second of her reasons for making the journey. She sat up in bed, leaned across towards him and stroked his hair.

"Look…" Her voice was soft, like velvet, and almost a whisper, "… the party needs a springboard, and any inside information is going to be vital at the next set of local elections. If we do well there, the next step will be a full scale campaign on Westminster. Now, are you with us? You seemed to be leaning that way in Nottingham."

"I'll have to think about it. You can't expect me to make a snap decision just because you come down here with some pre-planned strategy." He felt nettled at the sudden return to business.

"How long? I'm not staying down here forever."

"Twenty-four hours."

"All right. Tomorrow evening, back here, about eight o'clock." They kissed again, and his mind was whirling with the sensations of her, her body, and the perfume that she wore.

It was true that Marshall did feel used – he was human after all. The more he now thought about his earlier plans for resurrecting their relationship on a permanent basis, the more it made sense to go along with what Beverley wanted. This might also have the effect of getting Watkinson off his back – he had been getting too curious recently, and a plan to take on the BDP on two fronts could put Steve back where he belonged, temporarily at least.

"And you think that you can rely on the woman?" Watkinson stared at Marshall over the tops of his spectacles.

"Rely yes; trust… I'm not entirely certain at this point." Marshall decided to conceal the previous relationship. "She and the party will do all that they can to progress. If that means using personal contacts with a civil servant, me, then she'll do it without a flicker of conscience."

"You're sure that she knows nothing of your real job?"

"Absolutely. My other friends up in Derbyshire believe that I'm in the Department of Work and Pensions. She'll have picked it up from them. There's no reason for any of them to think otherwise."

"And Morse?"

"He'll be up there for another three months or thereabouts. He's been accepted as part of the local branch, and I'm getting regular reports on what they're doing. We could end up with a two-pronged strategy. I hadn't expected that."

"All right. That's good work, Steve. You're meeting her again tomorrow?"

"That's right, and I'm going to fall in with their plans. We need some disinformation to feed to them. Can I leave that to you?"

"Yes. I'll see the Cabinet Secretary later today."

Watkinson watched the retreating form of his number two, and started to wonder, faintly, whether he had misjudged the situation. Marshall was a very able deputy, and the security service was, by its very nature, clandestine. Was he in danger of misreading the man and reacting wrongly to his instincts? The shooting of Gerald Montgomery had looked like a protective act; the woman in his grasp was certainly in danger, and the man had been at the heart of the failed assassination attempt in Sussex. Left unchecked, Montgomery may well have taken Watkinson as his next target. Marshall had prevented that from happening... He shook his head – there would be time to look again at the whole scenario; for now it was important to prepare the ground for derailing an extremist party before it gained too much credibility.

Beverley Drake cursed. She had been trying to reach Mike Summers, but all calls to his mobile had gone unanswered. Where *was* the man? She couldn't run the East Midlands area alone, and didn't have his level of contacts within the party. He had been at the committee meeting called by Robert Grafton (she knew that much) but no-one had heard from him since. She didn't like what she was about to do - it would be going behind his back - but there did not appear to be an alternative. She punched in a number to her mobile.

"British Democratic Party, how may I direct your call?" The voice was polite, efficient, and nothing like the public's impression.

"Robert Grafton, please."

"Who shall I say is calling?"

"Beverley Drake, East Midlands."

"Hold the line, please."

Beverley had met the head of the party, briefly, at a fund raiser in the Derbyshire village of Holtby two years earlier. The event was planned as an annual gathering on the property of a local farmer sympathetic to party ideals. Opposition in the area had been vociferous and, on one occasion in Hakeham, violent. Grafton had called time out on the following year's plan, and moved it to a location in the West Midlands.

"Beverley, what a pleasant surprise. How are things in Derbyshire?"

The man either had an amazing memory, or he was stalling for more information – she could not make up her mind which.

"Mr Grafton…"

"Robert… please."

"Robert…" She smiled; he was good. "… there's a matter that I need to discuss with you, and I can't really do that over the telephone. Would you have some free time today?"

"Can you come over now? You know where we are, don't you?"

"Yes, I'm in London for a day or so. I can get a cab. I'll be there in an hour."

The sixteen mile journey across the city took Beverley Drake from Islington, across the Thames at Greenwich and down the A2 towards Bexley. The journey gave her more time to think. Summers' militant policies were well known to all at the local branch, but he had personally shied away from actual physical action. History had taught them all the benefits of using the ballot box as a means of achieving their ends, but it had also shown them the way not to go once that aim was achieved. Britain in the twenty-first century was a world away from Germany in the 1930s, and the British people had long memories.

"Miss Drake? Come with me, please. Mr Grafton is waiting for you." The receptionist, a woman in her forties, accompanied Beverley up the stairs and into a small lounge area. "Help yourself to tea or coffee."

Beverley was standing with her coffee, looking out of the first floor window of a former wine bar onto Bexley High Street when Robert Grafton greeted her from the other side of the room.

"Nice to see you, Beverley. Shall we sit by the fire?" He was all smiles, and clearly did remember her from their previous meeting. "What can I do for you?"

"It's more what I, that is, we, in the East Midlands, can do for the party."

"Just what I like to hear! Didn't Kennedy say something remarkably similar? Come on, out with it, you've got me intrigued now."

She ran the scenario before him of using a civil service contact, Steve Marshall, as a means of getting inside the corridors of power, and giving the party a first-hand view of what was happening. He leaned forwards, the smile temporarily gone from his face. What she was proposing was something which the national party had never had access to, and the thought of an inside track at that level was of more than a passing interest.

"Would he be reliable?"

"I have him around my little finger." She smiled. "He'll do pretty much anything that I ask."

"You're a proper little Mata Hari, aren't you? When are you seeing him again?"

"Tomorrow. He's thinking over what I said to him for twenty-four hours, but I'm certain he'll fall in with us."

"All right, but let's not get in over our heads. I'd hate this to come out just before the next local elections." Grafton rose.

"There was just one more thing." This was ground of a much weaker status, and she knew she had to tread carefully.

"Okay. What is it?" He resumed his seat, and the smile magically reappeared.

"One of our members has vanished – actually it's our chairman, Mike Summers. He was down here a while back, but I can't seem to raise him now."

"I see." His face was full of concern. "I remember him at a recent meeting, but at the end he left with two other guys, and I didn't see him again. What's his mobile number?"

This, of course, was all for show. Mike Summers and his two colleagues had been disposed of shortly after the meeting by the heavies sent to follow them. They would lie undisturbed in separate locations at the bottom of the Thames, weighted down to ensure little chance of discovery. All items of identification removed, there was little likelihood of their being traced back to him.

"See what I mean?" She pointed at Grafton's phone. "No answer. What now?"

"Well, short of putting a trace on his calls, I'm not sure what we *can* do. The BDP don't exactly have much clout with the establishment, as you well know. Look, I'll ask around and check if anyone's been in touch down here. He may simply be taking a break."

Whilst this was not what Beverley Drake had expected, she had to concede that it was unlikely that anyone outside of the party would be too interested in the whereabouts of one of its more vociferous members. Thanking Robert Grafton for his time, she sighed and made her way out of the premises and back to her hotel. The only remaining task now was her meeting with Steve Marshall, but a chance meeting with another old acquaintance was to delay her.

For Robert Grafton, this had been a disturbing and quite unexpected development. Replacing Summers in the East Midlands would be easy enough, and the man's militant style was not something that was likely to appeal to the broader British public when it came to elections. However, to find someone taking the time and trouble to seek him out was a concern. Beverley Drake was no fool, and it might not take her too long to work out what had happened. Those kinds of ripples on the water were the last thing that he needed right now; with the promise of finance from a hitherto unknown source, it would be so easy to derail a plan which had originally looked doomed to failure for lack of funds. Whilst he was reluctant to lose committee members of any status, should her enquiries become more intrusive she would have to go the same way as her friend. Omelettes and eggs – it was always the same.

Marshall looked at his watch for the umpteenth time. Eight o'clock she had said, and it was now eight forty-five. He checked at the Novotel reception desk.

"Miss Drake's key is right here, sir. She went out this morning, and I don't think we've seen her since then." The clerk was suitably sympathetic, but could do nothing else.

He gave her another fifteen minutes, and then departed. Leaving a note at the desk was, he thought, not the best idea if someone else were to be involved. There were too many irons in the fire at the moment to risk exposure in another operation. He put this one down as a missed opportunity and returned to Thames House.

The buzzing of the 'new' phone in his pocket drew Marshall's attention from the file before him, and the caller display on the non-contract device had him smiling wryly. He sat there, momentarily, shaking his head and pondering his next response.

"I was there – where were you?" The statement to Beverley Drake was rather flat and impersonal.

"Look, Steve, I'm really sorry – I just got caught up." She sounded sincere... almost.

"Well, you seemed to think a meeting was important." He leaned back in his chair. "Perhaps it wasn't after all."

Marshall played her like a fish on a line for a while, knowing that she would give ground rather than let the opportunity of an inside track at Whitehall slip away. In the end she was almost begging for forgiveness.

"So... are you in or out?" The question, when it came, had a hesitant edge.

Steve thought carefully, making her wait for the decision. He was sure that there was a sigh of relief at his answer.

"All right." He leaned forward. "I'll do it."

13

The end of the year was marked by a sudden worsening of the weather, and the snowfalls which had blighted the eastern areas of the UK now found their way to the capital. The three months leading up to the New Year period had not been the best that George Watkinson could remember. He had given Barry Newman free rein on the investigation which he had set for the new recruit, and with a thickening dossier now before him, he found himself reading some very unfamiliar terms. He pressed a button on his telephone.

"Yes, Mr Watkinson."

"Shirley, could you find Barry Newman and tell him to report to my office, please?"

"Right away, sir."

There was no doubting the thoroughness of Newman's work, and the trail of his logic was impeccable. Nevertheless, there was a distinct trace of the IT specialist about the young man, and some interpretation would be needed if Watkinson were to see the wood beyond the trees. The knock on the door brought, he hoped, a cure for the headache which the papers were beginning to cause.

"Barry." He forced a smile. "Come in; take a seat."

Barry Newman looked at the dossier which his boss had been attempting to read, and frowned. He was still slightly uncertain of the man's demeanour, and the blank expression which had returned following the greeting had him more than a little worried. Watkinson picked up on it with his customary speed.

"No need for concern. This is a good piece of work; trouble is I need an interpreter. I think you'd better take me through it, step by step."

"Yes, sir." Newman pulled his chair forwards. "Well, the number itself didn't give me much of a clue, even though I tried everything I could think of on Google and a number of other internet search engines."

"Let me guess. You have other resources at your fingertips… right?"

"Something like that, yes. The length of the numerical string could have been almost anything, but once I started down the road of financial institutions, one or two things started to slot into place."

"All right, you have my undivided attention." Watkinson leaned forward across his desk. "Where's this going?"

"Some of the software I use isn't exactly…" Barry pursed his lips, "… off the shelf if you see what I mean."

Watkinson nodded and smiled inwardly. There were things about this young man which took him back to his own early days with the agency. Newman continued.

"I started inserting national codes to the front of the set of digits. They're freely available on all of the banking websites, but without a perfect match they're useless. However, I wrote an algorithm to search all of the country codes in conjunction with the numbers, and I got a hit. It's a banking IBAN number."

"And presumably this is the part of the story where I cover my ears and pretend that I can't hear what you say."

"That's right. The program hacks into all the major banks across the world looking for this particular set of characters, and once I got past the firewalls and encryption codes it was easy."

"So, where *is* the bank?"

"Switzerland, sir. It's a relatively small provincial bank called Thunervolksbank AG."

"And the account?"

"Well, that's where the trail goes a little lukewarm, and I'm still working on picking up the breadcrumbs which will lead me back to a source in the UK. I assume that *is* what you were hoping for from the start?"

"As I said…" Watkinson resumed his inscrutable demeanour, "… it's better that you don't have that information. I don't want to influence your search in any way. How far have you got?"

"Well, this is where the more technical stuff comes in, and I'm still running the program in the background of a number of servers across the globe. There are funds in the Swiss account, but they move in and out of it on an irregular basis, so there's no pattern. The amounts vary – some are large, some are quite small."

"You're not being monitored by the banks, are you?"

"No, sir. The program mimics those within the suites on each of the host servers, so the internal security systems aren't alerted. I've tracked a number of transactions to some common offshore locations, though, and that's where I'm now concentrating all my efforts. If the funds are finding their way back into the UK, they'll all end up in the same place eventually."

"So, where are these offshore accounts?"

"The usual places as far as we're concerned. The Cayman Islands, Bermuda, Liechtenstein, Monaco; anywhere that UK banking authorities can't properly monitor."

"But we can."

"Yes, sir. Well, that is… I can." He smiled, confident now that he was on solid ground as far as Watkinson was concerned.

"How long, then, before you have something conclusive?"

"Probably the next couple of days, maybe a little longer. I need to wind the program down properly to make certain that I don't leave any loose ends."

Newman had been very careful not to raise the expectations of his boss to a level where it would be difficult to manoeuvre if he made any errors. His cyber trail had led him across the world's banking system, and had indeed included all of the locations which he had mentioned. What it had not yet told him was the name, or names, attached to the accounts involved, and a new phase of hacking would be required to drill down to that level of confidentiality. His skills in the art of programming had been honed since his early teens, and he had yet to encounter a database which could not be cracked; it was merely a matter of time and patience. These qualities he had in abundance, but Watkinson did not – results were needed quickly and Barry was not privy to the reasons why. He looked at his watch; another late night was on the cards.

Sitting at his computer some hours, innumerable coffees, and a variety of sandwiches containing curious fillings later, he was alerted to the plethora of screens which were attached to his CPU by a flurry of activity on the programs which he had been running. He looked involuntarily at his watch – 1am. It had been four-thirty when he left Watkinson's office to instigate the latest round of hacks which he had set up into the bank accounts. In his haste, the coffee cup was sent flying, and the curses issued met with an unexpected reproof.

"This is what comes of late-night working, Barry."

Watkinson had approached unheard – an ability perfected over many years, and to the detriment of a number of staff no longer with the agency.

"Sir? I didn't hear you come in. Is there something you need?"

"Just being nosey." He nodded towards the screens. "Looks like you might have struck gold."

"I think so, sir." Newman smiled. His boss was obviously not as naïve with computers as he had believed.

"So, what's going on?"

Barry frowned at the data spewing forth across the twenty-four inch displays, and shook his head in amazement.

"Briefly, sir, these are all accounts controlled by the BDP and seem to generate all of their funding needs. Here…" he pointed at one screen, "… are a number of currency deals through a group of offshore banks, and there…" at another, "… a stack of options across all the world's stock markets. They're all high risk and the returns are considerable."

"And this means what?" Watkinson had his spectacles on and was staring intently over the young man's shoulder.

"Well, if you look here…" he pointed at a third screen, "… this is the controlling account in the Cayman Islands for the cash flows. At this point, some six months ago, the funding took a nosedive, and it seems to have been the result of a single transaction which went pear-shaped. It's almost as if someone else stuck their finger into the plan and got it burned. The funds held at another bank, the Chase Manhattan in New York, had suddenly doubled, were transferred out to a provincial branch of the Credit Suisse, and then simply vanished. The BDP appear to have a very serious cash flow problem."

"Hmm. Suddenly makes them a prime target for the Organisation."

"Sir?" Newman frowned.

"I think, Barry, that it's time to bring you fully up to speed on exactly what it is that's been going on."

Watkinson sat down at Newman's side and, over the course of the next hour, gave him a fairly detailed rundown of the events of 1992 and the chase for the hidden Nazi files which had almost brought the political structure of Britain to its knees. At the end of the monologue, Newman sat bewildered at the facts which his boss had revealed.

"So, someone within Thames House was working for the other side." It was a statement rather than a question, and Watkinson looked long and hard into the eyes of his young recruit before speaking again.

"It's my opinion that, although we all believed the Organisation to have been dismantled, certain elements of it escaped capture, and that we still have a source amongst our number working at the very same plan which existed back then."

"Any ideas who it might be?"

"None." As far as it went this was the truth, and George had spent many hours pondering the subject without coming to any firm conclusions. "Suffice it to say that if what you've turned up is true, the BDP needs a substantial injection of funds if it's to retain its credibility in political circles. Don't misunderstand, their aims sicken me; however, they are a properly constituted political organisation operating freely within a democratic society."

"So, the funding?" Newman's eyed narrowed.

"Let's just say that I know where the Organisation obtained much of its finance. Its aims, however, took a body blow, and it had to regroup. We're almost thirteen years down the line – thirteen years of a vast amount of cash lying dormant… somewhere. It's been gathering interest all of that time, and now just may have the kind of outlet which the Organisation needs to fulfil its aims."

"A dictatorship?"

"Precisely, and just the kind which brought Germany to its knees in 1945. This time, however, there'll be a far more subtle outcome and we need to be ready to counter it."

"So, I need to find out where the Organisation finances are going." Newman paused momentarily. "I'll run the same programs I've been using on the BDP."

"Good. If we can show a link between them, it might be enough to blow the whole thing wide open and scupper any plans the BDP have. Get back to me as soon as you have anything."

14

The engineering company run by Gerald Montgomery in the West Midlands had survived his demise in 1992, and was currently operating successfully in an otherwise sluggish regional economy. It was the location chosen by Marshall for rallying the Organisation hierarchy which had been resurrected at the cottage on Tewkesbury's St. Marys Lane. Those assembled were the very same fresh-faced and enthusiastic individuals. He looked into the eyes of each one and saw an identical fervour which had fuelled his own desire back then. That had been before the darker aims of the group had taken a hold. It was now all about power; power to control, to influence others and events, and, above everything else, an all-consuming drive to rule. There was a hushed feel to the room – the very same room from which Montgomery had made his ill-fated flight to Nottingham and his death; a death meted out to him by Steve Marshall himself.

"You have before you details of where we're going over the coming four years. I trust you've all read the document."

Heads nodded and all eyes focused sharply on Marshall. His presence, almost messianic in its projection, held them in an awed silence. He continued.

"Very well. Anything said at this meeting should be relayed back down to each cell in the Organisation's structure. There must be no loose ends this time, no-one taking matters into his or her own hands. The mistakes of 1992 will not be allowed to derail us for a second time. You all have certain tasks to perform and, make no mistake, failure will be treated without mercy."

There was a hushed murmur around the room as glances were exchanged. Marshall was quick to dispel it.

"If there was a time for anyone to doubt their commitment, this is it."

"Mr Marshall." The voice was that of a blond haired, blue eyed man in his mid-thirties. "I think I can speak for all of us that there are no doubts as to the direction in which we are moving. It's simply a measure of the trust that we all place in you and the rest of the leadership which drives us on."

"Good, because this is the point of no return. Our aim is to hijack the British Democratic Party, gain a foothold in Parliament, and take control of Britain. Once there, society will be transformed on a scale not seen since the end of the Second World War."

"What will happen to their leadership?" A woman of similar age and appearance. Marshall looked around the table – it had not occurred to him until this very moment that all represented what the Nazis regarded as the ultimate in Aryan supremacy.

"They'll be given a choice. Join forces with us and reap the benefits or suffer the consequence of anyone else opposing our wishes. Look at it this way; they're broke and we have money. They have policies which are broadly similar to our own, and their aims are almost identical – almost."

"The Jews?" The woman again.

"There'll be no second Holocaust. The Jewish community is vital to the well-being of the British economy, and this is a factor which the Third Reich completely failed to understand. It proved to be its downfall."

"What about the timing?" Another voice from the far end of the table, confidence now growing with each question posed.

"There's a general election coming and we need to be ready. This government is becoming increasingly unpopular, and, with our backing, the BDP will feed upon the fears of the British electorate." Marshall ticked off the policies on the fingers on one hand. "Immigration, policing, defence, the budget deficit, employment – just five areas where politicians have let them down consistently since they assumed power. The BDP will offer an alternative strategy which will put this country at the forefront of Europe within ten years."

"Have they agreed to it?"

"The BDP?" Marshall smiled. "They don't even know yet, but they will, and without our funding they'll have nowhere to go. Their leader, Robert Grafton, is already drooling at the sort of finance which we can provide. Carefully played, he won't know what's hit the party until it's too late. "

"What if something goes wrong?" Yet another member of the gathering. "I mean, it did in 1992, Montgomery, Timson, and Mason all died. What if something happens to you?"

Marshall had not anticipated this level of intensity from his audience and was, for the moment, caught somewhat flat-footed. His quick-thinking rescued the situation, but it required the revealing of a part of his planning that he would rather have kept under wraps. However, the question had been posed, and now was not the time for prevarication.

"In that eventuality there are a number of others at the top of the Organisation, one of whom will step in and assume command. Our structure dictates that the fewer who know their names, the better it is for all. Once we take control everything will become clear, but for now rest assured that nothing will be allowed to stand in the way of our success. That much, at least, we learned from the events of 1992."

This appeared to quell any fears which may have been lurking beneath the surface, and the meeting broke up. Marshall watched them all as they left the car park outside the factory. Their fervour was not in doubt, and the Organisation's entire future now rested upon the shoulders of them and their like. His peers, at the pinnacle of the Organisation's structure, could not complete the work without the belief and trust of those further down, and his rallying call had come at just the right time.

Marshall's portrayal of Robert Grafton to those in the West Midlands lacked some of the detail which could have alarmed them all had it been included. He was a shrewd politician with an eye for the half-chance. From the founding of the BDP in 1982, he had been at the forefront of policy and policing. From its truculent beginnings, the party had acquired a reputation for strong arm tactics – an impression fuelled by inclusion within its early membership of some of London's more violent factions of football supporters.

That the party could not continue along these lines and also appeal to the ordinary voter became clear to him very quickly, and a section of its membership was set up, along the lines of Oswald Moseley's black shirts, to enforce internal discipline and maintain, at the very least, a veneer of organised respectability. It had been a long road to eject the thuggish element but success had been achieved, and with a modicum of success coming the party's way at the last local elections, Grafton had felt that a springboard was there to be used. The shortfall in funding had happened suddenly, and had caught them all totally unprepared. Steve Marshall's offer could not have come at a more opportune moment. It had, however, rung warning bells in his ingrained suspicious nature, and the knock at his door brought one of his trusted lieutenants into the room with a file in his hand.

"Is that what we've been looking for, Ian?"

"I think so, Robert." Ian McIntosh was another founder member, and there existed a bond between the men borne out of years of struggle to establish the party in the political mainstream.

"What have we got, then?"

"Marshall is MI5. No doubt about it."

"You think we're being set up?" Grafton leaned forwards, a look of grave concern on his face.

"Either that, or this Marshall guy has another agenda up his sleeve and he needs us to pull it off. How much did he give us?"

"Half a million, and it was all in cash."

"Untraceable then. Clever, that. Anyone snooping into his bank accounts won't be able to track it to us. What do you want to do?"

"I'm not sure. We need Marshall's money. Let me think about it."

"Okay. Anything else you want?"

Not for the moment, but make sure I can reach you quickly."

If Robert Grafton believed that he had enough on his plate, the events of 6th April 2006 were to set in motion a train of events which would open up the way for him to fulfil a long-held political ambition. The Labour government's majority was wiped out at the polls leaving it without a mandate to govern. Still the largest single party at Westminster, it was now faced with the real possibility of a surrender of at least a portion of its control by the necessity to share power.

That possibility turned into something definite when, following weeks of horse-trading, it signed a coalition agreement with the Liberal Democrats and other minor parties which secured a ruling majority, albeit very small, in the House of Commons. Amid a media frenzy, all of the party leaders smiled for the public and shook hands on the deal – it was an agreement fraught with conflict from the outset, and doomed to failure within a short space of time. For the moment, however, Richard Parker, the sitting tenant of 10 Downing Street, was out of danger and remained in office.

15

With dawning of a new year, George Watkinson was engaged in a hunt of quite a different nature. It is now April 2006, and whilst his conversation with Steve Marshall about Christopher Morse had not overly concerned him until it turned in the direction of a possible crime, he was now in a much more serious frame of mind. He had decided upon the need for help from within the traditional realms of law and order, and there was only one man to whom he felt that he could entrust the case – Dennis Marks. With impeccable timing, the voice of his secretary, Shirley Mann, broke the silence.

"Sir, Superintendent Barnes and Chief Inspector Marks are here to see you."

"Thank you, Shirley. Would you show them in please?"

Watkinson rose from behind his desk, and strode across the room to greet the two detectives as they entered. He had, of course, kept a close watch on the careers of both over the years, as it was policy within the department to be aware of the strengths, and any potential weaknesses, within the traditional policing agencies.

"Ah, gentlemen, please come in." He waved them to a group of leather armchairs surrounding a roaring fire. "Drinks?"

Both declined the offer and, safe in the knowledge that this part of the building at least was free from any listening devices, Watkinson came straight to the point of the requested visit.

"Chief Inspector, I regret the ordeal that you were forced to endure last week. It was none of our doing, but there is a matter to which I would like you to devote some attention."

Marks smiled. He knew from past experience that these 'matters' to which Watkinson referred were never quite as straightforward as they appeared to be. He tried a diversionary tactic.

The DCI had, over the past month or so, been the subject of an IPCC investigation which would normally have heralded the end of the career of the officer in question. It had only been due to the tenacity of his DI, Peter Spencer, and the willingness of Superintendent Barnes to listen, which had resulted in his being cleared of all suspicion.

"What will happen to Martin Ponsonby?"

Ponsonby had been the solicitor at the heart of the allegations, and for a while seemed to have Marks within his power. Watkinson's influence, in the end, had been the deciding factor in burning his fingers.

"Ah, yes, our delinquent lawyer friend." Watkinson, not in the least side-tracked from his true intentions, was nevertheless inclined to cut Marks a little slack. "Oh, he'll go back to doing what he ought to do without treading where he really doesn't belong. He was in over his head and now he knows that. He's aware of the fact that we'll be watching him; I don't think there will be any trouble from his quarter in the future. "

"We should focus on what MI5 want from the Met." Colin Barnes pulled the conversation back onto the track which Watkinson was treading.

"Indeed, Superintendent. This…" he pushed a photograph across the table to Marks, "… is a man in whom we would like you to take an interest."

"Who is he?" Marks stared at the snap, and frowned.

"Christopher Morse, and that's all that you need to know right now. I'll make sure that a file is sent to you within the next few days."

"Not one of yours, is he?" The DCI suddenly stiffened, acutely aware of the problems of becoming involved in the undercover world of espionage.

"Not anymore, and he's started to carve out a name for himself in the criminal fraternity. You'll find all you need in the files."

"Very well." Marks' tone was reluctant, but he didn't really see that he had too many options. "I'll need to take my own team into the investigation with me, and they'll need to be properly briefed."

"That's fine by me." He turned to Barnes. "Superintendent?"

"No problem from the Met's point of view." He shook his head and turned to Marks. "Who did you have in mind?"

"Peter Spencer – he's my right-hand man. I'll need a DS as well. You took Wallace back from me, remember, Mr Watkinson? She was a good sergeant."

"I do, but she never really worked for you. Any names I should be aware of?"

"Just one, and she has a first rate pedigree. Came through Hendon and transferred to CID soon after joining the Met. I've heard very good reports about her."

"It'll have to be cleared with her superior, but I'm sure Superintendent Barnes will be able to help there. What's her name?"

Now it was Marks' turn to smile; the name, when it was announced, caused eyebrows to rise on the faces of both men.

"Chloe Warner."

"Chloe Warner? Isn't she…? "Watkinson looked at Barnes.

"My sister." He smiled. "Yes, she is, and I'm sure that she'll be delighted with the compliment. It'll have to go through the proper channels, though. We've always kept our careers quite separate, for obvious reasons."

"I'll take that as arranged then, shall I?" Marks was happy at having the final word, and, as the briefing closed, he wondered just how he was going to explain it all to his long-suffering wife, June.

The meeting had lasted a mere fifteen minutes, but now that this particular ball was rolling, Watkinson allowed himself the satisfaction that, whatever Morse was up to, he would be aware of it in time to snuff out any links back to the department. Back at his desk he leaned forward, rested his chin on his right hand and stared out of the window. He frowned; Morse had been the mole within the department who had almost brought the country to its political knees. He had no tangible links, at present, to anyone operating inside MI5, but the fact that Steve Marshall was now proposing to use the man as a means of infiltrating the BDP did raise the beginnings of a concern at the back of his mind. He pressed a button on his desk phone.

"Shirley, get me the file on the British Democratic Party, please."

"Right away, sir."

Now, he decided, would be a good time to take an uninterrupted look through the papers which he had been accumulating. The plan to use Morse as a mole was tactically sound (the man had experience after all) and he was highly expendable, but the more Watkinson went over the matter of the Nazi files, the more convinced he became that he had missed something. He was as certain as he could be that the net had failed to catch all of the

Organisation hierarchy, and one figure of authority left out there was one too many. The door opened and Shirley Mann walked in.

"Thank you, Shirley." He took the folder. "How is Lewis these days?"

"Still Pete, sir, and won't answer to any other name. You know how these Yorkshire men are." She smiled.

Lewis 'Pete' Mann and his wife had made the journey south when the pit closure program decimated the Yorkshire coalfields. His father had been amongst the first batch of Bevin Boys to be conscripted into the mines from 1943 to 1948, and Lewis had followed in the old man's footsteps. Having trained as an electrician, he and Shirley moved south to the Kent coalfields in 1985 when the Barnsley Main colliery finally closed. Now 55, he had retired and, with the redundancy package, had set up his own electrical business which he ran as a hobby. His gruff exterior hid a sensitive core, and he and Watkinson had hit it off almost immediately at a weekend gathering of staff and family.

"Indeed." He returned the gesture. "Would you make some tea, please?"

"Yes, sir."

The file was up to date. He pored over his deputy's notes, rationale, and tactical plan - it appeared faultless. Not a stone had been left unturned - this was a scouting mission and, trusting no-one else to carry out the work for him, Steve had taken on the task for himself. Watkinson nodded - he would have done exactly the same.

He sighed. There was that feeling again, and he had trusted his instincts for too long to go against them now. Something definitely was not quite right, and he had only the technical skills of Barry Newman to help find out what it was.

16

Dennis Marks' particular brand of policing had made him something of a celebrity at New Scotland Yard. Fresh from a rare victory over the IPCC, albeit with the help of the man now seeking his assistance, he was as close to becoming an untouchable officer as it was possible to be. In his mid-fifties, a successful investigation by the Commission's leading inquisitor, Eric Staines, would have finished him both professionally and personally. He had been with the force all of his working life from the age of eighteen when he first set foot inside the Hendon Police College. His rise from the rank of sergeant in CID had been one of unparalleled progress, and the team which he now headed was the envy of most of the force. Not even a more than close encounter with the security services had derailed his career. Nevertheless, previous dealings with MI5 had left him with a less than confident feeling about his personal safety, and the type of involvement now suggested by George Watkinson would take him and his team to a new level of interaction with the service. He was by no means certain that he had the right to ask that of them. He had been scrutinising the file on Christopher Morse for a quarter of an hour when Peter Spencer knocked on his door and walked in.

"You sent for me, boss?" He sat down with the easy manner of a friend as well as a subordinate.

"Yes. We have a job, and I need you to take a good, long, hard look at this dossier before you commit yourself." He slid the file given to him by Watkinson across the desk.

Spencer scanned the papers quickly, despite Marks' comment, and emitted a low whistle as he closed the file.

"So, what is this guy, a murderer or a spy?"

"Hard to say at the moment." Marks leaned back in his chair. "And I'm not going to speculate until the final member of our team arrives."

"Groves?"

"Perhaps he'll be involved at some point, but we'll also have someone else on board to help with the workload."

"You'll be lucky to replace anyone as good as Wallace."

DS Sandra Wallace had worked as part of the squad investigating the background of Michael Roberts, a covert agent within the security services. That she was actually working for Watkinson was not revealed to Marks until the very end of the case. Her return to Thames House had been a disappointment to both of them.

"I wouldn't be too sure of that." Marks smiled over the top of his glasses.

"All right, who is it then? They'll have to be outstanding." Spencer sighed; the DCI loved these games of cat and mouse, and he just couldn't compete.

"Chloe Warner."

"What?" Spencer's eyes opened wide. "Isn't she…?"

"… the sister of our Superintendent? Yes, she is, and on a steep learning curve."

DS Chloe Warner was a rising star in the Met, and the half-sister of Colin Barnes. Her childhood had been spent during the years of his pursuit of the serial killer Peter Tremayne. The knock at the door interrupted their conversation; Spencer rose from his seat and held his breath at the figure now entering the room.

"Sir." She addressed Marks directly without a sideways glance. "DS Warner reporting for duty."

"At ease, Sergeant." Marks smiled. "You might strain something."

She looked at Spencer, blushed, and the three of them laughed; the ice had been broken. At five feet seven, Chloe Warner's physique belied her strength, as many at the training school were able to testify. She had made it her goal to emulate, at the very least, the achievements of her famous brother. Spencer's initial reaction on seeing her was a testimony to her appearance. She had shoulder length jet black hair, brown eyes and the well-rounded face of Penelope Cruz. Her voice, soft on first impression, had an underlying steel which was becoming a hallmark of her career. She was not a copper to be toyed with.

"Down to business," Marks continued. "This is DI Spencer…" he pointed to the right, "… and should you wish to join the team, we will function as a unit without the hindrances of rank. Understood?"

"Yes, sir."

"Right, and it's 'Guv' if anything from now on. Take a seat. The documents on the desk will require signatures before we go any further, and nothing will go on either of your records if you choose to decline."

Spencer and Warner glanced at each other with raised eyebrows as the requirements of the Official Secrets Act hit home. Neither hesitated beyond this, and the papers were returned to Marks' desk drawer. With instructions that they were to remain undisturbed, the DCI laid out the details of the task which George Watkinson had set for them. Both sat in silence as the story surrounding the career of Christopher Morse, and his fall from grace, was related to them.

Spencer, with his rise in the ranks, had been aware, through the grapevine, of an incident some years earlier which had resulted in an operative within the security services being involved in covert operations, but the details were almost non-existent and he, like many of his colleagues, had put it down to a certain amount of gossip. Warner, on the other hand, came to the matter completely fresh.

"So, what are we being asked to do... guv?"

Marks pulled two identical files out of his drawer and slid them across the desk. He waited for Spencer and Warner to flip through their contents, and sat back in his chair. They both looked up from the paperwork simultaneously.

"The man we are being asked to investigate, Christopher Morse, is a former operative of MI5. He left the department some time ago under something of a cloud, and the details of what happened have not been divulged to me at the moment."

"Will we be given that information at some point?" Spencer had glanced back at his file, and now looked up again.

"Maybe, maybe not. The point is that we are currently looking for a man answering to his description in connection with the death of a prostitute."

"Is he the main suspect?" Warner this time, keen not to be seen to be taking a back seat.

"He is *a* suspect, but by no means the only one. The woman in question was working for a pimp by the name of Rocky Martin, and he hasn't been seen on the streets since the body was discovered. Morse, because of the file given to us, is going to be the easier of the two to track. Before we go in mob-handed, though, I want to know more about his background. Just because MI5 have supplied the information doesn't mean that it is necessarily one hundred per cent correct."

"How long do we have?" Spencer closed his file and replaced it on the desk.

"Clear your desks of all other work; this one takes top priority." He turned to Warner. "Your transfer is already in the process of being arranged with DCI Farrington, so you'll need to hit the ground running, I'm afraid."

"Yes, sir. My brother did warn me that there would be times like this. I didn't join the force to sit around pushing pencils."

"That's what we like in this squad, Sergeant. Now, I'd like you to meet George Groves. It's more than likely that he'll be involved at some point, so Peter will take care of that whilst I update George Watkinson on where we are."

17

Whilst Steve Marshall was under no illusion that Grafton was a man whom he would not be able to trust, he was, nevertheless, completely unaware of the investigation which the man was undertaking into his background. Had he known of the link which had now been made to Morse and the infiltration of the Midlands branch of the BDP, his briefing with the ex-MI5 operative would have been undertaken on a far more serious level. They met at the Newport Pagnell services on the M1.

"We'll sit over there." Marshall indicated a table in the corner of the Welcome Break cafeteria.

"You look a little tense." Morse smiled at his attempt at humour. "You all right?"

"Let's just stick to the plan, shall we?" Marshall's instincts were telling him that all was not well, but he could not put his finger on anything in particular.

The resurrection of a relationship with Beverley Drake, whilst providing another opening into the BDP, had also complicated the plans he had for using the party to further his own aims. He was now playing several hands of poker at a table filled with opponents, any one of whom could bring him down.

"Okay. Summers has gone missing and Ms Drake seems more than a little concerned. There's a rumour up there about something going on between the two of them."

"I see." This came as a shock to Marshall, but went some way towards explaining her lukewarm greeting at their earlier meeting. "How are you progressing with the infiltration?"

"So far, so good. No-one appears to suspect anything, and I've been accepted into the group. Summers seems to have been the inspiration, but without a lot of the physical stuff that the party built its reputation on. He talks the talk without necessarily walking the walk."

"So, what's the story with the Drake woman?" Marshall had recovered his poise after the initial surprise of Morse's statement. He had been a specialist at first impressions and Steve had no reason, so far, to doubt his opinion.

"Committed to the cause from what I can make out, and has been at the centre of the East Midlands operation for some five or so years. Seems she might have been playing fast and loose with Summers and another guy, but I can't get any information on him at the moment; he's disappeared off the radar."

It was clear that Morse had no idea of Marshall's earlier relationship with Beverley Drake, or of their recent meeting. His reference to 'five or so years' did make Steve wonder, however, whether this had been her way of purging him from her system. He needed to deflect the conversation.

"Any news on what they might be planning?"

"Well, apart from a kind of party get together at the farm of a sympathiser in Derbyshire, they seem to be keeping their heads down at the moment. It was by invitation only, and faced a lot of opposition amongst the residents. The local council are powerless with stuff like this on private land as long as no laws are broken, and the BDP always bend over backwards to stay within guidelines."

"All right, let me know if there's any more on Summers, and keep an eye on Beverley Drake. If Summers has been taken out she could well be the one to step into his shoes, and we'll need to be aware of anything that we can use if she takes control."

Steve Marshall walked back to his car on the southbound side of the M1 deep in thought. As he accelerated down the slip road and onto the main carriageway he was snapped back to reality by the sudden blaring of the horn from a rapidly approaching HGV. With no time to brake before the filter lane ran out, he gunned the engine and eased in front of the vehicle by the narrowest of margins, leaving the driver in his wake, horn blaring once more and lights ablaze. The shrill tone of his mobile refocused his thoughts, and he hit the hands free button.

"Marshall."

"Steve, it's George. You all right?"

"Sorry. I'm on my way back now – just left Morse, and I'll update you as soon as I get back. Can't talk now – too much traffic."

"Okay. Couple of hours?"

"I'll be there."

Watkinson's call had Marshall looking back over the events of the recent past. Beverley Drake's reappearance had, initially, distracted him from the plan of hijacking the BDP. Her status as an officer of one of its branches put their relationship in an entirely new light. Now it seemed that she and Summers may have had something going, it made him begin to wonder at her motives all along, and her failure to turn up to their pre-arranged meeting rankled. That she knew of his cover as a Whitehall civil servant was not a huge concern, but he would have to play her very skilfully to ensure that it remained intact. The coming meeting with George Watkinson was also something which would need to be handled carefully.

<hr />

"Come in, Steve. Tea? Coffee?"

George Watkinson was all smiles as the two of them sat down to one of their frequent briefing and update meetings, and Marshall, in his normal frame of mind, would have read nothing out of the ordinary in his boss's demeanour. Now, however, with his circumstances becoming more complicated by the day, he found himself analysing Watkinson's every phrase and expression. Shades of self-doubt were beginning to creep in where only confidence had previously existed.

"Tea, please." He smiled in return and sat down.

"Okay, what's the situation with Morse?"

Over the next hour or so, Marshall gave chapter and verse on the progress of Christopher Morse's successful infiltration of the East Midlands branch of the BDP. He went into great detail of the new identity and the cover story at Chromex, fully aware that Watkinson would have consulted his notes in the file. His account of the meeting with Beverley Drake was more succinct, and he saw nothing to be gained by anything more than the briefest of outlines to his plans in that direction. She had the potential for usefulness in another area – a scheme to which it would be disastrous to alert MI5.

He did, however, relate a false account of a chance meeting with Robert Grafton – something which seemed to please Watkinson. It was, he said, the briefest of conversations at the BDP headquarters where he had witnessed the leader delivering one of his noted speeches.

"And that's about it. Morse has gone back to the Midlands where he'll continue to observe and, hopefully, become more involved in policy. Now we just wait to see whether he'll have any influence further up the party ladder. Grafton did intimate that they were going to be in need of some new ideas if the BDP are to succeed in their aims. I left that meeting before he could become suspicious."

"All right. It looks like you have your finger firmly on the pulse, but be careful with Morse; let's not forget that he almost brought us down once before. It would only take one slip back into drink and drugs and we'd be seriously compromised."

"There are no concerns on that score. I made it clear that we have him over a barrel. One step out of line and things will get very hot underneath him."

With the meeting now closed, Marshall headed home. The message on his answering machine added one more complication to an already problematical situation. He recognised the number immediately and it was not one which he could afford to ignore if his plans were to remain on track.

'Hi Steve. Sorry to drop on you out of the blue, but Sandra and I have a few days coming to us, and we thought it would be a great idea to pop down to London and have you show us the sights. We could be down there on the first train from Derby on Saturday morning. Let us know of it's all right.'

"Blast! Just what I needed right now." He thumped the wall in frustration, picked up the receiver and made a call which he hoped he would not regret.

"Sandra Miles."

"Sandra, it's Steve…" He got no further.

"Hi Steve! Wait while I get Peter." She was gone, and he had no chance to interrupt. Miles was there in an instant.

"So, are we on for Saturday?"

"Peter… look, I'm so sorry, but I have to work this weekend, and there's no way I can get out of it."

"Oh, I see." Miles' enthusiasm faltered. "Beverley seemed to think it would be a good idea."

It was clear that arrangements had been initialised without Marshall's knowledge, and this would have to be handled carefully.

"Right, well no, actually it isn't. I have to go up north, and it'll keep me out of the capital for a few days. She ought to have said something to me first."

"Okay, well if that's the case, so be it. You'll let us know when you get back, won't you? I suppose we could still come down and see her, though. Sandra's keen on meeting up again."

"Yes I will, but I'm not certain when that might be."

The conversation had been a little stilted and Peter Miles was no fool; he would have picked up on Marshall's less than convivial demeanour, and it was anyone's guess what interpretation he may have put upon it. He wouldn't be the first person to be caught out in a lie, even if it were only in the imagination of someone else. There was no way of telling what may or may not get back to Beverley, and that could derail another part of his plans. The uneasy feelings were now beginning to stack up, and the fictitious trip up north was now fast becoming a reality which could yet extricate him from a rapidly deteriorating situation. He called Watkinson.

"Yes, Steve." He looked at his watch. "You're working late, aren't you?"

"Not really. I'm back at home, but there's just one thing that I forgot to tell you. One of Chris Morse's contacts in the Midlands gave him the name of someone organising things for the party up in Yorkshire, and I thought I'd take a few days up there to check out the lie of the land."

"All right. When will you be leaving?"

"First thing on Friday. I'll make sure that nothing can lead from me back to base, and I'll be gone for three days at most."

"I'll see you on Monday, then. You can bring me right up to date at that time."

Now a little easier, Marshall packed a bag ready for the trip safe in the knowledge that he would be out of the firing line with Beverley and the Mileses, and that he would also have time alone to work out the next step in the plan.

18

It was unusual for Steve Marshall to ring George Watkinson at his home in the Surrey countryside. It was also out of the ordinary for him to let a field trip slip his mind in the middle of a briefing. The suddenness of the call had the head of MI5 thinking back, once again, to the issue of the Organisation in 1992 and the trap set for the burglar, Graham Poundall, over the Nazi files. It had been Marshall who had set up the CCTV hardware; it had also been Marshall who had organised the capture of the sniper in Watkinson's own back yard. Steve was also the one to shoot and kill Gerald Montgomery when MI5 were at the point of apprehending him. Watkinson frowned; was this all too much coincidence, or were his instincts kicking in once more?

"Who was it, dear?" Marjorie Watkinson noticed the concerned look on her husband's face and rested her hand on his shoulder.

"Hmm? Oh, nothing for you to worry about. Just something from work." He kissed her cheek and smiled as she walked back to the kitchen. She was worth her weight in gold, and had provided a port of calm in his sea of troubles on many an occasion.

"Well, go and wash for dinner. Harriet and John will be here soon."

Stopping off in his study, Watkinson pressed the concealed catch which released one of the paintings decorating its walls. Behind lay a safe built into the wall of the room, and which housed some of the more private papers which he deemed unsafe to leave at Thames House. One of those bundles, still bound in its aged, wartime style of wrapping, contained the details of original members of the Organisation brought back from Germany by Roger Fretwell.

"Odd." He spoke out loud to himself, a rarity for the head of MI5. He left the room and stopped at the top of the stairs.

"Marjorie!" He shouted, loud enough for her to hear him from the other side of the house.

"What is it, dear?" She came into the hall, drying her hands.

"Have you moved anything from my desk?"

"No, dear. Lost something again?" She smiled from the bottom of the stairs, but the expression froze when she saw the look upon her husband's face.

"I do not lose things, Marjorie. I thought I'd put a bundle of papers back into the safe, but it isn't there."

"No point in my asking about their importance, is there? Shall I help you to look?" She had started on her way up, but was halted by a hand raised before her.

"No, I'm afraid you can't. The papers concerned are highly sensitive, and I thought that they'd be safer here than back at the office. Now they're gone."

"Well, who else knew that they'd be here?" She frowned, now suspecting that they may have been burgled.

"As far as I'm aware, I'm the only one who had access to them. They certainly never left my office before I brought them here."

With his wife now returning downstairs, Watkinson replayed the sequence of events which had led him to bring the documents home. The office at Thames House had been broken into by Graham Poundall – a man subsequently killed by Christopher Morse. Morse had been exiled and was now under the control of Steve Marshall. Marshall had been the one to set up the covert surveillance which had trapped the burglar, and Marshall had seen Watkinson conceal the files in the safe at the office.

"No!" George hammered the table with his fist. "Surely I can't have been so stupid!"

He now recalled that he had inadvertently let out to Steve Marshall that he did not consider Thames House a safe place for the files to remain permanently, and that he intended taking them off site until a more secure location could be found. It had to be him; but why? What possible reason could Marshall have for stealing them?

"Of course!" He slumped into an armchair.

Montgomery was looking for a way out. They had him cornered, and the woman was out of his grasp. There was no need for a kill, and a bullet to the shoulder would have brought him down. It was Marshall who had fired the fatal shot, and Watkinson had believed all along that the woman's, and possibly his own, life had been saved in that instance. He had never, for one single moment, considered any other possibility. Maybe, just maybe, the shot which killed Montgomery had been to silence him. He picked up the phone.

"DCI Marks."

"It's George Watkinson. Assemble your team and get over to my house as soon as possible, please. Your case has just expanded, and each of your members will now need to be fully briefed. This is no longer a simple murder case – it's a matter of national security."

"Very well, but I'll have to clear it with the top."

"I'll do that. Just get over here, please."

With Marks and his team of Peter Spencer, Chloe Warner, and George Groves all now assembled and seated in his lounge, Watkinson had suggested to his wife that she might like to consider going to her bridge club for the evening. Marjorie accepted all this with the seasoned grace of the wife of the head of the secret service, and took her leave of their guests. George watched her down the drive, and turned to the squad before him. This was arguably the greatest risk he had ever taken.

"I've asked DCI Marks to drag all of you over here at such short notice because we're now faced with a situation of the gravest danger. MI5 cannot, by reason of the individuals involved, take control of the case which now lies before you, and under the cover of the current murder investigation I'm going to disclose further information which will expand the operation into an area which I'd originally decided to keep separate."

"Is the Morse case just a blind?" Marks placed his file on the table.

"Not at all. The killing of the prostitute is still an on-going investigation which I need you to bring to a conclusion."

"So, what's the new case?" The DCI frowned. His earlier encounters with the head of MI5 had left him with a less than easy feeling, and the shooting of Michael Roberts still brought a chill to his spine.

"We have an internal issue." Watkinson sighed and shifted in his seat.

"A criminal case?" Marks pushed gently.

"Yes… and no. I appear to have been burgled, but the items taken have no value outside of the security services. They cannot, by their very nature, be sold; the person taking them has run an enormous risk."

"So, you want a full forensic sweep of the crime scene, samples taking away for analysis, and a list of suspects." Marks was taking notes as he spoke.

"Forensics would be very helpful, though I doubt that you'll find any." Watkinson noted Groves' raised eyebrows at that last remark. "As to a list of suspects, I can make that fairly easy for you; the man you will be looking for is my second in command, Steve Marshall."

"Marshall? But I thought the two of you…"

"Were close friends as well as a team?" Watkinson finished the sentence. "Yes, until right now that was exactly as I'd envisaged the situation. However, when you've eliminated all other possibilities, whatever remains, however implausible, has to be the truth."

"Conan Doyle." Groves took this opportunity to have his say. "Holmes was the finest literary detective, and would never have ruled out basic forensic evidence."

"I agree, Professor. However, I have analysed all of the available data, and can come to only one conclusion. Steve Marshall has been in on the case of a set of Nazi files right from the beginning, was involved in their recovery, and knew that they'd be here."

"So, what's his angle?" Marks reassumed the initiative.

"It's a long story, and one which I was keen to get you involved in from the start, but it wasn't the right time then. Things have since changed. You'd all better settle down for the evening."

<hr />

Marks put down the glass of malt which he had been cradling since Watkinson finished speaking. The room was silent, and the eyes of his team were all now pointed firmly in his direction. Watkinson sighed and finished his glass before pouring another.

"I did some early checking on Steve's story concerning Morse's involvement in the prostitute's death, and it seemed to hold up. Now I have my doubts."

"Our investigation is coming to a similar conclusion." Marks replied.

"Forensic evidence at the scene didn't exclude him from the earlier stages," Groves chipped in, "but the fatal blow couldn't have been delivered by Morse."

"Really?" Watkinson leaned forwards.

"Yes. You see, the blunt force trauma was caused by a heavy metallic object, from both left and right. There were two blows, either of which could have been fatal, but they were definitely delivered by someone left-handed. We know from the files handed to us that Christopher Morse is right-handed."

"I see. So Marshall was holding the case over him like some Sword of Damocles. He had Morse over a barrel, he told me that, but I clearly put the wrong interpretation upon it."

"It would appear so." Marks again. "Whether your ex-operative would have been in a state capable of realising the deception remains open to question."

"I doubt it. When Steve found him he was already an addict and an alcoholic." Watkinson leaned back in his chair and shook his head. "I did wonder whether Marshall was instrumental in creating Chris's condition. You see my dilemma, don't you?"

"Where is Marshall now, sir?" Peter Spencer had been listening all of this time, but a lull in the conversation gave him his chance.

"Yorkshire, Detective Inspector. On a scouting mission, and I never saw it coming. It's a large county and I can give you no leads as to his exact whereabouts."

Watkinson's telephone interrupted any further explanation, and a hushed conversation took place at the far end of the room. When he returned, their host's face wore a careworn look.

"That was one of my staff. I've had him tracking a number of financial transactions across the world for the past couple of weeks, and it looks as though he may finally have made a connection."

"Is it a part of our brief?" Marks stepped in.

"If it wasn't before, it certainly is now. We were concerned at the direction which the Organisation was intending to funnel its funds. Barry, the guy at the office, succeeded in tracing them to a small provincial bank in Switzerland. It looked as if the trail had gone cold, but there's been a withdrawal of half a million pounds sterling. It would seem that a similar amount has now found its way into the coffers of the BDP. There's just too much coincidence between the two events. I know that Marshall has met, albeit briefly, Robert Grafton. It's time to put out a description of my deputy, DCI Marks. Bring him in."

"What about the other two you mentioned, Summers and Drake?"

"Summers has apparently gone missing, but Beverley Drake has contacts with Robert Grafton and may have been to see him. Beyond that I can't help."

"Very well." Marks stood up and the team followed suit. "I'll get back to you as soon as we have anything."

19

"All right. We're working with scarce resources, and we can't divulge any of what George Watkinson said to us to anyone else at the Yard. We have to deal with the Marshall situation ourselves, but Morse is still wanted in connection with a murder enquiry, so let's get a warrant for his arrest and circulate a description. According to MI5 he's in the East Midlands. Chloe, get onto the Derbyshire Constabulary at Ripley. We know he's on their patch, so they can pick him up for us. Oh, and circulate Marshall's registration number to the Yorkshire police."

"Guv."

"Peter, we need to track down Beverley Drake and Mike Summers. Don't rule anything out, and don't assume that either is still alive. You might try starting with Missing Persons."

"Okay. Where will you be?"

"I'm going to have a chat with our Mr Grafton. If Drake went to see him, as we're led to believe, she may have let something slip. I might even let out that Morse was working for MI5, and see if that rattles him."

"What do you want from me?" Groves, keen not to be left out, interjected.

"A full and complete autopsy on that prostitute. Make sure that nothing has been missed. I believe we now have her pimp in custody as well. See if you can get anything of a forensic nature from him. Chloe can help you with that."

Geoff Marsden was tired… so very tired. Working up in Yorkshire was not what he had in mind when leaving British Gas; his employment with them had spanned a period of forty years since being apprenticed at the age of sixteen. Now on the wrong side of fifty-five he was quite happy working for himself, and his name had spread around the trade as someone who could be relied on, but he had become a victim of his own success and the current job was a perfect example. The contract in Thirsk was, it had to be said, a highly lucrative one, but the twelve hour shifts were beginning to take their toll. A daily trip from his home in Derbyshire was out of the question, and although his long-suffering partner, Cath, would rather have him back there, she was philosophical enough to realise the benefits that the job was earning. He was on his way back to weekday lodgings in Helmsley when his mobile rang.

"Geoff, it's Cath."

"Owd on while I pull in." Having pressed the button on his Bluetooth, he pulled into the entrance to a farm track halfway up the one in four incline which was Sutton Bank.

"'Ey up gal, what's up?" The broad Chesterfield accent was always on his tongue, and it never failed to bring a smile to her face.

"What time will you be back home tomorrow?" Friday was usually the day which Geoff reserved for an early finish, and this week was no exception. Today being a Thursday, however, he had one more shift to complete.

"'bout teatime, duck." It was always 'duck', and she was never sure whether or not he was being serious.

"Don't you 'duck' me." She laughed. "I'll 'duck' you if you're not back on time tomorrow. We're out with Lynn and Philip, and I don't want you making us late."

"All right, my love." The switch of tack caught her momentarily off balance, and he ended the call without another reproof.

He yawned and stretched, filling the front of the van with his burly six foot frame. A headache had begun to irritate its way across his forehead, and he still had a fair distance to travel before he could rest for the night. Sutton Bank, also known as Roulston Scar, lies in the Hambledon district of North Yorkshire, and is one of the most treacherous routes for the unwary traveller. The remainder of its incline loomed threateningly before him, and he did not relish the thought of starting up again right now – he looked at his watch. Through its cracked face, he was just able to discern that it had stopped at precisely ten-thirty.

"Bugger!" He cursed. "Should've took it off before I got under that old boiler." It was evidently broken.

Marsden looked out at the darkness and guessed it was around one in the morning – the latest shift had been a particularly difficult one, and an hour in the van snatching forty winks would not go amiss. Setting the seat back as far as it would go, he crossed his arms over his chest and dropped off. Unaware of the passage of time, the roar of an engine and the splintering of wood brought him out of the arms of Morpheus with a start. The receding sound of running feet also had him wide awake and wondering what he had just heard.

He stumbled out of the van and, with barely focusing eyes, looked up and down the incline, but in the pitch darkness of an unlit stretch of road, he could see nothing which related to the sounds that he thought he had heard. Shaking his head, and convinced that it had been a dream brought on by his virtual addiction to strong cheese, he got back into the van, started the engine, and headed for Helmsley and the promise of a warm bed. As he rounded the next bend, and totally out of sight and hearing, the car which had left the road only moments earlier exploded in a fireball so intense that the tree into which it had careered erupted into the same inferno.

By the following morning, all Geoff's thoughts of the previous evening were long gone.

Chloe Warner, true to her training and an almost fanatical drive to succeed where her brother had gone before, was like a terrier when it came to investigative police work. Not only had she submitted Morse's description to the Derbyshire force, the Nottinghamshire constabulary had received a duplicate set of documents on the ex-MI5 operative. Not one to sit back and wait for results, she was on the case two hours later for updates from both counties.

The West Bridgford police in Nottingham were the first to respond with a sighting of him some time before at a riverside pub in Nottingham, talking to two known members of the BDP. From there, she managed to track him to Woodville, and a meeting house frequented by the party which had been under observation for a year or more.

With an address supplied to her by the managing director at Chromex in Longlea, she alerted the Nottinghamshire police, and arrangements were made to have him picked up as soon as he returned home.

"One down, one to go." She sat back with a self-satisfied smile across her face.

"Success?" Peter Spencer entered the office at that precise moment, and she updated him on progress. "The guv'nor will be pleased with that. Well done." The churning of the fax machine had him turning towards the wall. "Hey, look at this."

"Bull's-eye! A match to Marshall's car. What else does it say?" She was out of her seat in an instant.

"Looks like we may have hit a dead end, though. I'll get the boss."

Marks read the report from the Yorkshire police with a deepening frown etched across his forehead. A parcel delivery van, travelling down Sutton Bank, had pulled up at the side of the road where a section of wooden fencing had been smashed. Down in the valley, and some hundred yards from the road, lay a burned out vehicle embedded in the side of a large oak tree. The registration plates had been badly damaged in the conflagration, but what remained, together with the VIN number, was enough to confirm that it was the car which belonged to the MI5 operative. George Watkinson would need to be informed, and Marks was at Thames House within the hour.

"No doubt about this, then?" Watkinson removed his glasses.

"None at all. The number checks out with DVLA, and I've sent George Groves up there with his team to carry out the forensic search of the area. Any resistance from the locals and I've referred them to your office. Hope you don't mind."

"No, and I'd have been disappointed with any other action. How long before we get all the stuff back down here?"

"Probably tomorrow, and I've cleared an area back at the Yard. Access will be restricted to my team and you. We'll work around the clock on the car and the body found inside."

"It's bound to be Steve… isn't it?"

"I would have thought so, but you know Groves… 'I'll know more when I get it back to the lab'…I can't get any more out of him at this early stage in any investigation. They're all the same."

"Well, carry on with the rest of the background checking until then, but I'd like to be alerted as soon as anything arrives down here."

"Will do."

20

Beverley Drake packed up her papers as the last of the branch committee left the upstairs room at the Midland Hotel in Longlea. It had been twelve months since Mike Summers' sudden disappearance, and despite repeated calls to BDP headquarters, she could get no satisfactory answers from Robert Grafton. He had seemed, initially, very concerned when she first broached the subject at their meeting in London, but with the passage of time any mention of Summers' name had received less and less of a welcome response. Grafton's last reply to her e-mail had been brusque and business-like – quite unlike the man she had been led to believe he was. Christopher Morse came back into the room at that moment. The intervening year had seen his elevation to the local committee, and his reliability and dedication to the cause had become noted.

"You all right, Beverley?" He reached into his pocket, took out a pack of cigarettes and offered one. She shook her head and pointed to the 'No Smoking' sign on the wall. He put them away.

"I can't get Mike's disappearance out of my head. It was just so unlike him."

"Went to see Grafton, didn't he?"

"Yes, last May. He was at a party meeting when new funding was announced, and that was the last anyone saw of him. I keep asking for information, but I'm getting nowhere."

"Missing persons?"

"The Police? Don't make me laugh. They're about as likely to take us seriously as a bunch of Forest supporters on the rampage. I did consider it at one point, but it would be pointless."

"What now, then? Just forget him? That doesn't seem right." Morse continued the probing as Marshall had instructed.

"No, it's not, and I need to find out what happened. There's something very wrong about this. Mike wouldn't have just vanished without telling any of us up here. I'm going back down to London to see Grafton again for myself. Mike had no family that I'm aware of, so we can't even use that line to involve the police in a missing persons search."

"Who's running things up here until you get back?"

Beverley Drake looked hard and long into Morse's eyes. He had been in the party for only a short time but had shown himself, to all the local members, to be committed to the cause, and he was by far the most able of those currently on the committee.

"You will. The remainder of the members will follow your lead in the absence of Mike and myself. Just don't do anything that might alert the authorities. Right?"

"Right." He nodded – this was just what Marshall had said would happen if he played his cards right. Now firmly established, he would be a hard leader to shift if anything were to happen to Ms Drake.

<hr/>

Beverley Drake's train was approaching Bedford when her Outlook e-mail alerted her to a new message. Flipping open the top of the laptop which she carried on her party trips, she scanned the inbox. The new item was from a colleague in London, another party member with whom she had been at college. An officer serving within the vice squad at New Scotland Yard, he had fallen in willingly with the request for information about Tom Harriman, but she had, in the light of Summers' disappearance, forgotten all about the matter. That request had been some months earlier, and she now had the answer. She cursed out loud as the full implications of the information started to dawn on her.

"I beg your pardon?" The voice of the man opposite shook her back to the reality of the current situation.

"Sorry." She shook her head. "Family news – bad I'm afraid. You'll have to excuse me."

Picking up her bags and laptop, Beverley made for the buffet car and a little more privacy. A table at the far end of the carriage provided her with the opportunity she needed to rectify a problem which was now staring her squarely in the face. She read through the text of the e-mail once more.

'Bev,

Sorry this has taken so long, but you wouldn't believe the security I've had to hack to get to the stuff you needed.

Your Tom Harriman is actually a guy named Christopher Morse, an ex-MI5 operative. According to my source, he was kicked out of the security services a few years back for some double-dealing, but it looks as though they've found another use for him.

You need to be very careful around him. I have no idea who his handler is, but you can bet that he isn't about to do us any favours.

Justin.'

The message had been encrypted, and could only be accessed by Beverley herself with a password. She stared out of the window as the train approached Luton – there was no doubting her next move. The car was empty, and the buffet closed; with no-one to overhear, she dialled a Longlea number and gave instructions to the recipient for the disposal of Tom Harriman. Leading the branch committee was a subject which would now have to await her return. The train pulled in at St Pancras a little over half an hour later, and after the cab journey across London once more, she was at the head office of the BDP, where a surprised receptionist led her to the office of Robert Grafton.

"Beverley." He frowned. "I was just on the point of going out for something to eat; care to join me?"

"Thank you, but no. I have to get back to Nottinghamshire urgently. Something's come up and I'm afraid it can't wait, so I'm going back first thing in the morning."

"Party matters? Anything I can help with?"

"No, I can handle it. What I came down here to talk to you about is Mike Summers."

Grafton took off the coat which he had donned and sat down again, waving her to the chair opposite.

"I thought we'd been through this. I have no idea where he is."

"It's been a year now, and not a single word from him. His last instructions to me were to hold the fort while he was down here at the last meeting. We were all expecting him back within a few days. Did you see him?"

"Well, yes." Grafton shifted in his seat; he was not accustomed to being interrogated, and the feeling did not sit well with him. "We'd been running into a financial corner as you may be aware, but a new investor had come forward and I presented the matter to the members present. Mike was none too pleased at what he regarded as a sell-out, but that's him all over."

"So you argued?" She pressed the point, not seeing the dangerous waters into which she was sailing.

"Not at all. The BDP is like any other political party, and we don't all agree all of the time. No, Mike voiced his opinion and then left. I've no idea where he went, and the meeting broke up shortly afterwards."

There was an awkward silence, and Beverley stared into the face of the party leader. His expression remained blank, his eyes soulless, and the smile across his thin lips was that of a very dangerous man. She stood up suddenly and he was caught, momentarily, unawares.

"I don't know what to do, then. I had thought of filing a Missing Persons report, but the police are hardly likely to spend too much of their time and resources on one of our officials. It may be my final chance of finding out what happened to him. I'll have to go now; thank you for seeing me at short notice."

"Any time. Where are you staying? Can I offer you a lift?" Grafton rose and escorted her out of the office and back to reception.

"No, it's all right. I can get a cab; the Novotel's near St Pancras and it would be taking you right across the city."

He watched her as she turned left and walked back up the High Street. Returning to his office, he picked up the phone and barked out a command to Polly Harris, the afternoon desk clerk. "Get Williams and Stokes on the phone and put the call through to me straight away."

Beverley's earlier call had set wheels in motion back in East Midlands, and when Morse opened his door in the early part of the evening, he was pleasantly surprised to be faced with two of the party members, and an invitation to a night out in Nottingham. With no indication of anything untoward, he picked up his coat, locked the door, and followed them down the path. On the journey to the Phoenix Park tram terminus, he took the opportunity to check his voicemail and message box. There was nothing from Marshall, and he hadn't heard from Steve for the past three days.

Whilst not worrying, it was, in the circumstances of his assignment, odd. They approached the tram stop and he put the mobile away.

It was almost one in the morning that his body was discovered. Roy Middleton had had a remarkably unsuccessful evening's fishing in the canal close to the Trent Navigation, and he was packing away his gear as the line on his rod suddenly tugged.

"Oh no! Not now!" He cursed, ready for the short trip home.

Dropping the bait basket, he picked up the rod from its rest and began to reel in. The drag on the line was considerable, and he was not aware of any fish in the Nottingham waters which could exert such force. Nevertheless, he continued with the effort. His first sight of the body was as it emerged from the cover of the bridge leading across the canal to the Navigation pub, and it had him heading for the now closed alehouse and a call to the emergency services.

"Have you touched anything?" The Detective Sergeant looked up from his notebook.

"You're kiddin'. That's a dead man in there." Middleton pointed to the water where a team of officers were dragging the corpse to the bank.

"All right. We'll take it from here. You'll not be going far from this address, will you?" He tapped a page in the book.

"No, why?"

"We might need you again – this could have been a murder, and your evidence might be vital."

"Just my luck! A wasted night fishing, and all I catch is a flaming corpse."

The sergeant smiled and shook his head as Middleton strapped his fishing gear to the pushbike he had stowed nearby, and rode away.

"Sir! You need to see this." The call was from one of the uniformed constables who had brought the body out of the water.

The back of Morse's head bore what looked like a scar caused by some kind of weapon, and the sergeant was on his radio immediately, chasing up the forensic team which should already have been there.

"Looks like another long night, constable."

At the same time that Christopher Morse was meeting his gruesome and untimely end, Beverley Drake was walking back to her hotel after a meal at a nearby restaurant. All calls to Steve Marshall's mobile had gone unanswered, and his voicemail kicked in once more.

"Steve, it's Beverley… again! Why aren't you returning my calls? This is the last time *I'm* ringing *you*. I need to speak to you urgently." She cursed him in frustration and rammed the phone back into her bag.

"Blast you, Marshall! Why are you never around when I need you?"

She never heard the van which pulled up at the side of her. Any scream was muffled by a huge hand across her mouth whilst another dragged her inside the vehicle. The entire act had taken only a moment, and there had been no-one on the street to witness the abduction.

"Please! What do you want?" Her hands were, by now, tightly bound.

"Shut up!" The voice was harsh, and had a cockney accent.

"I have friends… friends with money. If it's money you want, I can get it. Please… what do you want?"

"You to shut your bleedin' mouth!"

The rag now placed in Beverley's mouth was sealed in place by a length of duct tape, and all further attempts at conversation ceased. Her eyes darted back and forth in the dim light of the back of the van for some idea as to the intention of her captors. Save for the sound of the only voice she had heard, there were no other clues either to their identity or their purpose. That purpose was not to be very long in becoming apparent.

21

Although Beverley Drake's unexpected appearance at BDP headquarters had caught Robert Grafton on the wrong foot, his experience as party leader and a track record for dodging the issue had stood him in good stead. Now, with her hopefully out of his hair, he found himself able to get on with the business at hand, and was presently sitting in a recording studio in the heart of London where his maiden appearance before the British viewing public would be aired.

The level of success achieved at the latest local government elections now entitled the party to an official platform to air its views and policies. This was a fact which did not sit well with the established parliamentary groups, but with no legal way of preventing BDP progress, they were all compelled to sit on the side lines and hope that he made a hash of it.

"Just a little to the left please, Mr Grafton." The makeup girl was putting the finishing touches. "We want you looking good under the studio lights."

Grafton smiled. In truth, he was a little nervous – this was the chance that he had been waiting for since 1982, and he could not afford to make any mistakes with the world looking on. Opposite him would be one of the BBC's top political editors - a man famed for taking no prisoners.

"Five minutes, Mr Grafton." A young man smiled as he popped his head around the dressing room door.

"All done, Mr Grafton." The makeup girl stood back and reviewed her work.

"Thanks." He smiled and swallowed to moisten his drying throat. "Do you have a glass of water, please?"

There was a hush in the audience as he took his place under the lights, and opposite Marcus Davenport, the presenter. All eyes focussed on Grafton as he sat down and crossed his legs. This was the pose which his trainer had taught him was the correct one to adopt. He appeared, on the face of it, relaxed and at ease; Davenport smiled inwardly – he had faced them all in his time, and a minor fish like Grafton in the large pool that was modern day British politics was going to be an easy ride. Half an hour later, his demeanour had changed considerably.

"Well, thank you Mr Grafton. I'm sure that we all understand where your party is positioning itself." Davenport's tone was brusque and condescending; he had singularly failed to get beneath the skin of the BDP leader and had, in the end, allowed himself to be outflanked by an expertly coached opponent.

The champagne flowed freely back at party HQ later that same evening as Robert Grafton took centre stage in a minor celebration. He had outplayed an expert in his own field and the entire nation had witnessed the event. His calm, relaxed demeanour held the audience entranced as he played upon all of their fears. Davenport's questions had become more and more barbed as he sensed the initiative slipping away from him, and the entire interview had been a triumph for Grafton's reasoned approach. Even unscripted questions from the audience had not fazed him. He had quickly spotted the 'plants' within their number, and was ready with well-rehearsed answers to obvious baiting. There was a ripple of polite applause as he rose from his seat at the end of the broadcast, and one or two came forward for an autograph. Davenport gathered up his notes as the floor manager approached. His mood was sombre – things had not gone according to plan at all.

"What happened there? I thought you were going to demolish him and the group of right wing thugs he calls a party."

"I have absolutely no idea. It's been so easy to derail people like him in the past. You have to admire him for the preparation – maybe I'm losing my touch."

"He had the audience eating out of his hand at the end. Did you see the looks on some of their faces? If he keeps this up, there'll be some interesting elections results on the horizon." The floor manager walked away, shaking his head.

Davenport was not so dismissive. The heads of the three major parties had convened a meeting for later that day, and his presence had been requested. It had been intended as a congratulatory social to celebrate the burying of the BDP in front of the TV cameras. Now it was more likely to descend into a kind of witch hunt. He finished his glass of water and returned to the dressing rooms.

"I, Felicity Partington, being the Returning Officer for the Burnley constituency, hereby declare that the votes cast in the election for each candidate were as follows. John Patrick Green, Labour, ten thousand eight hundred and ninety-eight; Elizabeth Margaret Johnson, Conservative, four thousand and nine; Colin Lomas, Independent, four thousand nine hundred and eighty-seven; Alice Wright, Liberal Democrat, six thousand five hundred and seventy-eight; Harry Parsons, UKIP, three hundred and one; Robert James Grafton, British Democratic Party, twenty thousand four hundred and eight."

The eruption of noise inside the counting room at Turf Moor could have easily been mistaken for that of the home crowd as they cheered a winning goal out on the pitch. Felicity Partington waved her hand and the noise abated; she continued.

"I hereby declare that the said Robert James Grafton is elected to serve as Member of Parliament for this constituency."

Grafton's tactics at the by-election had been faultless. His campaign had centred on the fears of the British public across all political and social lines, and had completely outflanked all of the other major parties. The swing had been massive, and the majority substantial. As the noise slowly died, he took the microphone from the Returning Officer, smiled his thanks, and stepped forward to address those present.

"I would like, firstly, to thank all of my opponents for a good, hard fight, and to say to those who have tried, over the course of the past few weeks, to smear our policies that they have been rejected by the people of Burnley."

A raucous cheer greeted that last statement, and amid a waving of party scarves and banners, Grafton smiled again as he milked the applause. He raised a finger, and the room fell instantly silent.

"The BDP will continue with its policies of returning Britain to the forefront of world politics, and we intend to restore our nation to the respected position which it once occupied. Our manifesto for the last election will remain in place for the next, and you, the voters of this constituency, in rejecting the tired and care-worn policies of days gone by, have clearly shown that the party has touched on the wishes of the silent majority. We will not let you down. Thank you."

The room erupted once more as Grafton and his entourage left the stage. At the exit door, the BDP leader turned once more, waved to those watching his every move, and left the building. The stage had now been set. Another night of celebration followed, as the reality of the threshold upon which the party now stood finally hit Robert Grafton. His address to those present was, unsurprisingly, very upbeat.

"Compared to our last performance in the previous year when we polled just over four thousand, this was a massive result. Our share of the vote was just over forty-three per cent and the majority was nine thousand five hundred and ten. Whichever way the other parties look at it, we caned them all. The really impressive statistic was the turnout; from fifty-nine per cent then it rose to over seventy-one this time. This means that the voters have listened to us, they like what we say, and they've got off their backsides to come out and support us."

There followed a loud cheer, and Grafton raised a hand to quell the enthusiasm.

"Let's not get too excited just yet. This is one result at a by-election where sitting candidates usually get a bloody nose only to return at the next general election. However, if this result _were_ to be repeated across the country as a whole…" He paused for dramatic effect, "… you could be looking at the next government being the British Democratic Party. That day could be another four years away, and we'll have a lot of work to do in the meantime to make sure that the message gets across the entire country. Tomorrow morning's papers are going to make very interesting reading. Thanks to you all."

He raised a glass, and the room erupted again.

Had Grafton been privy to the political manoeuvrings within the Labour Party, he would have had much greater cause for celebration than he could possibly have believed. A year of turbulence within the Coalition had been the catalyst for those in the Cabinet to make their feelings known to Prime Minister Richard Parker. His style of leadership, stylish and charming in 1997 and 2001, had hardened with the shackles tightening around his ability to rule by the Coalition Agreement. The Press painted him as a kind of socialist Thatcher clone in the last days of her premiership, and feelings ran high that it was time for a change. He was rocked by a vote of No Confidence from within his own party and forced to resign.

The handover of power to his erstwhile friend and Chancellor of the Exchequer, Mark Barrowman, was acrimonious in the extreme, and Liberal Democrats at the heart of the government were now beginning to look elsewhere for allies more willing to listen to their voices.

22

Dennis Marks had headed down to the lab as soon as he got George Groves' message. The vehicle and its contents from Yorkshire had arrived, and were presently being processed. The pathologist had been at work since early in the morning when he received a call from a member of his staff alerting him to the gruesome delivery. The car was in a separate garage area, but Groves himself was hunched over the remains of a corpse when the DCI entered the room.

"Is that all there is left of him?" Marks' face was a mask of disappointment. "I assume that it *is* a bloke."

"I'm afraid so; but yes, you are correct in thinking that this is the male of the species. No need to be so despondent though - he can still tell us all sorts of things."

"Such as?"

"Well, time of death, cause of death, identity… Get the picture?"

"Go on, then." The DCI pulled up a stool.

"You have to understand that the body is very badly damaged by the fire which consumed the vehicle, but there was still enough of the internal organs remaining to give me a rough estimate of when the crash occurred."

"Yes, yes." Groves was meticulous in his routines, and there were times when Marks could have shaken him.

"Right. We know from the parcel delivery chap that the car must have left the road sometime either late last Thursday evening or early the following morning."

"Why not earlier? That van can't be down that road every day." Marks frowned.

"Because he was on an early run from Helmsley to Thirsk, and saw the car still smouldering. When he went down the slope to take a look he burned his hand on the vehicle frame. Any longer than that and it would almost certainly have been a lot cooler. There was also this." He held up a plastic bag containing a mobile phone.

"How on Earth did *that* survive the fire?" Marks rose from his seat, took it, and turned it over in his hand.

"The driver found it in the grass as he made his way back to the road. Don't worry, he was clever enough to pick it up using a handkerchief."

"Hmm, there's a number of missed calls." Marks pushed another button through the plastic. "Voicemail... have you checked these out yet?"

"No." Groves sighed and shook his head – typical of the DCI, everything needed all at once. "It's on the list. I'm focusing on the body at present. I assume that you'll be needing identification at some point."

"Yes... please." The sarcasm was not lost on Marks, and he sat back down on the stool.

"Facial recognition is out of the question – too much skin and muscle loss. Clothing is all but gone, so there'll be very little there for me to go on. However..." He raised a finger, noticing the crestfallen look on Marks' face, "... dental and DNA records should pinpoint who it is we have on the slab. I've already taken X-rays of the jaw and samples of bone marrow and I should have some results back..." He looked at the clock, "... around lunchtime."

Another figure entered the room at this point, and neither Marks nor Groves were entirely surprised to be faced with the presence of George Watkinson.

"Is it Marshall?" He came straight to the point.

"Impossible to say at the moment but you can tell us if it's his car, and there's this mobile phone which was found at the scene." Groves passed the bag over.

"We'll soon find out." Watkinson took out his own and pressed a speed dial button. The phone in the bag rang out.

"It would seem that you're right." Groves frowned, not relishing another interruption. "I need to dust it for prints, and DCI Marks did find a number of missed calls and voicemails."

"Some of those could be from me – I've been trying to contact him, but I didn't leave any messages. I'd be interested to know who the rest were from."

Groves sighed once more. Marks he could handle, but when the head of MI5 put a rush on things, the smart thing to do was to go along with him.

"I'll dust it for prints now, but please bear in mind that our friend over there…" he nodded towards the slab, "… has very little in the way of fingers left."

"That's all right, we have records of Steve's fingerprints, DNA and dental records back at Thames House."

"Excellent!" Marks brightened at the prospect, and now that Groves had finished with the phone, Watkinson accessed the voicemail messages. There were six – four of them from the same source.

'Steve, it's Beverley… again! Why aren't you returning my calls? This is the last time I'm ringing you. I need to speak to you urgently.'

"Beverley…" Watkinson stroked his chin.

"Beverley?" Marks frowned, questioningly, and turned to Groves, who shrugged.

"Hmm? Oh, sorry, yes, Beverley Drake I believe. Steve was trying to get an inside track on a political organisation, and she's someone who looked a good bet. He knew her from some years ago I gather."

Groves stiffened. He walked to the far end of the room where the refrigerated compartments held some of his 'work in progress'. He traced a finger up and down the individual drawers until he came to the one he was looking for. Pulling the tray out onto a trolley, he raised the covering sheet.

"Beverley Drake." He announced.

There was a stunned silence as Watkinson and Marks walked over to where he was standing.

"She came in yesterday and I did the autopsy right away as there was nothing else waiting. Cause of death was drowning."

"So that puts her time of death after that of Marshall?" Watkinson mused.

"Yes. I suppose whoever killed her didn't expect the body to surface quite so soon. She was found on the banks of the Thames at Richmond Lock. Whatever was weighing her down must have pulled loose – the ligature marks on her ankles suggest that she had been tied to something fairly heavy."

"Richmond Lock? That's the second body that's been fished out at that place. One of our chaps was found there a while ago."

"Oh, that's not all. I have another one you've not seen yet, and he came in at the same time as she did." Groves opened another drawer further down the range. The body was badly decomposed and had clearly been in the waters of the Thames for much longer than Beverley Drake. "Police divers searched the waters when she popped up, and there he was, weighted down with the same kind of stuff that I suspect was used on her."

"ID?" Marks shrugged his shoulders and shook his head in a resigned manner, expecting the stock answer. He was to be surprised this time.

"Whoever searched him before he was dumped, missed this." Groves held up a plastic bag.

"What is it?" Watkinson took out his glasses and stared at the contents.

"It's very faded, but I managed to dry it out and enhance the text. It's a membership card, and I found it in a small inside pocket of his coat. *'British Democratic Party'*, apparently."

"That's the link!" Watkinson slammed a fist against the metal cabinets. "This chap whoever he is, is a member; Beverley Drake was the area secretary up in the East Midlands, and Marshall was investigating the whole organisation." He paused. "Oh my God!"

"What?" Marks and Groves voiced the same question together.

"It's only just occurred to me that Marshall may have been getting too close and someone took him out."

"Excuse me, sir."

The door opened and they were interrupted by Kevin Henson, one of Groves' assistants.

"Yes, Kevin."

"We've had a call from the Nottingham police in reply to a request put out by DCI Marks. They've pulled a body out of the canal at the Trent Navigation on London Road. ID is confirmed as being a chap called Tom Harriman."

"Thank you, Kevin, but what...?"

"Harriman?!" Watkinson was across the room in an instant. "Are you certain?"

"Yes, sir." Henson stepped back from the imposing form of the head of MI5. "They got details from Chromex in Longlea, the firm where he worked."

"Who is Tom Harriman, and why is he so important?" Marks stepped forwards as Watkinson turned around. Henson left, sensing that his job was done.

"Tom Harriman was the cover name for one of our operatives that Steve Marshall had working inside the BDP. His real name is Christopher Morse, and that's another link."

"Morse?" Groves piped up. "Isn't that the name of the suspect in the killing of that prostitute you mentioned at our initial briefing?"

"Yes, and it looks now as though we've got more on our hands than we bargained for. All right, can we get back to Marshall? What about the car? Can I see it?"

The three of them moved to the garage area where the Audi involved in the accident was being processed. Watkinson walked all around the vehicle, frowning; he paused at certain points and shook his head. Most of the paint had been scorched from the bodywork, and the number plates were almost unreadable. The registration however, etched into the surface of each of the windows, was still there, and he pointed to it.

"Yes, we identified the car from records at DVLA, and the VIN number confirms it. That's definitely Steve Marshall's car." Groves picked up the file lying on a nearby table and handed it to Watkinson, who gave him a puzzled look.

"How did the mobile phone survive the inferno? I mean, if the heat was enough to strip the paint and wreck the number plates, the phone should have fried."

"As I told DCI Marks, the mobile was discovered by the parcel delivery man. It was lying some way apart from the wreck, and intact - the grass would have cushioned any impact. I'm assuming that he was trying to use it when the car went off the road; apparently the driver's window was down at the time – it must have flown out as he struggled for control."

"Hmm, Steve did tend to drive with that window down. I still can't believe that he's gone. Were there any witnesses?"

"No." Marks stepped in. "It's an isolated spot and a treacherous incline. Once a car's out of control you're in serious trouble. Looks like the impact with the tree caused the fuel tank to explode."

"Is that usual?" Watkinson looked doubtful. "I've seen it in films, but that's just for spectacular effect, surely."

"Ordinarily I'd agree with you." Groves said. "However, the fuel lines were fractured, probably as a result of the rocky terrain. There was a scorched trail leading back to the road suggesting that may have been the cause of the explosion."

"I see. So this was simply a tragic accident, then."

"For the moment, there's nothing to suggest anything else, but once we've taken the car apart properly I'll be able to give you a clearer picture."

"All right. Well, if there's nothing else I'll head off back to base."

He had turned towards the door once more, when Groves' assistant, Henson, entered again. He looked at Watkinson anxiously before walking over to the pathologist.

"Professor Groves." He used the formal terminology – someone had obviously clued him in to the identity of their visitor.

"Yes, Kevin, what is it?"

"We've received a positive ID on the other body pulled out of the Thames."

"Go on." Watkinson had returned to the centre of the room, and Henson smiled nervously.

"Well, the fingerprints we took from the corpse weren't perfect, but there were enough partials to come up with a close match."

"Who is it?" Marks this time, and Henson backed away slightly under the onslaught.

"New Scotland Yard have sent us this." He handed over the file and disappeared. Watkinson opened the buff folder and his eyes stared in amazement.

"Michael James Summers." He flipped through the papers and turned back to the trolley holding the body. "Head of the Derbyshire branch of the BDP and noted hardliner. Now, what would *he* be doing at the bottom of the Thames?"

23

Robert Grafton was basking in the glow of the morning papers and their headlines. Try as they might, the tabloids had been unable to find fault with what he had said in front of the TV cameras. Now the result of the Burnley by-election had made them all sit up and take a serious look at what his party had to offer. It made very hard humble pie for them to chew upon.

'Grafton Cooks In Lancashire Hot Pot!' – The Sun

'Right Turn Up' – Daily Mirror

'Burnley Voters Commit Thuggee!' – Daily Star

He smiled and shook his head. Who *did* they employ to write this rubbish? Despite the crudeness of the headlines, all of the political commentators on the inside pages were forced into a situation of paying some kind of tribute to the way in which the party had run its campaign. Grafton had stuck to the advice given by his political advisors and kept away from the old party lines of anti-Semitism, racial abuse, and gay bashing.

"Yes, Jennifer?" He pressed the light now flashing on his desk phone.

"There's Detective Chief Inspector Marks here to see you, Mr Grafton."

"I see. Could you show him up, please? Oh, and could you arrange tea and coffee?"

"Of course, Mr Grafton."

Robert Grafton frowned. DCI Marks was a name that was familiar to him. One of The Yard's top detectives, and a man reputed to have beaten a case brought against him by the Independent Police Complaints Commission. There were not too many who could boast of that. The frown changed dramatically to a smile as the policeman entered the room.

"Detective Chief Inspector, please take a seat. Would you like some tea?"

"Thank you, no." Marks sat down and took out his notebook. "This isn't a social call, I'm afraid."

"Very well." Grafton glanced towards the door. "That'll be all, Jennifer."

He returned to the other side of his desk and cleared away the newspapers which he had been reading. Marks looked up from his notes.

"Do you know of a woman by the name of Beverley Drake?"

"Yes, I do. A very talented individual and a leading light in our East Midlands area. Highly committed to the cause as well."

"No longer, I'm afraid. She was fished out of the Thames a day or so ago. Now, why would she be down here, all that way from home?" Marks looked up.

"What?" Grafton remained seated, and put on an act of supreme surprise. "She only came to see me recently." The last statement was designed to take the wind out of Marks' next question. It succeeded.

"I see." The DCI flipped to another page in his notebook, momentarily side-tracked. "What would that be about?"

"A personal matter as it turned out." Grafton leaned back, sensing that he held the initiative. "It appears that a friend of hers had gone missing." He scratched his head, feigning thought. "A chap called Mike Summers."

"Another of your members, I understand."

"That's right. He's the leader of the Derbyshire branch."

"Indeed." Marks noted Grafton's use of the present tense. "Well, I have some more bad news for you. He too has been found in the River Thames, and very close to the spot where Ms Drake was discovered."

"Good Lord! This is terrible. What must their families be going through?" Grafton kicked himself for that slip, and Marks was on it in a flash.

"They have no family, as I'm sure you must be aware. You *are* the party leader after all. Summers and Drake were two of your officials, and their files would have told you that."

"Yes, how stupid of me." He smiled and tried to pass it off. "We've had a lot going on just recently."

"The election result – yes, I suppose you must be feeling very pleased with that."

"A small step forward, Chief Inspector, nothing more. What is it that they say? *'A week is a long time in politics.'* We'll be old news in seven days' time."

"Was Summers down here in London for any particular reason?"

"Yes. He was at one of our periodic meetings. This one was important as we'd secured a new source of funding for our election campaigns. It was a very successful gathering."

"Did you speak to him directly?"

"No, there were so many people in the room, and I simply didn't have the time to get around to everyone. I think he left before the meeting broke up, although I can't be certain."

The questions were not taking Marks in the direction he had planned when first setting foot inside the building, and he could sense that Grafton was coasting through what was, after all, a serious line of investigation. Time to ruffle a few feathers.

"What do you know of Ms Drake's relationship with a civil servant by the name of Stephen Marshall? I gather she discussed him with you."

It was a typical Marks gamble based on information which Watkinson had supplied, and the question startled Grafton. The DCI picked up on it immediately and pushed on without waiting for an answer.

"You see, the gentleman in question has been found dead in Yorkshire in what could be seen as suspicious circumstances. Are you aware that he was a secret service agent working undercover?"

The tide had now turned, and Grafton's manner became decidedly uncertain. This was a question which he had not anticipated, and his reply was somewhat ragged.

"What are you trying to infer, Chief Inspector? That I might have known something about their deaths?" The voice held more than a trace of anger, and all of the meticulous training which Grafton had been given had flown out of the window.

"Well, did you?" Marks, back on the front foot, leaned forwards.

"Of course not! I'm the leader of a political party, not a murderer."

"I never said they'd been murdered. Only that they were dead. Marshall's is the only one that appears suspicious, and he was found in North Yorkshire. That's quite a way from your back yard, isn't it?" Marks concealed the lie expertly.

Grafton had been outmanoeuvred and he knew it. Now it was down to damage limitation. He sighed, leaned back in his chair, and smiled at the detective before him.

"I don't like telling tales, Chief Inspector, but I knew this would end in tears. Beverley and Mike were in a relationship and things were, how shall we put it, going through one of those rocky periods. I knew that they'd argued, and Mike was down here to try and get his head around what it was that he needed to do. When he disappeared, Beverley came knocking on my door for advice."

"So, you knew her socially." It was a statement, not a question.

"Not as such. We'd met at one or two party gatherings, that's all. She must have thought that she could somehow enlist my help in finding him. I told her the same as I've told you. He was at the meeting and then left – I saw nothing more of him after that."

"I'm struggling to see why the two of them should have ended up at the bottom of the Thames, Mr Grafton."

"Inspector." Grafton, feeling that the pressure had eased, relaxed a little. "Have you considered the possibility of a third party to all of this? Someone related in some way to either of the deceased?"

"Go on."

"Well, Mike Summers was not a monogamous male. I'd known him for some time, and there was always a woman involved somewhere. Perhaps you should be looking for a jealous husband. Have you checked him out for partners in his past?"

"Not yet, no."

"Beverley Drake." Grafton shifted the conversation smoothly. "I confess that she came to me with a story about a civil servant whom she knew. That would, presumably, be your Stephen Marshall, and she'd restarted a relationship with him after a gap of some years – I gather he originally came from Derbyshire. This looks to me like a case of a tangled web which went badly wrong for the two of them – three if you include Summers."

"Really?" Marks stared hard into the eyes of Robert Grafton, but the BDP leader had regained his composure, and sensing that the interview was at an end, he stood up.

"Mr Grafton. This looks to me, a simple policeman, like a straightforward case of murder, and both victims seem to have links to the British

Democratic Party. I'll check out your theories, but if they do come up blank I'll be back here, and this time the questions will not be so pleasant."

Dennis Marks sat in his car outside the offices of the BDP and pulled out his mobile phone. Peter Spencer was quick to pick up at the other end.

"Any luck, boss?" He knew of Marks' intentions towards Grafton and was eager for some information.

"Not yet, Peter. Get me whatever files you can muster on Robert Grafton, and contact George Watkinson as well. There's more to this guy than meets the eye, and I thought I had him on the ropes at one point."

"What happened?"

"He's a politician. They're all the same – give them a crack to squeeze through and they'll take it. Something tells me he's more involved in our body count than he's letting on. I'll be back at the office shortly; we'll call in on George Groves and see if he's come up with anything new."

George Watkinson was at the lab with Groves when Marks and his team arrived. He looked up at the DCI as he entered and raised his eyebrows. Marks shook his head.

"Thought I had him at one point, but he's been well trained. We're going to need something pretty damning to prove that he's involved in any way." He glanced at Groves. "Anything new, George?"

"I was just explaining to Mr Watkinson. The car exploded as a result of ignition from the electrical system when it came into contact with petrol fumes from the fractured fuel lines. There was a point of impact on Marshall's skull consistent with it meeting the windscreen. That wasn't the cause of death, but it would certainly have rendered him unconscious – highly fortunate in the circumstances. From that point the car became an inferno, and we only have what there is now because the tank wasn't full."

"How do you know?" Marks asked

"Because the fuel level indicator had jammed at just under half way – the heat generated by the fire would have done that."

"Positive ID?"

"Yes. The dental and DNA records supplied by MI5 match those we took from the corpse. Can't be sure about fingerprints, but when you put them together with the rest of the evidence, I'd say that it's pretty conclusive. It was Steve Marshall in that car."

"This sounds too clean cut," Watkinson stepped in. "I only have Steve's word that he was up there on MI5 business, and he hadn't briefed me on the details. That in itself wouldn't bother me too much, but when you put it together with everything else that we have, well, it just feels wrong."

"I agree," Marks interjected. "I've been in this game too long now not to trust my instincts. My gut tells me that there are some loose ends hanging around, and I hate the darn things. We've got four corpses which all seem to have a common theme – all are related to activities surrounding the British Democratic Party and Robert Grafton. It's just too neatly wrapped up. Chloe," He looked at Warner, who had remained in the background until now, "find out when we can get Morse's body back down here. I'd like George to give it the once over. You never know, Nottinghamshire may just have missed something that he won't."

From a day which had promised so much, they all returned to their respective bases with far less than had been anticipated at the outset. For Robert Grafton it had been a narrow escape from a corner into which he had appeared to be painting himself. Marks was not a happy man, and that should have sent a warning signal to the BDP leader.

24

"I suppose that just about wraps it up then." Marks sat down opposite George Watkinson at Thames House.

"From your point of view, yes. The initial brief was to chase down Christopher Morse, and that's come to a rather quicker conclusion than I'd envisaged. The rest of the matter was a bonus, strangely enough. Your team should be able to return to normal duties now, but none of this can ever reach the outside world, you understand."

"Of course. What about the Organisation? You were coming around to the idea that Marshall had something to do with that, weren't you?"

"Indeed." Watkinson looked out of the window and across the Thames. "There'll be someone else to step into those shoes, and it'll be down to us here to find out who and where they are. That's a matter that I would be reluctant to have the Met become involved in."

"Well, here are the files you gave us at the beginning. There's only one to come, and I'll call in and see George Groves for his later today."

"Very well." Watkinson stood up and shook the DCI's hand. "Thank you for all the help; it's just a shame that we couldn't nail it all right down."

"You know where I am if the need ever arises in the future."

—————⊂≫————

Marks was disappointed to find Groves missing from his lab when he called for the file. Kevin Henson, the pathologist's assistant, was cleaning up at the end of the day and smiled as the DCI entered the room – his presence did not seem to upset the young man in the same way as Watkinson's had.

"No George, Kevin?"

"No. He's gone up to Yorkshire, Chief Inspector. Something that was bothering him, I gather."

"I see. All right, it's just odd that he didn't mention it to me."

"I think it was a sudden impulse, and he couldn't find you."

"When you hear from him again, could you ask him for the file? He'll know what I mean."

"Of course."

George Groves, at that very moment, was standing half way down Sutton Bank in North Yorkshire with his opposite number in the region. William Blount pointed to the taped-off area at the side of the road.

"That's where the vehicle veered off, and there's a scorched trail all the way down to the oak tree across there." He indicated a badly charred tree some hundred yards to the right.

"Something bothers me about this whole thing." Groves sighed. "I mean, I can go with the fractured fuel lines causing the explosion, and broken brake pipes preventing him from stopping the car, but why not simply bail out? He would have suffered cuts and bruises, but nothing more."

"Yes, we thought about that, and the only explanation I could come up with was panic. The distance isn't that far when you take into consideration the speed that he must have been travelling, even across this terrain. You'd need to be thinking clearly and fast in order to take action like that. Was he drunk?"

"Tox screen results came back negative for both alcohol and narcotics, but the body was badly burned and he had been out here for a while." Groves stepped off the road and under the tape – Blount followed.

"When you look at the state of the ground, all these rocks embedded in the surface, it was sort of surprising that the car made it all the way down there, but with no contradictory evidence we couldn't come to any other conclusion. He was simply out of control and locked in."

"You said earlier that there were tyre tracks in the farm entrance back up there. Did you get anything from them?"

"Yes." Blount pulled out a notebook. "We took moulds, and the treads relate to an all-weather tyre, a 215/65 R15, that Volkswagen use on their Caddy range of vans. We put out an appeal in the local media, and a gas fitter by the name of Geoff Marsden responded. He'd parked up to take a call from his partner, and he's not entirely certain what happened, but it puts the time of the crash at around one in the morning. He couldn't be more precise as he'd broken his watch."

"How did he know, then?"

"He'd left his last job at Thirsk at around half past midnight. The distance is around ten miles, and it would have taken him about half an hour to get here at that particular time."

"At least that gives us a more accurate time of death. What about that fencing at the side of the road?"

"It's made from ash – very hard and durable. The pilings are three feet down, and set in one-to-one concrete. He must have hit them with some force. Why do you ask?" Blount frowned, concerned that he and his team may have missed something.

"Oh, just something that I found in the car when we got it back to London." Groves noticed the expression on his face. "Don't worry yourself, the conditions up here wouldn't have allowed you to spot what I did."

"What was it?"

"Fragments of burned wood. Very small following the fire, and I assumed that they'd come from the impact of breaking through the fencing. That's one of the reasons I wanted to take a look for myself."

"What were they?"

"Not ash, that's for sure." He looked around once more. "And yet there's nothing else between the road and that tree which could account for it. I may be looking too deeply, but it's so out of place that I can't simply ignore it."

"What does DCI Marks think?"

"Dennis? Oh, I haven't said anything about this to him yet. I don't want to set him off on a trail which might lead up a blind alley. I'll have to bring it up when I get back, though."

Groves shook his head once more, and they returned to the road. All of the evidence gathered from the vehicle led him to believe that this was an accident. Perhaps Marshall had simply fallen asleep at the wheel; maybe he had been trying to answer that final call to his mobile when he lost control of the car – there were a number of possibilities. If it weren't for the fractured fuel lines, he would have been very suspicious of the whole thing. The engine compartment had been the prime site of ignition, and the flash would have sent a jet of flame all the way back to the petrol tank – an explosion had been inevitable, so why the wood fragments in the foot well?

"Well, thank you, William. I'm not sure whether this has helped or not, but I'm grateful for you bringing me here." The drive back to York and his return train journey to London gave Groves plenty of opportunity to reconsider all of the findings, but by the time he arrived back at the lab the next morning, he was still certain that something had been missed.

Steve Marshall's funeral took place a week later. With conclusive evidence that it had been him at the wheel of the Audi when it went off the road in Yorkshire, there was no reason to delay the ceremony. Groves had put the final touches to his report after returning from his own trip up there, and copies of the documents had been forwarded to Watkinson at MI5. No comments had been forthcoming from Thames House, and the gathering at the Eltham crematorium comprised those who knew and worked with Marshall. George Watkinson read the eulogy, a generalised tribute to a hard working civil servant cut down in his prime, and after a brief chat with those friends who had managed to make the trip, he started to make his way back to the car park.

"Dennis, a quick word." He had spotted Marks at the back of the chapel, and they stepped to one side as the rest of the small crowd passed by.

"Yes." Both glanced around to ensure that they were not overheard. "I thought we were done."

"Almost. There's the small matter of the break-in at my house recently, and I'd like you and your team to take a look before we finally close the book on all of this."

"The papers?" Marks had been briefed privately on the contents of the safe at the Watkinson home, and fully realised the importance of the dossier which Roger Fretwell had managed to keep secret for so many years.

"Indeed. It would be highly embarrassing for them to get into the wrong hands, but I need the job doing with as little fuss as possible."

"All right, I'll keep the four of us together later today and let you know when we can make the trip without arousing too much suspicion at the Yard. Groves is over there; I'll talk to him first." Marks nodded towards the flower garden where the pathologist was in conversation with a woman – someone the DCI had never seen before.

"Very good. I have to go now; there's the question of Steve's replacement to be addressed, and it isn't something that I can afford to delay too much."

Marks watched Watkinson leave the car park, and strolled over to the display area where Groves was still in conversation with the woman. She looked to be in her late forties, and had dark brown shoulder length hair. Her tanned appearance suggested that she was not a UK resident, and as he got closer her accent became clearer.

"Ah, Dennis." Groves smiled. "You may be interested to meet Amanda Pietsersen."

"Pietersen?" Marks shook her hand. "South African? I wondered when I heard your accent."

"Yes, Chief Inspector, and I've heard all about you from your colleague, Professor Groves."

"Amanda is Steve Marshall's aunt." The look on Grove's face told Marks that there could be more to this than met the eye.

"His aunt? I thought that he had no living relatives. George Watkinson told me…"

"Stephen's boss may not even have been aware of my existence. I've known of my nephew's work at the Ministry of Work and Pensions for a while, and it was nice to see that the head of the department could make the effort to be here." She took a pack of cigarettes from her handbag and lit one.

"So you're…"

"His mother's sister, yes." She laughed and shook her head. "Family disputes. Mavis and I had a serious falling out when Stephen was very young – too young to even notice that I was no longer around. It was only when he grew up that we re-established contact."

"May I ask what the cause of the argument was?" Marks pushed gently.

"Politics I'm afraid, and it got in the way of the entire family. I fell in love with, and married, an advisor to the right-wing National Party in Pretoria.

Jan was a very kind man, but mother and father could not reconcile to his views on apartheid. Even when the party disbanded I was still seen as an outcast amongst western society. Jan died last year, and when I heard news of Stephen's accident, I felt that I had to come."

"How long have you been over here?"

"I flew in two days ago; when Mavis died I would not have been welcome, but I was determined to be here on this occasion."

"If you wouldn't mind my asking," Groves interrupted, "what was the cause of your sister's death?"

"Cancer. Stephen had told me that Mavis had been ill for some time, and was not responding to any conventional medicine. When her condition became terminal, the consultant told her of an experimental trial and she jumped at the chance."

"Where did the trials take place?" Groves led the way to a bench and the three of them sat down.

"As you probably know, Stephen originated from Derbyshire, and Mavis was being treated at the Derby City Hospital. It became clear fairly soon that the procedure wasn't working. According to the consultant, any treatment tailored to an individual's genetic makeup was not going to be helpful in her case, but Mavis, being Mavis, decided to continue to take part in the trials for the sake of future sufferers. Stephen told me he was immensely proud of her."

"Where does all of this lead us?" Marks' interest was aroused, and his gut was telling him that a lead could be staring him right in the face. He stared at Groves for an answer.

"Results of clinical trials will be on record at whatever hospital carried them out, and they remain there for reference as long as they are needed. Sometimes that can be years."

"So that means…?"

"It means, Dennis, that a person could compare the records of sisters and see just how close the DNA matches. In the case of Mavis and Amanda their records will show a very strong link."

"And therefore you'll be able to compare those to the…."

"Well thank you, Amanda. It's been a pleasure to meet you on such a sad occasion. If you're ever in England again, please look us up." Groves smiled, pulled Marks by the sleeve, and they left Amanda Pietersen getting into the taxi booked to take her back to her hotel.

Groves watched her all the way, and then took a small plastic bag and a pair of tweezers out of his inside coat pocket. Picking up the cigarette butt she had discarded at the side of the bench, he placed it inside the bag, sealed the top, and put it back into the same pocket. Marks had watched all of this with mounting interest, and raised a questioning eyebrow as Groves turned to face him.

"Oh, just a fancy I had. Nothing to get excited about."

"Come on George, you never do anything on just a whim. What's going on, and what was all that DNA stuff about?"

"I've told you before, Dennis, I'll let you know when I'm sure." He smiled knowingly and Marks shook his head in frustration.

"I'm damned if I'll let you go without telling me what could possibly be interesting about that woman's cigarette end and her dead sister's DNA. Unless..." His eyes widened.

"Now, now. It's just a butt; nothing more."

"Yes, but what you're saying..."

"Is nothing, Detective Chief Inspector, and neither should you. Dennis Marks goes on hard evidence, and at the moment he has none. That's right, isn't it?"

"Yes." Marks was stumped and he knew it. The chances of getting an opinion out of Groves right now were zero.

"I suppose it's asking too much as to whether our friend from MI5 is happy right now." Groves changed the subject, and Marks let him off the hook.

"The case is officially closed, but he does want to see the four of us at his Surrey home as soon as possible. I told him I'd try to get us all down there straight away, so it looks like there's another busy week coming up. We'll have a chat about it when we get back to the Yard."

25

For Robert Grafton, the news of Steve Marshall's death had come as a significant blow. He recognised his benefactor's face from the press releases, and was still unclear how a civil servant could be the source of so much money. Now, in early autumn, that was no longer his main concern and with the half million which Marshall had donated fast running out, there was a need for a fresh injection of funds to finance another push towards the next general election.

His sources had made him aware of the police presence at the funeral, and that fact puzzled him. The deaths of Morse, Summers, and Drake could not be traced back to him, and the perpetrators had all been provided with sufficient remuneration to ensure their absence from the UK for the foreseeable future. There seemed to be no point in Marks being there, unless there were factors in the background of which he was not aware. The DCI had been clear in his threat to return should fresh evidence point him in the way of the BDP, but that was now extremely unlikely. His thoughts were interrupted by the buzzing of his telephone.

"Yes, Jennifer."

"Mr Grafton, there's a gentleman on the line, and he says he needs to speak to you right away."

"What's his name?"

"He wouldn't give it, sir. I did ask."

"All right, put it through, and you can take an early lunch." Grafton sighed – cold calls irritated him, and he made a mental note to replace his receptionist at the earliest opportunity.

"Mr Grafton?"

"Yes, who is this?"

"Someone with your interests at heart now that your benefactor is no longer with us." The voice was deep and flat, and had a northern edge to it.

"I have no idea what you mean."

"Of course you do, and I have no interest in any of your denials. The stakes for which we are both playing are far too high for nonsense like this. We need to meet." His tone remained even, and Grafton's attempts to deflect the conversation were failing.

"What's in this for you?"

"The same as it was for Mr Marshall. Yes, I'm aware that you must know his name by now, but he wasn't the only one capable of providing the necessary funding for you to win the next General Election. You *do* want to win the next General Election, don't you?" It was the first time that the voice had changed its pitch, and Grafton was taken by surprise.

"We do. What's your angle? Marshall never explained his."

"That's why we need to get together. I find discussing matters like this on the telephone tiresome and inconvenient. You never know who might be listening in."

"We're quite safe now. I've sent our Girl Friday off to lunch. So, where do you propose we meet?"

"There's a pub called the Pilot Inn near the O2 Arena; know it?"

"River Way?"

"That's the one. Be there in half an hour."

"All right." Grafton put down the phone.

His naturally suspicious nature was ringing all of the alarm bells, but the party needed funds, and since there were no other outstretched hands this one could not be ignored. He had noted the stress placed on the reference to the General Election, and maybe, just maybe, this guy had an inside track on the workings of the party funding mechanism that the BDP were yet to realise. The bar at the Pilot was not full when he arrived, and a raised hand from a corner had him making his way over to that table. Drinks were already there.

"How did you know?" He pointed at the glass.

"Mr Grafton," He leaned forwards, dropping his voice, "we in the Organisation know many things which escape the attention of the general public, and I include you and your party in that statement."

Grafton looked at the man before him – a man whose name he had yet to learn. His height, he guessed, was around five feet ten; he had black hair, swept back from a broad forehead. His grey eyes appeared soulless, and he sported a full beard and moustache. A broad grin revealed a set of teeth which reminded the BDP leader of the smile on the face of the tiger. The paunch around his middle suggested someone accustomed to the good life, and he decided there and then to take whatever it was that was on offer.

"I know what Marshall wanted, but what's your angle?" He sat down and took a pull on the pint before him.

"No different to that which my predecessor outlined to you."

"You've taken over?" Grafton put the glass back down.

"There are always people ready and willing to step up to the mark. Steve Marshall knew that, and his demise, tragic as it was, can't be allowed to derail the plans."

"I still don't know your name."

"My apologies." The outstretched hand was taken. "Adrian Lawson – Steve and I worked closely together. You could almost say that our aims were identical."

"All right, what now?" Grafton's wary tone did not escape the ears of his new ally, and Lawson smiled again.

"You, Mr Grafton, are running out of funds. We know that; we know many things. The half million which Steve organised is quickly being spent, and you're going to need a whole lot more to finance the sort of success that the Burnley by-election gave you."

There was no doubt that this Adrian Lawson held all of the cards, and Grafton, skilled politician though he was, had no answer when it came down to the cold, hard, subject of cash. The BDP simply did not have enough fee-paying members to be self-sufficient, and it had lost many of its traditional backers due to a shift in policy which had seen a change in its profile. No longer were they portrayed as the bully boys of the British right wing, and Grafton's committee had selectively rid themselves of the kind of person adopting that line – Mike Summers had merely been the latest of those casualties.

"What do we do, then?" It sounded like capitulation, and Grafton writhed as the words came out.

"No more than you already are doing, but with a lot more money behind you. Our organisation is more than happy, as long as you follow an agreed path, to take a back seat and see you transform this country. We're familiar with your policies, and the British public up in the North West obviously liked what they saw. We - that is, *you* - need to get them understood by a wider representative circle now, and I have the finances to ensure that that happens. Are you interested in a couple of million?"

"I'd be an idiot not to be." He sighed. "It'll have to go before the committee first, though. I make no decisions off my own bat; it's not like the early days any more – we have a constitution and I'm not about to circumvent it."

"Staying within the law, eh?" Lawson's smile had vanished, and Grafton felt a cold sensation running down his spine. "You're not beyond a little weeding out where it's needed though, are you?"

"Meaning?"

"Oh, just a few names that I could mention. People who've stood in the way of progress; eggs which needed to be broken in order to make an omelette. You know."

"I'm afraid I don't." Grafton was feeling hot under the collar, and this meeting was fast becoming a place where he did not want to be, despite the promises made.

Lawson leaned closer once more, and Grafton was unable to resist a similar movement, "I know what happened to those three." He whispered. "Shall I remind you of their names?"

"That won't be necessary." He moved back into his chair. This man held every card in the deck, and Grafton knew that he, himself, was powerless.

"Very well. Just stick to the plan, and no-one need ever know of any involvement which you may, or may not have had in their fates."

Back at the BDP offices, Grafton had recovered his composure sufficiently to take stock of what had been said to him. He was over a barrel – there was no doubt about that – but all he had to do was persuade the committee to accept a further two million (he repeated the figure to himself, *'two million!'*) in funding for a concerted push on the British electorate. He buzzed reception.

"Yes, Mr Grafton."

"Jennifer, put a call out to all members of the central committee. There'll be an extraordinary general meeting tomorrow evening here in the main room. Got that?"

"Of course, Mr Grafton. Right away."

Adrian Lawson's journey north, after the meeting with Robert Grafton, had taken him up the M1 to Birmingham. He now stood, looking out onto the car park, at the window of the boardroom of FM Engineering. The room had changed very little since the day, in 1992, when Gerald Montgomery had made his dash for freedom from Watkinson's cavalry. That flight had taken him to Nottingham and the fatal shooting at the city's Midland Station which had seen Steve Marshall assume control of the Organisation. He turned as a group of younger people entered and took their places at the table in the centre of the room.

These were the same faces, albeit considerably older now, that had been present at the cottage on St Mary's Lane in Tewkesbury where Marshall had given his rousing speech to rally the troops. He knew their names, and was familiar with each of their files; all had pedigrees going back to the secret documents which the Fretwells had hidden all those years ago. They looked at him expectantly, and hung on his every word.

"You'll all know by now of the unfortunate death of Steve Marshall. He'll be sorely missed, but don't doubt for a minute that this event will not, in any way, halt the progress which has been made. I met with the leader of the British Democratic Party earlier today, and he, Robert Grafton, has graciously accepted our offer of funding for his party's activities."

There was a smattering of laughter around the room, and Lawson raised a finger – silence fell immediately.

"Don't take the man lightly. We need him and his organisation if we're to fully achieve our own ends. His is the acceptable face of our intentions; never forget that. He's no fool, and will see right through us if we don't take great care with our planning. Down to business; there's a set of files before you, each one representing your own particular geographical area. Read them thoroughly and ensure that you're familiar with all of the objectives in detail. You'll see the amount of funding which has been allocated, and I need not remind anyone remotely considering what could be done with the money, that a less than pleasant fate will be waiting for those stepping out of line. The name of Miranda Farnley is in there – look her up; she'll be a lesson to you all."

The meeting ran on into the evening, and after a final session of questions and answers, those whose missions were now to carry the Organisation upon its predetermined path departed the building and headed home. Lawson watched them all as they left and pondered once more the fatal blow which Gerald Montgomery had tried to inflict. The attempt on

Watkinson's life in 1992 had brought about not only his own downfall, but had also seriously compromised the entire structure. It was an error which would never be repeated. He looked at his watch – it was now almost ten o'clock. The flat upstairs would suffice for tonight, and he would make his way back south in the morning.

26

George Groves stood up and stretched. He rubbed his aching back and winced, picked up his forensic kit and moved from the hallway to the lounge where Marks, Spencer, and Warner were carrying out their own searches for clues.

"This is back-breaking work, Dennis. I usually have a team of six with this type of stuff."

"You'll just have to make do with us amateurs." Marks smiled. "We've dusted every surface, just like you showed us, and the box over there is full of the prints we've found. It's down to you now, old man, to sort the wheat from the chaff. George and Marjorie gave us samples of theirs, but some of the others must belong to friends, and there's no way that Watkinson will allow us to spread the net in that direction."

George Watkinson chose that very moment to appear at the doorway, and stood at the threshold surveying the scene. Groves turned as he coughed to attract their attention.

"You can come in; we've just about finished in here now." The pathologist fastened his case and took off the pair of latex gloves.

"Did you find anything?"

"We couldn't find any sign of a break-in," Marks shook his head, "and from that point of view the whole place is as clean as a whistle. We've dusted every outside door and window, and the prints we found are in Professor Groves' bag. They're all marked with the location where they were found, so it's down to the lab team now."

"The lab team?" Watkinson frowned.

"There's no need to be concerned." Groves chipped in. "I need help to analyse the samples, but my staff won't know where we found them. That's still between the five of us here."

"So, all of the windows and doors are still secure?"

"Yes," Marks said. "We found no evidence of any damage, however slight, which might indicate a forced entry at any point on the property. There were none of the tell-tale footprints around the windows, and to be quite honest, whoever did break in would need to have been Santa Claus coming down the chimney."

"And still those papers are missing." Watkinson sat down – they all followed suit.

"You're absolutely certain that you left them upstairs in your study?" Marks asked.

"Positive. I remember placing them back into the safe."

"Could your wife have moved them?" The DCI trod very carefully.

"Marjorie rarely goes into my study." Watkinson shook his head. "We've been married for thirty years and she realises the importance of some of the stuff I bring home. No, she would have reminded me if she had seen anything left out on the desk, but she wouldn't have gone in there."

Marks had to admit that, in all his years on the force, he had never been in a 'locked room' scenario before. He did not doubt the fact that Watkinson had brought some papers home and had worked on them in his study. The questions posed had been merely formalities, but it seemed impossible for anyone to have entered the house, let alone the room upstairs, without leaving at least some trace of their presence.

"You mentioned Steve Marshall in connection with the papers. You had stated that he knew you'd brought them here." Marks had no notes of that meeting, but remembered the conversation.

"I did, and I'm now more convinced than ever that he may have had some involvement. My team are turning his flat over at the moment, so you can forget about that end of things. If the papers are there, I'll know about it very soon. I just can't see him having come here himself."

"What was the name of the burglar you told me had broken into Thames House?"

"Graham Poundall, but Morse killed him. We know that for a fact because there's a confession on file – one of ours I might add, not yours."

"Murder? Why weren't we told about that?" Marks scowled – concerned at the sudden revelation of some kind of cover up.

"It was an internal matter, and one which we chose to keep within the department. I'm sorry if it offends your professional ethics, but that's the way the security services operate. I think you must be aware of that after your run-in with Eric Staines at the IPCC."

Marks nodded slowly. That investigation had almost cost him his career, and brought home to him in sharp focus the secretive workings of the internal discipline routines within the Metropolitan Police. He sighed; there was nothing more that the four of them could do at the Watkinson home and, taking their leave, they all returned to London. They had been gone only a quarter of an hour when Watkinson's mobile phone rang. There was a brief conversation, after which he put on his coat, told his wife he would be out for the rest of the day, and left.

"Okay, Barry. What have you found?" Watkinson walked in through the front door of Steve Marshall's flat.

"It's upstairs, sir. We were taking the floorboards up and one of the guys moved a step ladder we'd been using to get up into the loft area." The two of them made their way upstairs to the front bedroom.

Like the rest of the apartment, Marshall's bedroom was panelled, floor to ceiling, with some of the finest oak that Watkinson had laid eyes upon. Polished to a fine degree it, like the rest of the property, exuded an aura of well-heeled comfort. Marshall was, it had to be said, well paid as number two to the head of MI5, but Watkinson's questioning glance betrayed a feeling that this was one item beyond the scope of the salary which he drew.

"I see." His comment was brusque. "It would appear that I'm not the only one with a secret safe."

"No, and had it not been for the fact that Martin dropped the ladder we wouldn't have spotted it. The panel splintered just above that line there." He pointed to a faint break in the surface of the oak.

"Impressive, it's practically invisible. Have you tried to open it?"

"No, we're waiting for the locksmith. Hold on, that looks like him now." Newman looked out of the window to see an older man with a tool box coming up the path.

The safe in Marshall's upstairs room was, to all intents and purposes, invisible. The gap in the panelling was so fine, and so expertly crafted, that it was no more than the width of a human hair, and yet, when released, would have swung freely and noiselessly away. The locksmith stood momentarily in wonder at the workmanship, before setting about destroying what had taken much time and expense to create. Now faced with the metal safe behind its protective screening, he set to work.

Watkinson and Barry Newman paced the room for almost half an hour before the craftsman turned to them with a smile on his face.

"That's it." He announced, turning the recessed handle and swinging open the door.

The interior of the safe itself, at only twelve inches square and ten inches deep, was quite small. It nevertheless contained a stack of paperwork from top to bottom, and Watkinson had the room cleared of all staff apart from Newman and himself before he emptied the contents onto a plastic sheet which had been spread on the floor. The bulk of the documents were of no interest to them, being a collection of personal correspondence – passport, bank statements, and a variety of utility bills, and it was not until they had almost come to the end of the pile that Watkinson stood up.

"Sir?" Newman stopped what he was doing.

"This, Barry, may be just what I was looking for." He held up to the light a small, yellowed, piece of aged paper.

"What is it?" The younger man squinted in the sunlight to see what Watkinson was pointing at.

"A watermark, and a very specific one at that." He sighed. "I may have to resign myself to the fact that the rest of the papers, of which this was just a small piece, could well have gone up in smoke with the vehicle that Marshall was driving when it left the road in North Yorkshire."

"A dead end, then?"

"Perhaps. That would depend upon whether Steve would have had the chance to move the rest of the file somewhere else. If he did, we may never find it. Either way, I fear the papers may be lost to us now. I need to check something out before I can be sure."

"Are we done here, then?"

"Yes, I think so. Get the place tidied up and we'll move out." Watkinson looked down again at the small remainder of the files in his hand and smiled. The man he was going to see may well have a surprise coming.

Watkinson pulled up outside the house in St John's Wood Road just off Regents Park. With Lord's cricket ground as a backdrop, the location was one of the most sought after in London. He walked up the front garden with its immaculately manicured lawn, and rang the ornate brass doorbell. Times had certainly been good for the man whom he was about to see. A woman in her early sixties opened the door.

"Hello, Miriam. Is he at home?" The smile was genuine, and she, at least, was always pleased to see him.

"George. Won't you come inside? We were just about to have tea. Would you care to join us?"

"I'd be delighted, though whether Solly would think so remains to be seen."

"Go on in, and never mind that old fool. He doesn't know what's best for him sometimes."

The lounge was pretty much as Watkinson remembered it from his last visit – places like these rarely changed with time, and Wiseman was a stick-in-the-mud as far as alterations were concerned. His taste was impeccable though; a Turner above the Adam fireplace was supplemented by a set of Chippendale dining furniture at the end of the room, overlooking a spacious back garden. The lounge itself was carpeted in the finest Axminster and ranged by a set of dark brown leather Chesterfields. It was into one of these chairs that George sank, wondering whether he would be able to extricate himself at the end of his stay.

"Oy vey! Can't you leave an old man in peace at the end of his life? What did I do, Lord, to deserve what you inflict upon me?" Wiseman's pantomime had Watkinson smiling as the Jew came into the room. He managed to stand up.

"Solly, you old devil. Still managing to earn the odd crust then?" He looked around the lavish interior.

"Mr Watkinson, you have no idea of the hard time that Miriam and I have been through. It's all fake you know." The smile was as wide as the Red Sea, and they shook hands enthusiastically. "What brings you to our little backwater?"

"I'm off out now, dear." Miriam came into the room and placed a tray on the oak coffee table. "I promised to go into town with Hester. You'll be able to look after Mr Watkinson on your own, won't you?" The smile said everything, and she left the room.

"I tell you, that woman is worth her weight in diamonds!" He nodded as he watched her down the path.

"Remember this?" Watkinson pulled the slip of yellowed paper carefully from his wallet.

Wiseman went to the mantelpiece and put on his glasses. He took the paper and held it up to the light, turning it over as he examined it in minute detail. He sat back down and placed it almost reverentially on the coffee table.

"Where on earth did you get that? It's a part of that special job we looked at all that time ago." Solly's face was a picture of amazement.

"It doesn't matter where it came from, but can you be certain that this was the exact paper that we had back in 1992?"

"Come with me." Wiseman rose and Watkinson followed him. "Let's go down to my little workshop and take a look at the records."

The cellar workshop was another place which had seen little change during the intervening years. The smells were identical, and Watkinson sat in the very same chair he used when his host completed the commission for him back then. He waited while Wiseman rummaged around amongst some old box files.

"Not at the print works any more, Solly?"

"Oh, no." He replied. "The boys are grown up now, and run the place far better than I ever did. I go in once in a while, and they always seem very pleased to see the old man, but it's a youngster's world out there now, and people like me… well, we're past our sell by date. Ah! Here we are."

He pulled out a slim folder and blew the dust away from its surface. Unfastening the quarter inch pink ribbon which he used on all his files, he laid out the contents on a workbench and Watkinson rose from his seat to take a look.

"There, you see? The watermark is identical. It wasn't too hard to replicate that kind of stuff. As I think I told you at the time, things were pretty crude back in the 1940s, and paper and ink were of fairly basic quality."

"Yes." Watkinson held the torn off piece up to the dim light along with a full sized sheet from the folder. "I can't really tell, but I'll take your word for it that they're identical."

"It's the irregular impression of the image there." He pointed to the right hand edge of the stamped watermark. "I had to be careful to get the proportions correct so that the same fault appeared on the forgeries."

"You are a true master of the art." Watkinson shook his head in admiration. "But I really should have had you in jail a long time ago."

"You wish." The old Jew smiled. "You'd have had a hard job proving anything in a court of law. I tell you, there are times when I can't tell the difference myself amongst some of this old stuff. What chance do you think *you* would have had?"

"Can I take this?" He held up the full sheet. "I'd like to show it to one of our forensic team."

"Well…" Wiseman's demeanour changed, and his face suddenly bore a concerned frown.

"Don't worry, you old fool, I'm not going to come back looking for you. It may be just the clue I need in an old matter going back to the 1990s."

"The Nazi papers?"

"Can't say, sorry. It's all a bit 'hush hush', if you know what I mean." He smiled. It was good to get one over on the old sod for a change.

Wiseman smiled as he watched the spymaster get into his car and pull away, off the drive and back up the road past the test match ground. That was a close one, he thought; good thing Watkinson hadn't spotted the blank passports he'd been in the middle of preparing for the Americans.

27

The voice of the speaker rang out crisp and clear in the chamber of the House of Commons.

"Order! Order! The house calls upon the Right Honourable Robert James Grafton."

Robert Grafton's day had come. Three months and one day since his spectacular victory at the Burnley by-election he was here, in the Houses of Parliament, about to deliver his maiden speech. It would be a speech unopposed by any other member in the chamber, and would be delivered in an atmosphere of total silence from all those present – that was the tradition. It was customary to avoid all contentious and controversial issues, and Grafton's writers had been very careful in that respect. He rose from the back benches where he had been sitting for the past hour - the room fell still.

"Thank you for calling me to make my maiden speech in this debate today, Mr Speaker. I am deeply honoured to have been elected as the Member of Parliament for the constituency of Burnley in the recent by-election. The circumstances for it were remarkable, and it is only right to mention that many constituents and colleagues from across the House have commented on my predecessor John Green's intellect, his incredible attention to detail, and the kindness he showed to them."

"My constituency is a place with an interesting history. Burnley is a market town with a population of around 73,500. It began life in the early medieval period as a number of farming hamlets surrounded by manor houses and royal forests, gaining a market over 700 years ago. Its main period of expansion came during the Industrial Revolution, when it grew into one of Lancashire's most prominent Mill towns. At its peak, it became one of the world's largest producers of cotton cloth, and a major centre of engineering."

"As beautiful and as varied as my constituency is, what I care most about are the people. During the by-election, I met thousands of constituents from all walks of life, some of whom supported me and some of whom did not.

Regardless of their political affiliation, however, they were invariably polite. Their tolerance and decency reflect something very special about our society: a social conscience that values fairness, treating people as they would like to be treated, while recognising that different people have different needs and merits. As we know, both intuitively and from research, fairer societies do better, and *are* better for everyone. Of course, all political parties have claimed that they are the party of fairness, but I think most people will agree that actions speak louder than words."

Hansard recalls that the subject matter of Grafton's speech centred upon the plight of the unemployed – particularly those youngsters leaving school and college without the hope of a job. His criticisms were evenly spread amongst successive governments, and yet no manifesto pledges were made relative to policies of the British Democratic Party. Vague hints at what should be done were outlined, but in no more detail than those propounded by ranks of MPs before him.

His final words were no more controversial than those which had gone before, but those listening with more than a little care would have noted a steely edge to his voice as he came to his concluding statement.

"I promised my constituents that I would stand up for them. I believe that the Government's policies are deeply unfair and, contrary to their assertions, unwarranted. As history has shown, Governments set the tone for the culture of a society. The tone being set by this one threatens the country's sense of fair play and social justice. Thank you again, Mr Speaker, for calling me."

When he resumed his seat some thirty minutes later, it was to an undercurrent of comments from both sides of the House.

———❦———

The leader of the BDP was on a high. Not only had he carried the party meeting following his provisional agreement with Adrian Lawson, but he had now made his debut in the real world of politics. The funds promised, and now delivered, by Lawson were yet to be used, and as far as he could see this was to be a time of consolidation (as far as one member in the house could be regarded), and observation. He was not prepared for what was to come.

"Very impressive performance, Mr Grafton." Lawson raised his glass and the two of them toasted the maiden speech.

"Thank you, although I will confess to being a little apprehensive at the start." He looked around the room. Lunch at the Dorchester was a far cry from beer and sandwiches at the Pilot Inn on River Way.

"When do you plan to announce your party's manifesto? A General Election could be upon us sooner than you think, and you'll need to be prepared well in advance."

"Already at the final editing stage. The national committee have agreed on all major issues, and we go to the printers next month. From that point, I'll lead the launch at a press conference. Would you like to see a draft copy?"

"Quite unnecessary. I think we both agree where your party wishes to be, and I have a dossier on past activities, so we in the Organisation know precisely what it is that you want to achieve."

"Very well, although we're going to need a few more members in the house before any real progress can be made. There'll be at least one other by-election coming up before the next election, and we'll be in amongst the voters as we did in Burnley."

"Just keep eyes and ears open." Lawson smiled and, not for the first time, Grafton felt a chill running up and down his spine. "Here, take this; we stick to untraceable contact from now on. Make sure that you keep it topped up, and we stay away from landlines, e-mails – anything where we can be overheard. Understood?"

He slid across the table a mobile phone; the stakes had clearly moved up a notch, and their relationship was now assuming an altogether more secretive character.

"Sir, you need to turn on the television right away." It was highly unusual for Barry Newman to burst into Watkinson's office without knocking, and he made a mental note to reprove the youngster for it later.

"What the…?!"

"The BBC News Channel, sir. You'll miss it."

Newman picked up the remote and switched on the 32" TV at the end of the office. Flicking over to Channel 83, the news presenter was in the middle of a section of Breaking News.

'The House of Commons was brought to a standstill earlier this afternoon when three members abandoned their party's benches and crossed the house. In an unprecedented move, all took up seats adjacent to that occupied yesterday by Robert Grafton, leader of the British Democratic Party, as he made his maiden speech to the house. In a signed note handed to the speaker, they affirmed their intentions to resign the whips of their respective parties and serve as MPs for the BDP. Proceedings in the house were suspended for the day.'

"What is *that* all about?" Watkinson was out of his chair, all thoughts of a reprimand for Newman now forgotten.

"I don't know, sir. I picked it up as a headline on the main news bulletin. Is it unusual?"

"Not unusual, Barry. Winston Churchill did it twice. Three in one go though, that's extraordinary." Watkinson jabbed a number on his phone. "Wallace. Come in here, please."

"Right away, sir."

Sandra Wallace was one of Watkinson's senior operatives, and now in line for promotion following the death of Steve Marshall. She had served undercover on a number of occasions in the past, and was highly resourceful.

"What do you make of this?" He pointed at the screen, where a studio of political commentators had been hastily arranged to mull over the unusual events of the past half hour.

"One member from each of the main parties, all highly respected and all long-serving. I've done some digging around already, but there doesn't appear to have been any link between them until right now. There's certainly no hint that Robert Grafton either knew about it or was in any way behind it."

"Where is he right now?"

"We've been keeping tabs on him since Steve died, and he's been seen at the Dorchester with another man who goes under the name of Adrian Lawson."

"Background?"

"None yet. But I've got a team working on it."

"Good. Throw as much at it as you can, no expense spared. I don't like the look of where this might be going."

"What the devil's going on?!" An almost identical question now in the ear of Adrian Lawson.

Robert Grafton had been sitting at BDP headquarters catching up on the news when the story broke surrounding the activities in the chamber of the House of Commons. Lawson had given him the number of an untraceable mobile, and was now at the receiving end of what was bordering on panic stations.

"Calm down, Robert. You wanted a parliamentary party –you now have one."

"*You* did this? What right do you think you have to go tinkering with the BDP?"

"I believe that I have approximately two million of them at the last count. Don't you?"

Grafton was stunned. Yes, he wanted a presence in Parliament – it had been his dream for longer than he could remember. His desire to run the country ran deep, and a fervent, perverse, passion for what he regarded as 'right' burned within him with an intensity which none of his colleagues really understood. But this was *not* right – he had not achieved it; it had been given, served up on a silver platter, and he was powerless to do anything about it.

"Where the devil did they come from? Who are they? What on earth are you playing at?"

"One question at a time, please. They're all established parliamentarians – back benchers of repute, and not subject to the whims of party politics as such. They will give you and your party some credibility where it's needed right now. I'll tell you their names so that the BDP can officially adopt them and welcome them into its ranks. I suggest you convene an early meeting with all three, together with your committee. An official press release should be issued without delay. As for your final question, I'm kick-starting your campaign to become the Prime Minister of this country – now, I ask you…you *do* want to be the Prime Minister, don't you?"

"Yes, I do." The reply was somewhat muted, and Grafton realised for the first time that control over the BDP was starting to slip from his hands and into those of his paymasters.

"All right. Once you've convened the first meeting of your parliamentary party, you need to brief your newest MPs on the BDP manifesto. I think you'll find them to be easy converts to your philosophy. This is just the beginning."

"So, what are these people? Sleepers?" Grafton's question hit a momentary silence at the other end before Lawson replied.

"In a way. They've all been a part of the plan which the Organisation has been formulating over a considerable number of years, and are key to the success or failure of what you and the BDP are about to do. Keep your eyes and ears open over the next week or so – you may find that you have more of a political presence than you believed."

"Where is all this going?" Grafton's remark had Lawson smiling.

"All right, the news will be out soon anyway. This government is set to fall, and soon; my sources tell me of a back bench revolt."

"What?!"

"Just listen, would you?" Lawson interrupted. "Iraq and Afghanistan, expenses scandals, phone-tapping, that business with the Speaker just recently," He ticked them off on his fingers. "It's all coming to a head, and the Lib Dems are set to call timeout on the Coalition."

"A General Election!"

"Precisely." Lawson sneered. "A No Confidence motion's coming, and you need to be ready."

28

Dennis Marks and Peter Spencer were halfway up the stairs to the first floor CID offices when their progress was halted by the voice of George Groves from below. Catching up, he pointed silently to the office where the DCI had his base, and closed the door behind them.

"All a bit cloak and dagger, George. Where's the fire?" Marks sat down and Spencer leaned against one of the filing cabinets.

"Can we be overheard in here, Dennis?"

"No, I don't think so, but it never crossed my mind to ask. What's up?"

"First, the fingerprints we took from Watkinson's home came up with no matches on any of our police or Home Office databases, so that's a blind alley. We'll have to look somewhere else for any evidence of a break-in."

"And…?"

"Patience, man. I got the results on the DNA tests back from our lab. Remember the cigarette butt that Amanda Pietersen dropped at Steve Marshall's funeral?"

"Yes." The DCI leaned forwards, his attention now completely focused.

"Early days, but they don't even remotely match the records which Watkinson made available from the MI5 files."

"What?!" Marks eyes widened.

"Steady. As I said, it's early days. All I can say at the moment is that, on the face of it, there is no blood tie between the two of them. Either she is *not* his aunt, and is therefore lying for some reason which escapes me, or…"

"Or the body in the Audi wasn't that of Steve Marshall." Spencer finished the sentence, now engrossed in the conversation himself.

"Look," Groves continued, "All I have at the moment is two people who are definitely not related. Without a reference sample we have nothing concrete."

"And that sample is coming from?" Marks again.

"The City Hospital up in Derby, where Mavis Marshall underwent those clinical trials. That will be the benchmark against which I can assess the two other sets of records."

"How soon before we can get a hold of those?"

"I told them of the urgency, but you have to realise that those trials were a long time ago. The records will have to be found, and it'll take time; they won't jump when I click my fingers. It doesn't work that way."

"So we sit and wait?"

"I'm afraid so. I do have a contact name, so if we haven't heard anything by, say, the end of next week, I'll make another call and see how they're getting on with it."

"What if we involve George Watkinson? He should be able to flex a few muscles." Peter Spencer got one of Marks' legendary withering looks for his trouble.

"Not likely! First, it would send ripples out on some waters at MI5 which I'd rather not even dip my toe in at present; secondly, can you imagine the chaos it would cause at a provincial hospital if the weight of the security services suddenly descended upon them?"

"I agree." Groves came back. "What we, and I, need is for this to be allowed to run its course without anyone up there knowing what our true motives are."

Marks sighed in frustration. He did share Peter Spencer's enthusiasm for getting to the bottom of a key piece of evidence, but experience had taught him patience. It was a hard skill to learn, but the alternatives in ruffling feathers were almost always negative in the results they produced. The door opened suddenly, and Chloe Warner stepped inside holding an evidence bag – she was smiling.

"Yes?" Marks picked up on the look on his detective sergeant's face.

"This," She waved the bag, "could give us a new lead in the burglary."

"Go on." Marks leaned forwards again, and the others sat down. Warner had centre stage.

"I took a look around the back garden at the Surrey house whilst the rest of you were packing up. I wondered what approach I'd use if I were going to attempt a break-in, and the back garden seemed the best choice."

"Watkinson did mention to me some time back that a sniper had been caught down there. The guy led them to Gerald Montgomery in the end." Marks stared into space, his head resting on the fingers of one hand.

"Yes, guv. Well, there's a bramble patch down near the fence, and somebody had a problem with it. Here," She held the bag up and pointed to the end of a longish piece of the blackberry stem, "are fibre traces where the thorns caught on a piece of clothing."

"What's that, there?" Spencer pointed to a stain near the end.

"Blood, Peter. Brambles aren't the place you want to be without protective clothing, and someone must have caught a hefty scratch by the look of it. I sent a sample of it off to your lab, Professor Groves, and we got a match."

"So it's not the Watkinsons then." Marks was now at the edge of his seat.

"No, guv. The man we're looking for is Dieter Hahn, and I've been in touch with Interpol."

"Why?"

"Because he left the country about ten days ago. Records show him passing though Heathrow bound for Munich, although I'd think it unlikely that he's still there."

"Anything else?"

"No, I'm afraid not. There was a garden rake stashed behind the shed, and an area of soil which had recently been disturbed. Hahn clearly wanted no trace leaving behind. He couldn't have seen the brambles in the dark, though."

"All right, good work, Warner. At least we now know that there really *does* seem to have been a break-in. I'll inform Watkinson and see if he can come up with anything through his contacts on the continent."

The meeting now being at an end, Groves and Spencer went their separate ways, but Warner hung back.

"Sir?"

"It's 'Guv', Chloe." Marks smiled. "You have something else?"

"Not specifically, but there might be another angle on this."

"Such as?" Marks had risen from his chair, but now sat down again.

"Well, I've been seeing someone at Thames House, and he's a bit of a specialist in IT."

"You mean he's a hacker?" The DCI looked over the tops of his glasses.

"Guv. Anyway, he may be able to trace Hahn through his bank accounts. We might get a lead on whoever paid him to carry out the burglary."

"Bit of a long shot, a burglar having a bank account."

"Barry says it doesn't matter where the account is, he should be able to track it down."

"You've already asked him?"

"No, guv. We were just talking the other evening, and he was explaining how things are done. I would never release details of a current investigation without your permission. Thing is, if we can get clearance through Thames House, we might be able to follow the paper trail back to the UK."

"All right, but take it one step at a time, and make sure that this Barry takes it to Watkinson first. Clear?"

"Yes, guv."

Marks leaned back in his chair and smiled as the door closed behind his sergeant. Chloe Warner was ambitious, and her file was full of complimentary detail. She displayed an insight into investigative police work way beyond her years, and there had not been so much as a hint of anything negative in any of her assessments. Half-sister to Colin Barnes, she bore all the traits of the Yard's top Superintendent and was clearly following a similar career path. He checked his diary – the results of her exams were due out very soon; promotion to the rank of Inspector would follow, and at thirty-one she would be one of the youngest in the Met. His musings were interrupted by Peter Spencer's entry.

"Back so soon. Fancy a coffee?" Marks was out of his chair.

"Can do – my turn I think, and I'll tell you an interesting story while we're down in the canteen."

⎯⎯⎯⎯ ⋐⦀⦀⦀⦀⊃⎯ ⎯⎯⎯

"All right, you have my full attention." Marks put down his mug.

"Remember that gas fitter up in Yorkshire? The one who heard Marshall's car go off the road?"

154

"Yes, what was his name... Mar... something?"

"Marsden, Geoff Marsden. Lives in Derbyshire and was lodging at Helmsley while he was completing a contract at Thirsk." Spencer took out his notebook.

"Well?"

"Well, seems he remembered something else, and contacted the North Yorkshire police. It appears that he'd dropped off, and the sound of the crash had awoken him. This is where it gets interesting; he now thinks he heard the sound of running feet after the car had gone through the barrier and down towards that tree where it exploded."

"What?"

"My thoughts exactly. What would running feet be doing in the middle of the night on Sutton Bank in the pitch dark?" Spencer leaned back, picked up his coffee, and smiled.

Marks sat in silence for a while. Groves had cast some doubt on the identity of the body found in the car – he had known the pathologist too long to read him wrong on that score. There was now the appearance of an aunt from abroad of whom no-one at MI5 seemed to be aware, and three bodies all of which had links of some kind to Marshall. George Watkinson had expressed private doubts to the DCI of his second-in-command's recent activities, and there seemed to be a resurgence of some shadowy organisation from years earlier. The pieces in the puzzle didn't yet fit together, and Groves was the key.

"Penny for them?" Spencer jolted him back to reality.

"Hmm?"

"Thoughts. You were gone there for a moment or two."

"Sorry." He smiled. "We need to get a hurry-up put on those records that George is waiting for from The City Hospital in Derby. Our friend won't like it, but see if you can light a fire underneath someone up there, Peter. I'm going to read through the autopsy reports on those three bodies again."

Peter Spencer was back sooner than Marks expected, and the DCI closed the file on the desk in front of him. The fax copies of the reports of the clinical trials at the Derbyshire hospital left no room for any further doubt.

"Has George Groves seen these yet?"

"He wasn't at the lab when I went down there with them, but I left him copies with a message that I'd be here with you."

The door swung open at that very moment, and the pathologist walked in still reading the file which Spencer had copied for him.

"Pretty conclusive, isn't it?" Marks looked at Groves for the long-awaited opinion.

"I'd say so." He closed the folder and dropped it onto the desk. "Mavis Marshall and Amanda Pietersen were most definitely sisters. The reference sample from the hospital is indisputable unless there's been one almighty cock-up, and I simply don't believe that."

"So, the body in the Audi up in North Yorkshire could not have been that of Steve Marshall." Spencer joined in.

"No." Marks stated. "That sort of begs the questions of who exactly it was, and also where Marshall is right now."

29

The surprises were coming at an increasing rate for Robert Grafton and the BDP. Hardly a week had passed since the sensation of three long-established MPs crossing the chamber of the House of Commons to join his solitary presence in Parliament, and now, this very afternoon, at the end of Prime Minister's Question Time, a further six had followed suit. The timing could not have been chosen for a more dramatic impact. The house was beginning to empty as members returned to their respective committees and duties, when the Speaker called them all back to order.

He held in his hand a note, signed by the six individuals now standing between the two dispatch boxes, formally resigning their respective party whips and joining the now swelling ranks of the British Democratic Party. With a solemnity born of hundreds of years of political process, they turned and made their way to join Grafton himself and the three other new recruits on the back benches.

Sketch writers and other commentators had a field day and, amid the uproar, the Prime Minister and leaders of the other two major parties were quickly forgotten as all attention was focused on the now departing figure of the BDP leader and his nine MPs. It took Grafton a full hour to get back to his headquarters, and he was quickly on the telephone to the private number given to him by Lawson. The office door was closed, with strict instructions that he remain undisturbed.

"Just how many more are there going to be?!" He hissed down the line.

"Calm down, Robert. I did tell you that this was just the start. You can't have a voice in Parliament unless there are numbers behind you to reinforce your opinions."

"But this isn't the BDP doing it… it's you!"

"Makes no difference. As long as the message gets across to the voting public, the means are irrelevant. Just carry on with the manifesto that you have, and you'll see the results. By the way, the last set of local government figures was impressive."

"Yes." Grafton had calmed down. "Nineteen per cent of the vote across the country gave us second place on thirty councils and overall control of one."

"Can you imagine how *that* would pan out at a General Election?" Lawson's voice was hushed, almost conspiratorial.

"First past the post would probably not help too much. There are no prizes for coming second." Grafton snorted.

"Yes, but what if you could change the voting system? What then? Think about it – another few deserters to your cause and the British public will wake up. Once they realise what you're all about… well, who knows what you could achieve? Did you get your manifesto published?"

"We did… and circulated. With the money you gave us, we've been able to open more branches, and they've been handing it out on the streets. Let's face it, WH Smith are hardly likely to stock it, are they?"

"Right. Let it sink in for a week or so. There's a set of opinion polls coming up, so watch out for the results. You might be surprised."

"You can't influence them… Can you?"

"Of course not, but with the events in Parliament and the release of your manifesto, the tide is turning."

Grafton put down the telephone and reflected on what Lawson had said. It was true that the BDP could not possibly carve out a serious place for itself in British politics without the muscle which was now being placed within its reach. He still resented the actions being taken behind his back, and was very uneasy at the thought of outsiders, unvetted individuals, now flocking to the banner. There would be question marks against their true loyalties, and only with a mandate from the public at the next election would he be entirely happy.

⊂═══⫘═⊃

George Watkinson sat reading Barry Newman's report on the funding of both the Organisation and the BDP. He had scrutinised the dossiers before, and was combing them once again for anything which he might have missed. The initial half a million pounds had been withdrawn from the bank account which the Organisation believed was concealed at the Thunervolksbank in Switzerland, but all attempts to link it to a similar amount deposited by the BDP had failed. He buzzed for Newman, and the young man was in his office moments later.

"Are you sure that there's no way that these two amounts can be traced to each other, Barry?"

"Positive, sir. The withdrawal was made in cash, and the deposit in the BDP account a few days later was the same. The amounts don't match either, but some of it could have been withheld to cover expenses."

"I see. This picture from the Volksbank of the individual making the withdrawal is of little use as well – too grainy. Can we get it enhanced in any way?"

"No, that's the best that I could do, and we have some very sophisticated software. Sorry."

"All right. I want you to try to dig up as much as you can about this man." He slid a photograph across the desk. "He's been seen with Robert Grafton on a couple of occasions."

"Adrian Lawson."

"You know him?" Watkinson was amazed.

"Know *of* him, sir. I started making some enquiries when I saw him with Grafton. I hope you don't mind."

"Not at all. What have you got?"

Newman was back a little later with a file on the man they were talking about. He sat down and began leafing through a set of pages.

"He's thirty-eight and from Leeds. His parents are both dead and there are no other living relatives. He was an only child, and was educated at Leeds Grammar School. He studied law and economics at Aston University and graduated with a two-one. Since then he also qualified as an accountant, and is currently listed as CEO of FM Engineering in the West Midlands."

"FM? That's where we tracked Gerald Montgomery. What's his connection to the company?"

"None beyond being their Finance Director until Montgomery's death, after which he took control of the company."

"Go on."

"The company is awash with money – all legitimately generated. It seems that Frederick, the father, invested heavily at the start of the Dot Com boom and got out just before the bubble burst. He made an absolute fortune, and if you look at the cross-referenced note in the Organisation file, I managed to track down some of that money to the Volksbank. The two are linked, but as there's no hint of laundering we can't touch them. They even pay their taxes on time."

"Okay, back to Lawson. What's his connection to Grafton then?"

"All we have is the fact they they've been seen together on a number of occasions. We can't get a microphone near them because the meeting places are never the same, so we don't know what they're talking about."

"It's very odd that Lawson should appear shortly after Steve Marshall's death. Did *they* know each other?"

"There's no mention in Marshall's file of any connection to a man by his name, and from the information that I've dug out about Lawson, their paths were unlikely to have crossed in public life. Lawson has the usual records going back to his childhood; I know where his doctor is, his dentist, all his hospital appointments are documented, and I can track his employment back to the first job he took when he came out of university."

"Legends can be created without too much trouble." Watkinson sat back, he was clutching at straws now.

"Yes, sir, but at this level of detail it would have taken a monumental effort to build up such a profile. I even spoke to some of those contacts in his records, and they all confirm the details which we have."

"Nevertheless, he's been seen in the company of the leader of a right wing party – a party which has benefited from the sudden appearance of a considerable amount of finance. Keep digging, but take it steady. It there is a connection, we need to watch it closely; I'm quite prepared to let it run and see where it leads us."

"There was one other thing, sir." Newman shifted slightly in his chair, and Watkinson spotted the change.

"Yes, Barry. What has DCI Marks asked you to do?" He smiled.

"Sir?"

"There isn't much that goes on around the law enforcement agencies that gets past my nose. Come on, out with it."

"Well, it's not exactly DCI Marks, sir, but I have had an approach from a member of his team."

"And did she smile at you when she asked?"

"Yes, that is no, I mean…" Newman coloured up, took a deep breath and explained the information which DS Warner had asked for.

"I see. So this Dieter Hahn is, they believe, the man who broke into my house." Watkinson was now interested, and Newman continued with the brief.

"He could be, but I'll need to track his movement now that he's out of the UK. That means digging around for bank accounts on the continent. I know I've been doing that, but it was on your instructions, and I'm not prepared to take this on without official sanction." He sat back.

"You have it. I want that man back over here and in this building. If there is the slightest possibility that he can lead us to whoever commissioned the break-in we may yet be able to establish who's pulling the strings with the BDP."

Newman was on his way out of the office when Sandra Wallace passed him at the door. She placed a copy of the London Evening Standard before Watkinson.

"I suppose you've heard about this?" She pointed to the headline story blazoned across the front page.

"Another batch of defectors to the BDP. Yes I picked it up on the BBC News channel. It must be more than coincidence; fresh funding, success at the Burnley by-election, and now an actual party on the floor of the Commons. Barry's off on a chase for some German burglar – see what you can do to help; I get the feeling he's going to be needing it."

Dieter Hahn was very drunk. He had staggered from the U-Bahn on Munich's Brudermühlstraße at around midnight, and was now on an unsteady way home to his apartment at its corner with Thalkirchner Straße. He had been drinking at the city's Hofbräuhaus since early evening, and had run out of the day's portion of the fee that he earned for the job at Watkinson's home in Surrey. He was a well-known figure in the Deutsche Volksunion, and connections within the UK had contacted the neo-Nazi group to carry out the assignment. The fact that he was already in London at the time had been a bonus.

He stopped in the drifting rain to light a cigarette, and leaned against the wall of *Feichtner und Frey* away from the stiff breeze which was now whipping its way along the street. There were no witnesses to observe the white Mercedes van which pulled up alongside him, and Hahn was inside the back compartment, and unconscious, within seconds. When he awoke he was bound and gagged, and heading for Dunkerque. By the morning of the following day he was sitting in an anonymous room within Thames House, and facing the imposing figure of the head of MI5.

"Waß wollen Sie von mir!?" He tried to stand up, but quickly found any progress in that direction halted by the straps holding his arms and legs to the chair.

"Herr Hahn." Watkinson's German was flawless. "Wilkommen in Groß Brittannien. Ich heiße George Watkinson von MI5, und du, mein Freund, hast viele Probleme."

Hahn glanced nervously around the room. He was alone with this man and what looked like another operative by the door; the last thing he *clearly* remembered was the waitress serving him his final 'Maß' of Helles at the Hofbräuhaus.

"Das ist unglaublich! Ich bin Deutscher, und will sofort zurück nach Deutschland!"

"All right, enough with the formalities. I know that you speak perfect English, Dieter, so shall we get down to business?" Watkinson pulled out the chair opposite his captive and sat down.

"What do you want from me?" There was a Bavarian lilt to the voice, and he stared down at his bindings.

"Not very much." Watkinson signalled to the figure by the door, and the straps were removed. "Those were to prevent you from hurting yourself." He smiled.

"So, why am I here? You have no right to kidnap a German national from his home and carry him across Europe."

"I think, Mr Hahn, that I have as much right to do that as you did in entering my home and taking away some things which don't belong to you." He dropped a key onto the table in front of the German. "This would tend to explain the lack of evidence of a forced entry."

Hahn froze; it had not been explained to him that the house into which he was required to gain entry was that of the head of one of the British security services. He had heard of Thames House, and now believed that he knew where he was. No-one was aware of his presence in Britain, and his girlfriend would not be back at the apartment on Bruderműhlstraße until the end of next week – he would not be missed.

"I suppose a lawyer is out of the question."

There was a cough at the door, and Watkinson turned to the subordinate there as they shared the joke, laughing out loud.

"You Germans! And to think that we always considered you to be completely devoid of a sense of humour!" His face changed to a blank stare. "There will be no lawyers. Tell me who gave you the key and who paid you to do the job; you can go home as soon as we have them in custody."

"I cannot."

"Cannot... or will not? It's all the same to me." He shook his head and smiled condescendingly. "I've lost count of the number of guests who've sat in that chair and said the very things that you have; they all talk in the end. Oh, don't worry, there'll be no harm done to you; well, not physically anyway. You'd be amazed what a few nights without sleep will do for the unwilling tongue."

Hahn leaned back in the chair and folded his arms. There were a few moments silence after which Watkinson stood up, pushed his chair neatly back under the table, and walked to the door.

"What about me?" Hahn frowned at the retreating figure.

"You?" Watkinson turned. "Oh, you can stay here. I understand it's quite comfortable, and the food is safe to eat. I'll be back tomorrow... or the day after; it depends. Don't worry, my staff will keep you busy whilst I'm away, and perhaps then we can have another chat. Sleep well."

The door closed and Hahn was alone; he looked around the room. There was no bed, but a toilet cubicle was located just behind where he was seated; they clearly planned to keep him here for a while. He looked up – the room was lit by a bright, blue-tinted, fluorescent tube. It was set into the ceiling and protected by a metal grille - he would not be able to turn it off. The room was windowless and there was no clock. It had been daylight when he first arrived, but he now felt himself becoming temporally disorientated; this, then, was part of Watkinson's strategy. He would need to sleep, of that there was no doubt, but the man had said that eyes would be watching him. Rest was going to be a scarce commodity. With no more comfortable place than the chair he was using, Dieter slumped down and closed his eyes. He was woken almost immediately by the opening of the door.

"Mr Hahn." There was no 'good morning' or any other reference to the time of day, and the man before him held only a towel and toiletries. "With Mr Watkinson's compliments. I'll be back a little later to check in on you." He smiled and left.

Hahn sighed; this was to be the routine. Stay awake and they just watch, fall asleep and he would be woken each time. He was already tired, and despite all thoughts that he had at the start relating to withstanding the pressure, his resolve was beginning to flag even at this early stage.

30

"Look at that." Marks dropped the latest edition of the Daily Telegraph onto the desk in front of Peter Spencer.

Opinion polls had been showing, over the past few months, a rising trend of support for The British Democratic Party in general, and Robert Grafton in particular. Current standing for both had hit twenty-five per cent, and despite a round of dismissive speeches from both politicians and commentators alike, there was an undercurrent of unease pervading the corridors of the Palace of Westminster.

"He certainly seems to have seized the mood of the nation. There's a party political broadcast tonight, isn't there?" Spencer skimmed the front page, and turned to the 'Opinion' column inside.

"There is, and I think it'll be worthwhile taking a look." Marks shook his head. "I'm still convinced Grafton had something to do with those killings, but all we have is a set of tenuous links."

"We do know that it wasn't Marshall in the car up in Yorkshire now. Couldn't he be behind it somehow?"

"Possibly." The DCI sat down. "The trouble is, Watkinson may well be on our side, but he'll only release information when it suits his purpose. We have no idea what's actually going on there."

"What about this Hahn character that Chloe dug out? Did they manage to track him down?"

"Yes." Marks smiled grimly. "It would seem, however, that the man has vanished into the bowels of Thames House. She did find out from her friend that he was picked up in Munich by some of the German Special Forces, but that's all we have. The man committed a crime, and we should have him here."

"So, we're done then?"

"Until MI5 need us again, yes, I'm afraid we are. Unless we can establish a link between the killings of Drake, Summers, and Morse to someone in particular, they'll remain as open cases. Sometimes this whole thing just hacks me off."

"Seen this piece here?" Spencer folded the page and pointed to a section of the commentary.

"Still the migration continues." Marks read the snippet with a knot tightening in his gut.

Since the initial influx of new members to the parliamentary gathering on the benches occupied by the BDP, there had been a steady if unspectacular stream of MPs resigning party whips and joining their ranks. The number now stood at thirty-eight – a mere three short of that representing the Liberal Democrats, who had suffered more than the other two parties from the exodus.

"How is he doing it? I mean, the BDP have come from nowhere, and he's not exactly the statesman type, is he?" Spencer was nonplussed.

"This, Peter, is what democracy is all about, and it's the power of the ballot box which will decide his fate. What we're seeing at present is an artificial situation – a kind of protest against the established parties. By-elections have a similar impact, but this goes way beyond that; whether he'll be able to sustain the party's appeal at the next general election remains to be seen. I confess though, I am concerned."

George Watkinson looked at the calendar on his office wall. It had been forty-eight hours since the arrival of Dieter Hahn at Thames House and, as far as he was aware, the man had not had a wink of sleep during that entire period. Experience had shown sleep deprivation to be a very sharp tool in weakening the resolve of those from whom information was required. Gone were the crude, and often brutal, techniques of the 1950s and 1960s, and as he made his way down to the small, brightly lit, room where his guest awaited, he was confident that the German would now be more amenable to his requests.

"Good morning, Herr Hahn." It was the first time that Dieter had received any clue to the time of day since his arrival, and the use of the German form of address caught his attention immediately.

"Morning? But what day?" Hahn sat up from the slumped position he had occupied in the chair.

"The day is of little consequence, since you will be out of here immediately if you provide the information which I need." Watkinson sat down.

The contrast in their appearance could not have been greater. Hahn was dishevelled; he had not shaved for two days, and his clothes were badly creased. Despite the toiletries, his hair was unkempt and an unpleasant aroma surrounded him. His eyes were red from lack of sleep, and his voice carried a thick timbre. Watkinson sat before him, neatly dressed in suit and tie, trousers freshly pressed and a handkerchief adorning his top pocket. He removed a pair of spectacles from it, polished them slowly, and put them on.

"Down to business. Who commissioned the job at my home?" He leaned back and crossed his legs.

"I do not know." Hahn's words came out slowly, and with some effort.

"I see. Well, perhaps these may be of some assistance to your memory." From the folder which he had brought into the room, Watkinson produced a number of photographs which he slid across the table in a stack.

"I do not know the name of the man; we met only once and he did not tell me. He showed me the house, provided the key, and gave instructions. That is all." He was leafing through the pile as he spoke.

"All right. Take your time – you have it in abundance at the moment."

"Him!" Hahn stopped, pulled out one snap from the set, and jabbed his index finger in the middle. "He is the man! I would recognise the face anywhere."

"Very good, Dieter." Another MI5 subtlety; the kind of carrot and stick technique useful with children.

"May I go now?" Hahn's eyes widened in anticipation, and Watkinson weighed the German's request.

"Perhaps tomorrow. There are a couple of things which I need to check out first. I'll have a bed set up in here – get some sleep, I'm sure that you think you deserve it." The sarcasm was lost on Dieter, and his face relaxed in relief.

Back in his office, Watkinson heaved a sigh of disappointment. He had churned the issue of Steve Marshall over and over in his mind for quite some time. He had watched his number two's development from a raw recruit amongst many, had seen the young man's maturity manifest itself as each assignment stretched his abilities, and took pride in the fact that they had come to work so closely together. All that, it would seem, had been for nothing.

What was it that had changed? Could he have foreseen it in some way? Why had he been so blind with Steve when he had watched others so closely? Questions like these fuelled the self-doubt which was starting to occupy more and more of his time. A new, and more alarming, matter now came to the fore – where *was* Marshall? DCI Marks had released the findings from the Home Office pathologist, George Groves; there was now incontrovertible proof that the body in Steve's Audi was not that of the MI5 operative, and that, somehow, a substitute corpse had been placed there. He picked up the phone.

"I need you and your team again, Dennis." Watkinson poured two glasses of single malt and handed one to the DCI.

"I see." Ordinarily, Marks would have declined, but something told him that this was not the time or place. "To what end?"

"I have a guest downstairs…"

"Dieter Hahn, yes I know." Marks was unable to resist the interruption, and had Watkinson momentarily off guard.

"Ah yes, your detective sergeant; a very resourceful young woman who will go far - Colin Barnes' sister." Watkinson nodded.

"As you well know, since it was she whom I was allowed to recruit after all that nonsense with the IPCC." He folded his arms.

"Yes, that was very unfortunate. Still, water under the bridge now, and I am sorry – you should have been informed of Hahn's detention."

"He is a criminal after all, and since we at the Yard are the forces concerned with the criminal law, he should have come to us." Marks had felt for some time that he and the head of MI5 should be speaking as equals, and this was the point which he was now making.

"Indeed. He has, however, after a little persuasion, revealed to me the source of his instructions in carrying out that job at my home."

"Marshall?" Marks smiled a thin, knowing smile.

"Very astute, Detective Chief Inspector; Steve Marshall himself. Apparently they met only once, and Hahn has only a photograph as a means of identifying him - names were never mentioned. He had a key – that's why you didn't find any signs of forced entry."

"Well, you and I know that it wasn't Marshall in the burned-out car, so the question remains: where is he?"

"My thoughts exactly, and as a missing person is also a matter for the police, I am making an unofficial Missing Persons report."

"You want us to find him." A flat statement from the DCI, and Watkinson was left in no doubt of the irritation which Marks and his entire team were beginning to feel.

"Yes please, but I'm afraid I have nothing to hand over to you in the form of clues."

"All right. We had a statement from that Derbyshire gas fitter, Geoff Marsden, that he may have heard someone running away from the scene of the crash. I'll get onto the Yorkshire police and see if they have any reports of unusual traffic in the area that night."

"Good. Do you want to interview Mr Hahn?"

"Will you be making an official report of the burglary?"

"No, I don't believe I will." Watkinson smiled.

"In that case, I think the matter can be dropped. We're going to have enough on our plate without it." Marks stood up, finished the scotch, and left.

Dieter Hahn's world had been turned inside out over the past week, and as the Mercedes van pulled away from the Olympiapark he was left to rue the day that he became involved with the neo-Nazis in Munich. It took him an hour to get back to his apartment on Bruderműhlstraße, and by the end of the day he had packed up his belongings, hailed a cab, and left the area. Karin would be less than pleased when she returned from her latest shift with Lufthansa, but of the two he was more afraid of Deutsche Volksunion than he was of her.

31

"What do you mean you lost him?" George Watkinson thumped his desk in exasperation. "I give you a simple task of tailing someone, and you lose him. We're running a branch of the security services here, not Fred Karno's Circus. How did you manage that?"

Tirades from the service head were rare these days, and since the escape of Roger Mason, which almost cost the lives of Julie and Doug Martin in 1992, things had tightened up considerably. The chase for the secret documents which were missing once more had, he thought, ended on that day.

"We had him in clear sight in Hyde Park, but he dodged into the underground and, well, we lost him… sir."

"Get out of here, the lot of you! If I don't get a clear sighting of Adrian Lawson by tomorrow, you could all be looking for new jobs!"

A hurried exit of all six operatives almost had Sandra Wallace on her backside as they rushed past her.

"What!?" The angry outburst from her boss had Wallace on the back foot, and he regretted it instantly. "I'm sorry, Sandra; come in, please. What have you got?"

"My goodness, what did they do, steal the crown jewels?" She smiled, despite the force of the reprimand.

"No. I give them a simple assignment and they lose their man. There were six of them for heaven's sake!"

"Lawson?" She asked, a knowing look on her face.

"Yes." His eyes narrowed – he should have become accustomed to her intuition by now.

"Well, this might just put a smile back on your face." She placed a still photograph in front of him. "Taken an hour ago."

"How…?" He looked amazed.

"Oh, recruiting Barry Newman must have been an inspired move, sir. The man's an absolute genius with computer systems. He's borrowed, as he put it, the Yard's CCTV software to track Lawson across the city, knowing that you'd sent out a team to follow him." She shook her head in admiration. "Priceless!"

"Shirley." He buzzed his secretary, Shirley Mann.

"Yes, Mr Watkinson."

"Get hold of that group of clowns who just left my office please, and send them down to Barry Newman. He'll show them what they need to do next. You'd better let him know they're on their way as well."

"Straightaway, sir."

"Right, Sandra, what has our friend been up to? Any more contact with Robert Grafton?"

The trail on Adrian Lawson had, after the second of his appointments with Robert Grafton, gone somewhat cold. There had been no further meetings, and hence no chance to establish a consistent link with the BDP leader. It was almost as if the man knew that MI5 were watching him, and Watkinson wondered once more whether there was still a mole within the department, or whether he was just plain observant.

"There are gaps in the surveillance camera network, sir, and if he's as clever as I think, he could simply stick to those areas for any meetings and we'd be restricted to our foot patrols to pick him up there."

"And if what I've witnessed today is anything to go by, we're beaten before we start on that subject."

"Yes, sir. However, Robert Grafton doesn't appear to be so aware of the extent of our abilities, and Barry is also keeping tabs on his movements. If the two of them gravitate towards the same area, we'll be able to pick them up despite the lack of CCTV."

Not for one moment had George Watkinson regretted the recruiting of Wallace from the ranks of the Metropolitan Police, despite his current misgivings about Marshall. The youngsters now coming through, and they included Barry Newman and, hopefully, Chloe Warner, would form a formidable team for him.

As Wallace had suspected, Adrian Lawson was well aware of the surveillance placed upon his movements by MI5. The Organisation had its methods of detection, and it had enabled him to shake off quite easily the team which had been sent out to monitor his progress. His movements around the capital on the current occasion were for legitimate business reasons, being contract negotiations on behalf of FM Engineering, but it suited his perverse sense of humour to lead his trackers a dance across London before his pre-arranged meeting. By the time he emerged, the MI5 operatives sent on their abortive mission were gone.

"Robert? It's Adrian Lawson." The speed dial on the non-contract phone had Grafton picking up at the other end immediately.

"Where are you?"

"London, but we can't meet face to face any more – I have a tail at the moment, and any links between us are bound to derail things. You have a broadcast coming up, don't you?"

"Yes, it's tomorrow. Don't worry, everything's under control. We've timed it down to the minute, and the manifesto will be covered in detail. You know we've outstripped the Liberal Democrats, don't you?"

"I heard; forty-three MPs now, isn't it? There must be some very worried faces around Westminster these days."

"There was a meeting of the three main leaders and party whips last week."

"Sure you'll be ready?" There was just a hint of uncertainty in Lawson's tone, and the BDP leader was quick to dispel it.

"Positive. With the funds that have been coming our way, we'll be able to fight every single seat in an election, and we've got activists out on the streets almost daily getting the manifesto across."

Grafton and the BDP had indeed gone on the offensive. Sensing a change in the public mood following his spectacular appearance on the BBC's flagship political programme, the BDP leader had stepped up its profile. The combination of new regional offices, opened in late summer 2006, and a more subdued projection of the party's ideals was bringing out a broader cross-section of support than had hitherto been evident. Overall response to the manifesto had been positive, and it was this document which was to be the focus of the leader's attention at his first party political broadcast. It would go out on all major terrestrial channels, and expose the BDP to an audience of millions. Grafton had never been more ready for anything in his life, and this time there would be no interruptions.

The studio had been decked out exactly as he had wished. The funds provided by Lawson had been used for a multitude of purposes, but none quite so important as the fee paid to the set designers who were now watching from the wings. A bright backdrop portraying a study area lined with bookshelves enabled Grafton to stand out in his dark blue business suit. The large, rather grandiose, oak desk lent him an air of respectability, and a real fire crackling away in the background set the scene for the picture he was about to paint.

"Good evening. I am Robert Grafton, leader of the British Democratic Party." He smiled – the first of several during the ten minute slot which was allocated to all major parties.

"I'd like to talk to you briefly about our vision for the future of Britain." He turned as the camera angle changed, following the tell-tale red light atop the active shot.

"Did we tell him about that?" The question came from the producer in the control booth.

"No, Mike."

"The man must be a natural. Move the camera shot again and see if he picks it up – that could have been a fluke."

Back on the studio floor, Grafton had his eyes ready for every light change, and moved around the floor with the practised ease of a dancer in full flow. In the short slot, he covered all of the major policy issues from immigration to care of the elderly. The floor manager ticked off each item as Grafton cruised flawlessly through the entire manifesto. There was even time, at the very close, for him to seize upon a batch of that morning's front pages – a popular press which had clearly been given false information in an attempt to derail the broadcast with a crudely constructed smear campaign. In the end, it merely served to play into his hands, and he closed the allocated time with another of his now hallmark smiles. The shot faded, and Elgar's *Land of Hope and Glory*' provided the perfect overlay for an image of the Union Flag fluttering proudly in the breeze.

"All right, cut." The producer leaned into the microphone. "Very good, Mr Grafton."

The broadcast was the subject of scrutiny by all of the networked news bulletins later that same day, and each one gave somewhat grudging praise to Grafton for the professional manner of his performance. Analysis of his ten minute presentation was detailed and thorough, but none of the political experts could fault the content or apparent sincerity of the message. Telephone calls of support flooded the switchboards, and Grafton bathed in the glow of the knowledge that they were from potential voters right across the political spectrum. All he would have to do, it would seem, would be to stick to the plan and not allow himself to be baited into any ill-considered remarks. He was alone in the office after the now customary round of celebratory meetings, when the phone rang.

"Grafton." He frowned – the incoming call, by-passing the switchboard, had come direct to his desk.

"Highly impressive performance, Robert. You must be feeling extremely pleased." The voice was quiet and even.

"Who is this, and how did you get my number?" Grafton's direct line was, he thought, known only to a select few of the party's committee, and he did not recognise the voice at the other end.

"The 'whos and hows' aren't relevant. What is important is that we meet. I have some interesting information to discuss, and it'll be to your advantage to listen."

"That sounds like a threat." There was a knot beginning to form in the BDP leader's stomach, and he shifted uneasily in his chair.

"Not at all, Robert." There was the hint of a laugh, and Grafton balled his fist in frustration. "I'm aware of certain facts which, if not handled correctly, may completely destroy what you're trying to achieve."

"This sounds like some crude attempt at blackmail. Who are you?"

"That will become clear when we meet. Give me your untraceable mobile number – the less said on this line the better. We never know who might be listening in, do we?"

Grafton put the phone down. This individual, whoever he was, posed a threat and would have to be dealt with in the same way as all of the others before him. He thumped the desk, got up, and paced around the room. The man had told him to wait; told *him* to wait. Who did he think he was talking to? The mobile blared out and he stared at the display: '*unknown number*' it told him.

174

"Yes."

"Good, no tricks then. Be at the Albert Memorial in half an hour."

"How will I know you?"

"You won't – I'll be waiting. Don't be late – your entire future could depend on this."

The line went dead, and Grafton cursed. Grabbing a coat, he locked the office and hailed a cab. It had started to rain when he arrived on Kensington Road, and the weather was unseasonably cold. Dismissing the cab, he took shelter in the lee of the monument commissioned by Queen Victoria in memory of her dead consort. The dark coloured Vectra pulled up on Queensgate and the window rolled down.

"Mr Grafton." The voice was quiet, and the passenger door swung open. Moments later, they were heading west and back onto the Kensington Road.

The journey from Queensgate to Clapham Common took fifteen minutes and, despite Grafton's attempts at conversation, passed without response from the other party. He had no idea whether this was the man who had called him, or whether he was merely a messenger. A turned up collar, glasses, and a hat with a broad brim turned down were sufficient, in the darkness, to hide the identity of the driver. They pulled up on North Side, and Grafton followed his driver's lead to the bandstand in the centre of the park. Now under cover from the steady rain, the hat and glasses came off – Grafton stared in amazement.

"You! Weren't you supposed to be in Poland or somewhere?"

"Yes. Poland, the Czech Republic, Slovenia… I've been around since we took care of Mike Summers for you."

Tony Williams had been one of two leaving the meeting, following Summers and his group to the public house where they had vented their displeasure. Once separated at the end of that evening, he had been easy to subdue and dispose of; the other two followed soon afterwards.

"So, what is this…you want more money? I thought we'd paid you both very well for that service." Grafton snarled.

"Let's just say that it'll be sufficient compensation for what I'll reveal to you in exchange. Call it blackmail if you want, but you can hardly go running to the cops about it, now can you?" Williams smiled.

"How much?" Grafton closed his eyes and shook his head; they were soon open again.

"A couple of hundred thousand should cover it."

"Two hundred...? You bastard! I don't have that sort of money." Grafton grabbed him by the collar, but Williams merely smiled.

"Yes, you do." He eased Grafton's grip, and the BDP leader turned away momentarily.

"How do I know you'll stick to your side of it?"

"I give you all of the information I have, hard copy and digital, take a one-way trip to South America, and you never hear from me again." The smile was gone, but the voice remained with its cold, even tone.

"Say I agree. What next?"

"You're a Hammers supporter aren't you? Season ticket isn't it? There's the Fulham match coming up on the thirteenth. Be at the corner of Green Street and Tudor Road at two-thirty, and bring the cash in a rucksack. Just hand it over and go to the game as if it were nothing out of the ordinary. I'll be in touch on the Sunday, and I'll give you a time when we can meet again."

The journey back to the BDP office in Bexley was completed in silence, and as Grafton got out of the car Williams wound down the driver's side window.

"One more thing. Don't bring anyone along with you – it would be pointless attempting anything stupid. I have a timed e-mail ready to go to the desks of a whole host of tabloid editors – I'd hate to miss my appointment to cancel it each day, and I'm sure they'd all love to read the stuff that I've accumulated about you and your organisation."

He smiled, and Grafton's words of reply died in the noise of the car as it drove off down the High Street and out of sight.

32

The intervening time had been, for Robert Grafton, one of a period of self-doubt which he had not experienced for some time. His mind had, up to this point, been able to focus clearly on the objectives which the BDP had set down in its policy documents. Always on the lookout for an opportunity, he was outspoken in his condemnation of the BAE Bribery Scandal case when it hit the headlines, and had been equally vociferous when the Speaker was forced to stand down at the height of the MPs expenses row.

With these and other publicly aired political mishaps associated with the BDP's outrage, public opinion had, from that point in time, been steadily mounting in his favour. Now all of that was hanging by a thread because of one individual. There had to be a way of permanently silencing Tony Williams, but without knowing what it was that the man had up his sleeve, any pre-emptive action would be ill-advised at best and disastrous at worst. Not for the first time, the direct line in his office found the BDP leader in a less than equable frame of mind.

"Grafton!" The voice was waspish, the tone hard.

"Temper, temper. That'll do nothing for the blood pressure, and you do need to keep calm, Robert."

"Are you ready?"

"I am. West Ham, this afternoon, two-thirty."

The line went dead and, picking up the brown rucksack, Grafton made his way to the appointed location where he stood waiting for Williams. It was a big game – a sell-out, and Grafton's unease at carrying two hundred thousand pounds worth of cash amongst a crowd of just under 35,000 was only relieved by the tap on his shoulder which heralded Williams' arrival.

"Going in?" He smiled.

"Not likely." Grafton hissed. "Let's get this over and done with. Where are we heading?"

Another car journey across the city, and another open space where they could not be heard. Any attempt at surveillance would be useless on Wimbledon Common, and they sat down on one of a number of benches which dotted the area.

"All right. Here's the bag – want to count it out here in the open?"

"Not necessary. If it isn't all there when I get it somewhere less public, I'll just release all the documents I have to the papers." He looked into the rucksack and shrugged. "Seems okay; now listen, and make sure that you take all of this seriously. You and the BDP are standing on a knife edge right now. Adrian Lawson isn't the man you think he is."

The wind across Wimbledon Common had strengthened, and the drizzling rain of only half an hour earlier was now being whipped up into their faces. For Robert Grafton, it might just as well have been a blizzard blown straight from the Arctic Circle. He stood in silence at the end of Williams' soliloquy, his face a mask of deep concern.

"Where did you get all of this from? MI5 and the Yard have been sniffing around for ages – surely at least some of it should have come out before now. Are you the only one who knows, for goodness sake?" He snapped out of the trance which had enveloped him, and the questions came in machine-gun style.

"You get to hear some really strange stuff when you're outside this country. Some of it's wide of the mark, but there are so many things pointing in Lawson's direction that you just can't ignore them."

"Look, Williams, I have my own staff watching and listening for all kinds of dodgy things. We'd have spotted it a mile off." Some of the composure had returned, and Grafton reached out for the bag.

"Oh no, remember what I said. This," he pulled the rucksack away, "is the price for saving you and the BDP. Do you really think that you need Lawson now? I've seen the opinion polls – you're on course for a major impact at the next election."

"What about Marshall? Seems he didn't die in that car crash after all. You're not the only one with sources."

"Marshall was the one who pulled it all together. It's all in there." He tapped the dossier. "There was a guy called Michael Roberts some time back, and he was involved somehow. It was his father who helped with the liquidation of the Czechs at Lidice. There are links between MI5 and the Met way back then. Watkinson may have been the puppet master, and used Marks to flush him out, but it was Marshall who made the kill shot. Funny that; he was right at the centre of the shooting of Gerald Montgomery in Nottingham as well. Think about it – too many coincidences."

Grafton had to admit that Williams' story *did* contain far too many convenient links to be dismissed out of hand. Lawson had appeared at just the right time after Marshall's apparent death, to step into the vacuum and provide the funds which the BDP desperately needed.

"All right, what now? Do you just vanish?"

"Pretty much. Here's the dossier on Lawson," he handed over a bound folder, "and a flash drive with all of the details I managed to dig up about this Organisation which was started up in the UK after the end of the Second World War."

Grafton watched as the figure of Tony Williams made its way north towards Putney Vale Cemetery and the Kingston Road - within minutes the murky light had swallowed him up, and he was gone.

Barry Newman's initial brief of tracking the funds of both the BDP and the Organisation had, so far, borne very little fruit. The programs which he had embedded into the bank accounts used by both parties had continued to quietly and covertly monitor all transactions processed since the outset, but an alert which he had installed forced him to take them offline whilst an upgrade to the spyware could be written. The amended program had been installed and tested, and was now transmitting live data on a daily basis. The size of the transfers which he now saw had his eyes bulging.

"Five million?" George Watkinson looked up from the papers on the desk before him. "Are you absolutely certain of this, Barry?"

"Positive. The account details match, and authorisations for the transactions were in line with mandate requirements. I think someone screwed up."

"This could be just what we've been waiting for. It establishes a link between what Marshall started and Lawson is carrying on, and our friends at the BDP."

"As far as I can tell, sir, no laws or banking rules have been broken. The total was made up of a number of smaller amounts but they all track back to the bank account in Thun. The details were encrypted, but I managed to break the coding – from that point on it was quite simple."

"Do you know how many of these donations there have been?"

"As far as I can see, sir, only three - but this last one is the largest to date."

"It's a war chest. Grafton's building up to the next election and the Organisation are bankrolling him." Watkinson walked over to the window and stared out over the Thames.

"Sir?"

"A long story, Barry, but it means that things are now moving a lot faster than I believed. Lawson's Organisation was bent on subverting the democratic process way back in 1992, but we stopped them. Now it looks as though they're trying to use the ballot box as a means of achieving their aims. If we can't halt them this time, we could all be living under the kind of tyranny which brought the Germans to their knees in 1945. I wonder if that fool Robert Grafton knows that he has a tiger by the tail."

"What next, then?"

"Somehow I need to let Grafton in on what's waiting for him once he gets into any position of political influence. I can't prevent people voting for him, but we should be able to let one or two things out of the bag. I'm going to see Dennis Marks – he interviewed Grafton a while back, and I know he was none too pleased at the answers that he got."

"Detective Chief Inspector Marks." Robert Grafton's tone at seeing the DCI again was less than welcoming. "I thought we were done with the questioning."

"I did say that I'd return if I had anything new." He sat down without being asked, and fixed the BDP leader with an icy stare.

"Very well." Grafton sighed; he could play the game and Marks knew it. He was, however, unprepared for what followed.

The file on Michael Roberts, lent to him by Watkinson, slid across the desk. Grafton looked from it to Marks and back; he frowned – the Met had played games like this before, and a number of the BDP's early membership had been scared away by the bullying tactics of the time. He turned the folder around and opened the first page. Marks studied the man again as he leafed through the first dozen, but his face betrayed no trace of emotion, and when he looked up from the file the DCI was no wiser than when he walked into the room.

"This could all be a work of fiction; it's been done before. I remember the Birmingham Six and the Guildford Four – some of your people did hard time for those scandals." He sneered.

"Policing is more tightly controlled than it was forty years ago." Marks could have added '... and I speak from experience.' He chose instead to go on the offensive. "The man you just read about, Michael Roberts, was a fascist – an individual bent on subverting the rule of law to suit his own ends."

"Just what are you getting at, Detective Chief Inspector?"

"Mr Grafton, we know where your funding is coming from, and have tracked every transfer into the accounts of the BDP."

"And?" Grafton's eyebrows rose in a show of mock innocence. "I don't remember reading anywhere of a list of approved contributors to political party funding."

"This Organisation, as they call themselves, contains a lot of extremely dangerous people who will dispose of the likes of you and your party once you've served their needs. You know that MI5 are watching them, don't you? What makes you think that you won't get dragged down along with them once their game's up?"

"What game? Look, you've had one attempt to incriminate me and the BDP over the deaths of Summers, Drake, and Morse. If you had any proof at all of the involvement of me or any other member of the party, we wouldn't be sitting here discussing it, would we?" He closed the file and shoved it back across the desk.

"Very well, Mr Grafton, if you won't believe me, believe these." He pushed another folder, slimmer this time, across the desk.

Grafton opened the cover leaf, and a sharp intake of breath told Marks all that he needed to know - the pictures were of a farmyard outside a Czech village in the early 1940s. In the foreground lay bodies, all male, shot where they had stood.

"There were a hundred and ninety-two of them, some as young as sixteen. The Germans massacred them in retaliation for the killing of Reinhard Heydrich, one of Hitler's closest friends. The women were all taken away to Ravensbrück concentration camp, and the children were dispatched back into the *fatherland* to be 'Germanised'."

"I don't see the connection." Grafton had recovered from the initial shock.

"Tony Williams did."

"Tony?" Grafton shook his head.

"Williams. He was picked up at Heathrow yesterday with a one way ticket to Rio de Janeiro in his pocket. Started kicking off when the check-in staff wouldn't allow him onto the plane. He'd been drinking in the bar, and was unfit to travel."

"I don't see what this has to do with me."

"Well, that's where it gets interesting; he had a rucksack with ten thousand pounds in it. Security staff found it when they searched his luggage. Seems an awful lot of cash to be carrying around. The really odd thing is that he had one of your business cards in his wallet."

"Chief Inspector Marks, I give those cards out to many people – it's my job; I'm a politician." Grafton was becoming visibly irritated.

"That may be, but this Tony Williams was a fully paid up member of the BDP."

"Was? What do you mean *was*?" Grafton's surprise was genuine.

"He was taken to the local nick, but I didn't find out about it until they discovered him dead in his cell this morning. He'd choked on his own vomit."

"Well then, that's the end of it." Grafton smiled. "I can't see why we're even discussing the matter. Am I supposed to be responsible for that as well?"

"The fact remains that four people, all connected to you and the BDP in some way, have met their deaths in odd circumstances," Marks pulled out his notebook, "and now Tony Williams is dead with ten grand in his bag. He'd also been seen at the airport drinking rather heavily with another, as yet unidentified, man."

"Look!" Grafton stood up and jabbed the air across the desk. "If you have anything which ties me or my party to these people, spit it out and let's make this official. If you haven't, bugger off and leave me alone!"

"Adrian Lawson." Marks shifted his ground, and Grafton was caught cold – he sat back down.

"Who?"

"Lawson, your backer. The man who conveniently appeared from nowhere to step into Steve Marshall's shoes – odd that, wasn't it?"

"What's all this got to do with him?"

"Ask him for yourself." Marks had not missed the 'my party', and the slip by Grafton had been quite accidental.

"I've had enough of this. Get out! I'm not answering any more of your questions; the next time we speak it will be in the presence of a solicitor."

Marks closed his notebook, stood up, smiled knowingly at Grafton, and left the office. Having now set the cat amongst the pigeons, it remained to be seen what Lawson's next move would be once the details of the past half hour reached his ears.

33

"How long are you going to give them?" Marks sat down as Watkinson closed the door to his private office.

"That rather depends upon how badly you managed to rattle Robert Grafton. From what you've told me, he'd be on the blower to Lawson as soon as you'd left the building. We'll be on the lookout for any further movements, and my staff are under strict instructions not to lose him after the last fiasco."

"I read through their manifesto the other day, and it isn't surprising that they're starting to make inroads into the other parties." Marks sighed. "Withdrawal from the EU, cancellation of all foreign aid, increases to the defence and policing budgets, reductions in Whitehall costs, a complete review of the criminal justice system... and that's just the tip of a huge iceberg. Grafton's saying precisely what middle England wants to hear, and they're all listening to him."

"He's dangerous." Watkinson frowned – he was doing a lot of that these days. "I also understand that the BDP propose full proportional representation if they get in at the next election - that could scoop them the entire Liberal Democrat vote. When you think back to what Hitler achieved in the 1930s, it makes your blood run cold at the very thought of it."

Support for the BDP had, in the past week, surged in the opinion polls, and their rating now stood at 25% of the individuals questioned. Whilst not sufficient guarantee of seats to cause problems under the current system, it could, as Watkinson was well aware, be the springboard from which the party could launch a successful bid for power.

"The trouble is I'm sure that the four killings we investigated are, in some way, all linked to Grafton. If I could prove at least some aspect of complicity it would ruin his chances at the ballot box."

"Yes, we lost one of our operatives right at the start of all this." Watkinson said. "He was getting close to something when he vanished. We fished him out of the Thames a few weeks later, and all he had on him was a number."

"A number?"

"Bank account code as it turned out – Barry Newman traced it back to a provincial Swiss bank in Thun, but it's as far as he got. We managed to establish the link between that and the BDP, but I'm buggered if we can do anything with it."

"What about leaking something to the press? You know how the tabloids love a whiff of scandal." Marks was on thin ice and he knew it, but with few other options it was a desperate gamble.

George Watkinson stared at the DCI for a few moments, weighing the pros and cons of what the detective had just said. With an IPCC investigation quashed less than a year ago, it would be highly unlikely that the internal disciplinary mechanism would be activated once more against one of the Yard's top men so soon. Marks' record was unparalleled within the Metropolitan Police, and with the weight of MI5 behind him he had become almost untouchable. It was still quite a risk that he was taking - one word in the wrong place and the entire thing would come crashing down. He opened a drawer.

"This was found in the apartment of Steve Marshall." He handed over a plastic bag containing the torn off piece of paper which he had shown to Solomon Wiseman. Marks help it up to the light.

"A forgery, I assume. Old paper like this could have been used to fabricate quite a story."

"Indeed, and one which only a select few would be capable of achieving."

"Wiseman, then?" Marks smiled. He knew the printer of old and was, on the quiet, an admirer of the man's skill.

"He identified it as part of a job which I commissioned some time ago, and I can only think of Marshall being aware that the papers from which it came were at my house. Our burglar is now back in Germany, but he told a good story before I released him."

"With Marshall out of the picture, it's going to be hard to establish any link at all to the current state of affairs. What's known about this Adrian Lawson chap?"

"Had one of my operatives working on that." Watkinson replaced the paper in his drawer. "All his details check out, and it's not as if he appeared out of nowhere. Unless I can find him connected to some illegal activity neither of us will be able to touch him."

"So, we're back to watching and waiting for Grafton to slip up?" Marks sounded disappointed.

"I'm afraid so."

The DCI stood up and put on his coat prior to leaving, but was stopped in his tracks by the ringing of his mobile phone. He listened with a widening smile on his face and then ended the call.

"That had to have been good news." Watkinson's voice bore just a touch of hope.

"That was my DI, Peter Spencer. It would seem that we may have our link after all." Marks sat down again. "It began at my first meeting with Robert Grafton at the BDP headquarters when I noticed where he banks."

"I don't see." Watkinson poured two coffees from the percolator across the room.

"I can read upside down, and whilst he was away from his desk, I saw some bank statements – personal ones – bearing a considerable balance. It's one of those things that make me suspicious; I didn't realise up to that point that he is a wealthy man in his own right."

"So?"

"It would seem that a rather large withdrawal was made a few days ago from that account, and in cash – two hundred thousand pounds to be exact."

"How did you come by this information?" Watkinson smiled. "I thought that was the speciality of the security services."

"It depends on who you know, and I happen to know a certain bank manager who wouldn't like details of his little habit to get back to his employers. Nothing serious, you understand, but highly embarrassing."

"All right, you have me hooked. What next?"

"I got a call to say that not only had Grafton withdrawn the cash, but that its make-up was very specific – ten thousand in Sterling and the rest in US Dollars."

"Dollars? Why Dollars?" Watkinson's eyes lit up as soon as the words had left his mouth.

"Tony Williams was on his way to South America; what better currency to use over there? I also persuaded my bank manager friend to list the serial numbers of the Sterling notes, and they match those that we found in Williams' bag. There's your connection – Williams got the cash from Grafton, and the only remaining question would seem to be 'why', and I think I know the answer."

"Which is…?"

"Blackmail. Williams had something on Grafton – something which would certainly ruin his political career, and all we need to do is find out what it was and where Williams was keeping it." His explanation was cut short by the mobile once again, and the smile broadened at the fresh news.

"There's more?"

"Spencer again. Amongst Williams' luggage was a laptop. Unfortunately the files on it are password protected, so *we* are unable to access them, but I feel sure that you have resources at your disposal which are more than capable of cracking them wide open. Barry Newman, for example."

"Get the thing over here and we'll have them open."

"Peter's already on his way – should be here in about half an hour. Any more coffee in that percolator?"

Robert Grafton, unaware of the speed with which wheels had begun to turn against him, had attempted to contact Lawson but discovered him to be unaccountably unavailable. Calls to the untraceable mobile went unanswered, and with the deadline given by Williams already past, he was fast running out of options. The man had clearly said that the automatic e-mail would be sent if he were not there to cancel it, and the BDP leader was staring down the barrel of some serious charges if Marks got hold of the information. It had been almost twenty-four hours since the blackmailer had left with the money, but there had been no widespread exposé of the information with which Williams had threatened him; the man had been bluffing and Grafton had no choice but to swallow the loss. He looked at his watch – he was going to be late.

The Prime Minister sat down and Grafton was on his feet in a flash, catching the eye of the speaker.

"The member for Burnley." Members previously on their feet resumed their seats and, after what had become a ritual haranguing of the BDP leader, the chamber fell silent.

"Mr Speaker, in the light of the circumstances surrounding the arrest of the Foreign Secretary's son, would the Prime Minister care to comment on any steps which he will be taking to address the issue which appeared in yesterday's press?" He held up the headline, to the dismay of the government front bench:

'Minister's Son in Late Night Drink and Drugs Bust'

Grafton sat down. The report had appeared in two of the Red Tops, and contained very little which was actually newsworthy, but a Whitehall source had hinted at an attempt to suppress publication although, again, little substance had been attached to that either. Nevertheless, it had provided the BDP leader with a chance to grab some headlines, and he took full advantage. To loud cheers from the opposition benches, and much waving of order papers, the embattled government leader rose and struggled through one of the most embarrassing episodes ever to afflict his party.

"Coming on well, isn't he?" Lawson turned to the man sitting to his right in the visitors' gallery.

He had deliberately kept a low profile for the past week, leaving Grafton to fend for himself as the pressure started to build. There would be no room for any faltering steps now that success was within the grasp of the Organisation.

"Mr Lawson," the accent was thick and deep, and from a man whose political affiliations dated back to the days before the fall of the Berlin wall, "one question does not make him a serious politician, and he will be of no use if the result of the British General Election does not run in your favour."

"I'm aware of that, but we're in a much better position now than we were back in 1992. Once the BDP are in power, we will merely move in, dispose of Mr Grafton in some typically British political way, and install our own people. The dream may have died a little in 1946, but Bormann saw it coming and made contingency plans – they are still holding up."

"Very well, but be assured that it is your neck on the British block if it all comes to nothing. I must go now; my plane leaves for Munich in three hours and I have business to conduct in the Landtag. Just because Germany is now reunited does not mean that we have to pander to the wishes of our liberal government. We will speak again."

His departure was unobtrusive and unnoticed, leaving Lawson to ponder the two stools which he was currently straddling. Kaufmann was one of the old school, steeped in the politics of the pre-war Reich, and had little use for progressive attitudes. A fervent opponent of modern day German ways, he and his Bavarian associates were driven by the ideals of Hitler's Deutsche Arbeiter Partei before the rot set in. The Deutsche Volksunion, on the other hand, saw Grafton and the Organisation as a means of purging Europe of the ails which the Third Reich had railed against; its aim was to purify, its goal ethnicity.

34

Barry Newman wore a smug, self-satisfied smile upon his face. It was a look born out of the confidence which had grown during his time working under George Watkinson. He had cracked the password protection on all of Tony Williams' files, and the results were there for Marks and Watkinson to see. Their less than enthusiastic response took the shine away from his satisfaction, and the disappointment was clear in his voice.

"I did what you asked. Is there something wrong?"

"No, Barry." Watkinson picked up on the inflection in Newman's voice. "This is perfect; just what we wanted."

"So, why aren't we celebrating?"

"The data is fine." Marks looked up from the screen. "It's just that we now have to establish a solid connection between what Williams put down in those files and the money which he was able to extract from Grafton."

"Isn't it obvious?" Newman was losing the thread of the conversation.

"Not in a court of law it isn't." Marks took off his glasses. "Grafton would state that the cash was to fund a valid political journey by a known member of the BDP, and a defence barrister would tear our case to shreds. We'd then be left with evidence tainted in any subsequent charge. The fact that Williams had a one way ticket to Rio would be dismissed by the defence as coincidental, that's all."

"So, what now?"

"Now," Watkinson drummed his fingers on the desk, "DCI Marks will return to Grafton and rattle his cage once more. We're getting close to an election in my opinion, and the BDP leader will have quite a lot on his plate. You never know what he might let slip now that the pressure's on."

Their conversation was interrupted by Marks' mobile, and the DCI remained silent as the contents of the communication sank in. His only remark was a curt 'thank you', and he looked at Watkinson and Newman with a knowing smile.

"That was George Groves. I think it may be well worth our while making the trip to his lab. You may find what he has to say rather illuminating."

"We know that the body in Marshall's car wasn't Steve." Groves leaned against the slab where the charred remains of the corpse pulled from the wreckage lay. "However, we had no idea just who *this* is."

"Just a moment." Watkinson interrupted. "I thought we cremated him."

"You," Marks grinned, "do not have the monopoly on subterfuge at MI5. I made arrangements to have him replaced with a suitable weight in the coffin. It's surprising what can be achieved when you have contacts in the right places."

Watkinson shook his head in amazement; this was something new from the DCI, and he was clearly trading on his untouchable reputation after the successful encounter with the IPCC and Eric Staines.

"You have something new then, Professor?" Watkinson looked from Groves to Marks, who was clearly in on some information which was yet to be revealed.

"Yes. I've been working on identifying the man, and the body *is* male, for quite some time. What fingerprints remained were of very poor quality, but the hands were sufficiently intact for me to take some impressions from the bases near to the wrists."

"Tell me that you've found a match."

"Well, that alone wouldn't have been enough." Groves wrinkled his nose. "When I took the DNA samples into account as well, things started to become a little clearer."

"Is he always like this?" Watkinson turned to Marks, who smiled and nodded.

"As I said," Groves continued, "I needed other evidence to support my findings. We know that the records you have at MI5 don't relate to Marshall, and that they therefore must have been planted. The question is, whose are they?"

Groves beckoned them over to a side table and opened a folder which had been lying there. Removing a piece of A4, he handed it to Watkinson and continued.

"I asked Sandra Wallace for a list of all operatives leaving the service within the past year; I'm sorry to circumvent you, but you seemed to be unavailable at the time. Anyway, leaving out the ones who clearly didn't match the gender and physical attributes of our friend over there, I narrowed it down to six. Of those, three are now living abroad and, as far as I can tell, are in perfect health. One is currently resident in a Berkshire nursing home, and another is currently with MI6."

"So… the final one?" Groves' sense of the dramatic was beginning to irritate Watkinson.

"Is there." The pathologist turned and waved an arm with a flourish. "One Frank Pearson. He vanished off the face of the earth some time ago."

"All right, how do you know that it *is* him?"

"Because a hand print which matches the partial taken from the corpse was found on the records I examined from your files at Thames House. Once I compared the DNA which I extracted from his bone marrow to that on the file, it was conclusive."

"Conclusive?" Watkinson narrowed his eyes.

"Well, almost." Groves raised a finger. "I needed, of course, a reference sample to confirm it, and discovered that our Mr Pearson was on the register of bone marrow donors. I have a contact there."

"You came by this information through the proper channels?" Watkinson asked.

"Best if you don't know the details; confidentiality of source and all that. I'm sure you understand. Anyway, it's Frank Pearson all right; all you need to do now is to establish how on earth he came to be in Marshall's car."

"We need to take a much closer look at Adrian Lawson as well. There are one or two things that are beginning to bother me about how he fits in with all of this. If Marshall had an accomplice to get his records switched at MI5, it stands to reason that there are others working in the background too." Watkinson headed for the door. "I'll call you if I find anything."

They stood in silence for a moment as the head of MI5 left the room, and Marks turned to Groves as he began tidying up.

"There's something else, isn't there? I've known you far too long to miss the things you *don't* say." Marks leaned back against the table.

"Not much, and I can't be absolutely certain, but there was evidence in the foot well of the Audi which I can't tie down to anything else that we found at the scene."

"Spit it out; you know how I hate loose ends."

"Well," Groves removed his gloves and sat on one of the stools in the lab, "when we'd done sifting through the rubbish on the floor of the car, I found pieces of charred wood – wood that didn't match to anything up there at the place where the vehicle was found. Once I managed to piece some of them together, they seemed to be a part of a strut long enough to hold down the accelerator pedal."

"All right, but we know that the body wasn't Steve's, and that he, therefore, is the most likely person to have put it there. What does the wood tell us that we don't already know?"

"That's what I can't understand. The gas fitter, Geoff Marsden, thought he heard the sound of footsteps running away from the scene. Let's face it; up there you'd need another vehicle and driver to get clear of the place. Why wouldn't Lawson have been that other person?"

Marks had not expected this, and although Groves could surprise him with the occasional leap of logic, it was not in his character to make suppositions – the man dealt in hard facts. It was, however, a set of circumstances which neither he nor Peter Spencer had considered.

"If that's the case, he'll be hiding Marshall somewhere until it all dies down. I need to have him in, whether Watkinson has him under surveillance or not. This is still a murder investigation, and Marshall is the only positive link that I can see between the four bodies that we have."

"You could do with finding out where Frank Pearson has been as well. Anything less than a deep freeze would have been very unpleasant."

"Guv, we got a hit on Marshall's cash card." Warner rose from her desk as Marks entered the squad room.

"What?" He flung his coat across the back of his chair and crossed to the window where she was standing.

"An hour ago at an ATM on the Mile End Road."

"How did you get this?" He looked at the printed report.

"My friend at Thames House. I asked him to look out for any suspicious activity." She started to blush.

"This friend wouldn't be called Barry, would he?" Marks tried hard to suppress the beginnings of a smile.

"Yes, that is no, he's not really… he's just… yes guv, it is." She gave in. "He accessed all of Marshall's bank details when we thought he'd died up in Yorkshire, and we've both been watching ever since."

"Very good, Chloe, your brother would be very proud of you. I don't suppose there's any chance of an ID?"

"Better than that, guv. The machine takes a picture with each withdrawal, and this is the guy." She pointed at a grainy shot. "Sorry, but it's not very clear."

Marks' smile grew even wider as he held up the photograph, and DS Warner stood in puzzlement at his reaction. He went to his office and came back with a folder – it was one of a number which he kept in his own filing system.

"Mickey Thomas." He dropped the file onto the desk. "I'd know his face anywhere, grainy or otherwise."

Michael Thomas was fifteen when his path crossed with that of the then DI Marks. The eldest of five children to a single mother, he had been a serial truant at junior and secondary schools in the area, and left full-time education at the earliest opportunity. He was a loner with enough of an unpredictable reputation to ensure that the local gangs steered clear of him, particularly following a run-in with one of their leaders which left the young man in question with three broken ribs and severe concussion. Marks had been involved as the duty Inspector, but with no witnesses to the assault, charges were never brought.

"How do you know him, guv?"

"One of the local bad lads." Spencer had just entered the office and now joined in. "Not really a hard case, and the guv'nor always saw something worth saving; that's why the file's in his office. What's he done, sir?"

"Theft." Marks waved the cash point report in front of Spencer. "Looks like he's somehow got hold of Marshall's cash card, and it won't be too hard to find him at this time of day."

"The Winning Line?"

"The Winning Line, Peter. Get your coat, Chloe, and we'll show you some of the local sights."

The Winning Line is an arcade on Bethnal Green in London's East End, and the location of choice for the youngsters of the Mile End Road seeking to while away their boredom and their cash. Mickey Thomas was a known and respected player of the pinball machines in the area, and always attracted a crowd wherever he indulged his obsession. It would not be hard to find him.

"Mickey!" Marks slapped the young man on the back as his admirers melted away. "How've things been?"

Thomas jumped visibly at the sight of three of the 'filth' – his lookouts had clearly failed him, and retribution would be swift once he got his hands on them.

"It wasn't me, Mr Marks. I've been here all day; ask around." He waved his arm at the now empty space where moments earlier a crowd had stood.

"Now, Mickey." The DCI's voice had that disappointed air. "Why would you think that I had something like that on my mind? We're just here for a little chat."

"Yeah, like I've heard that before. I ain't done nuffin'." He stood up from the seat he had occupied and tried to outstare Marks – he failed.

"Come into some money just recently, did we? Say a couple of hundred?" Marks rubbed his chin thoughtfully, and tried to look unconcerned.

"You know I'm broke, Mr Marks. Ain't got no job, and me mum lets me play down here with the child benefit. Once that's gone I'm done."

"So… this couldn't possibly be you, then?" Spencer joined in, pointing at the photograph which Marks had pulled from his coat pocket.

The young man stood silently for what seemed an age, and then suddenly made a break for it. He got as far as Chloe Warner, clearly believing her to be the weak link, and aimed a blow at her face. He connected with fresh air, and the next thing he saw was the ceiling as Warner flipped him over her right hip, using his momentum to carry him to the floor. With all of the breath temporarily knocked out of him, he had nowhere to run.

"Now, that was a silly thing to do, wasn't it?" The DCI strolled over and stared down at the confused form before him. "Our DS Warner is a judo black belt. I think we'll have a chat back at the Yard – you look like you need a nice cup of tea."

Once in the interview room, all pretence at being a macho man vanished, and Mickey Thomas' eyes flitted nervously around the place. He had been here before, and the last time had seen him end up with six months in Feltham Young Offenders Institute – a stretch which he had not appreciated.

"Right then, Mickey, get that cuppa down you and tell me all about the cash card you lifted from Steve Marshall." Thomas' talents were not restricted to the pinball table, and his reputation as a skilful pickpocket was well known.

"All right, but what do I get if I cough? It must be important for you lot to be involved." He had dropped the east end dialect and its truncated diction.

"Our undying thanks, and a clip round the ear if you don't play ball."

"You can't do that, Mr Marks. I got rights." He stuck out his chin.

"Mickey, you and I go back a while, and don't forget the hiding I gave you when you and your mates trashed that old bloke's flat on White Horse Lane. You were lucky – if your mother had found out, I'd have been the least of your worries that day."

Thomas stared at the floor. Marks was right; Sylvia, his mother, was handy with her fists when her kids stepped out of line. It was only when they got caught though, but many had been the night that one or more of them had gone to bed bruised. Social Services were neither welcome nor regular in the East End.

"It was too easy. He hadn't even got his coat fastened up. I was in Bexley High Street and he looked lost; he was crossing the road and all I had to do was bump into him. The lift was a piece of cake – idiot even left his pin number on a piece of paper inside the wallet I took. Can I go now?"

"No. Where's the card, and what did you do with the wallet?" Marks held out his hand, knowing that Thomas would still have the plastic on him.

"Here!" He grunted and threw the card on to the table. "Dumped the wallet in a litter bin; there was hardly any cash in it."

"Warner." Marks turned to his sergeant. "Take some uniforms and have all the bins in the Bexley High Street checked. They won't be emptied until tomorrow."

"Yes, guv."

"Now then, Mickey." He turned back to the young thief. "Is this the man?" He held out the picture Watkinson had supplied from MI5 records, fully expecting a positive ID.

"Nah, that weren't 'im. Never seen that bloke before in my life." The statement was true, and had Marks staring in disbelief.

Further questioning failed to shake Thomas' assertion that the man in the photograph was not the victim of his crime, and the detectives were forced to accept the story. Spencer excused himself from the room and was back moments later with another set of stills. There were eight in all, and he laid them out on the desk in front of Thomas. He was about to speak, but never got the chance.

"There! That's 'im! That's the bloke I nicked the wallet off." He pointed to the third one in the row, and the two coppers stared at each other in disbelief.

With Thomas now back on the streets after a caution, Marks and Spencer looked at the picture again. Mickey had been so certain, so adamant in his identification, that they had no option than to grudgingly believe what he had said.

"Did you?"

"Did I what, Peter?"

"Give Thomas a good hiding?" Spencer's face had showed a trace of concern, and Marks grinned.

"No. He was fifteen, drunk, and with a few of his mates he ransacked an empty flat where an old guy had died. The council were about to strip it out anyway, and he wasn't fast enough to get away. He thinks I did though, and that seems to have done the trick."

Spencer smiled in relief. There were still the odd times when the DCI could catch him unawares. Marks' face returned to its serious side as he gathered up the photographs.

"I think we need another trip to Thames House, Peter. This is getting a little too regular for my liking. We'll pick Warner up on the way; I don't think it matters whether she's found the wallet or not now."

35

Lawson had known almost immediately that he had been mugged, but by the time he checked his pockets the thief had disappeared down one of the side streets which led away from Bexley's main thoroughfare. It was too late now to worry about the consequences of losing the wallet; the chances of anyone realising the nature of the contents would be minimal without a police report of its being stolen. More fortunate was the fact that he had no longer been carrying the latest instalment of the funding which was being channelled towards the BDP. One million in cash suddenly appearing in the hands of a petty criminal might have turned a few heads if it came to the attention of the local plods.

He hadn't intended being south of the river at all and, but for Grafton's insistence on the money being delivered personally, would have been miles away from Bexley. Hailing a passing cab, he headed for the flat rented out under an assumed name in Finchley. The journey gave him time to reflect upon the BDP leader's plans. With rumours rife about an impending announcement from Westminster, the BDP had taken the lead in organising a series of open air rallies up and down the country.

The party had met with a series of well-organised protest marches which had seriously disrupted their plans, and at a particularly violent meeting in the centre of Birmingham, missiles were thrown at Grafton and his constituency candidate. True to form, however, he turned the entire fiasco to the party's advantage and, at a press conference called in more secure surroundings, rounded upon his opponents' tactics in attempting to subvert what he referred to as a properly convened and legitimately organised rally. The senior police officer in charge on the day was forced into an admission that no fault for the near riot could be attributed to the BDP. With similar instances happening at other locations, it became clear that a serious error of judgement had been made by those organising the protests, and Grafton's personal rating had risen sharply as a result. To the astonishment of political commentators across the country, he was, temporarily at least, more popular than any of the other three major party leaders.

In the House of Commons he was no less effective, and had participated in a series of highly focused attacks on the Prime Minister personally, and the government in general, for their handling of a series of damagingly high-profile issues. The Iraq War enquiry, suggestions for an impeachment of a former Prime Minister, and the shambles into which the MPs' expenses row had dissolved, all provided easy meat for his campaign.

───────

"I take it that you've seen these?" Watkinson slid a section of the morning newspapers across to Marks. Their meetings were becoming regular, and the DCI was beginning to feel more a member of the agency than a policeman with the Met.

"I have, and it grieves me that we can't find anything to nail him with. He's as guilty as sin of complicity to murder, but I just can't prove it."

"In that case, I may have some news for you." Watkinson reached into his top drawer and removed a document carrying the headed crest of the Foreign Office. "This came to Downing Street in the diplomatic bag."

"Warren Stokes? Who's he?" Marks was scanning the text for clues.

"Someone who wants to cut a deal with Her Majesty's government in exchange for his freedom. Here, give it back to me and I'll fill you in with the detail."

Warren Stokes had been the second of two men, the other being Tony Williams, sent out by Robert Grafton to follow Mike Summers after the meeting at BDP headquarters. Summers' death, and that of Beverley Drake, had been down to them and on the instructions of Robert Grafton.

"Stokes has got himself into a bit of bother with the Saudi authorities it would seem. I'm not sure how he got out there, but there was an incident a couple of weeks ago involving a local woman. He'd been out drinking and was involved in a car crash; the woman was killed outright, but the driver didn't die until a few days later. Under Sharia law, I understand that the family have the right to demand the death penalty, and that's precisely what's happened."

"How do we get involved then?" Marks was not sure where Watkinson was going with the story.

"He asked to speak to the British ambassador out there, and made a number of allegations against our friend Mr Grafton. He says he'll reveal exactly

199

what it is that he has if we can get him off the death penalty and back home."

"How do we know that we can trust the guy?" Marks' inherent scepticism kicked in.

"Because one thing that he did let out, just as corroboration, was the name of Tony Williams."

"Williams? That was the name of the guy stopped at Heathrow with all of that money in a rucksack. A dead end as it turned out and in more ways than one – he choked on his own vomit during a night in the cells at the Yard. The IPCC are holding an enquiry into the matter. God help the poor bugger who was supposed to be watching him."

"Yes," said Watkinson. "I'm aware of the circumstances, but how this chap could know without being involved beats me."

"Are we going to rescue him then?"

"The Foreign Secretary has already given the go-ahead, and negotiations have begun with the Saudi royal family. The entire thing's a bit of a fiasco, and they think that a suitable amount of cash compensation will settle the husband's feelings."

George Watkinson's revelations to the DCI were, as it turned out, considerably out of date, as a plane with the man on board had already left Riyadh airport. Stokes' presence in the kingdom was proving to be something of an embarrassment, coming as it had in the midst of a series of business negotiations with leading British companies, and both sides had deemed it essential that he be removed without delay.

"I need to question him as soon as he lands, then. If he can give us the link we need to Grafton, we could tie up the whole matter very quickly. You'd be more than a little pleased, I'll bet."

"Indeed." Watkinson poured two coffees. "We already have some tenuous connections to Adrian Lawson, and a joker in the pack like Stokes would solve all of our problems."

"Yes, and I might just have that playing card. We interviewed a petty thief earlier today – a young man who stole Steve Marshall's wallet and used the cash card."

"So?"

"So he couldn't identify Marshall as the mark. This is the man he took it from."

"Lawson? What would he be doing with..." He paused. "Are you serious?" Watkinson was not easily surprised, but Marks had him this time.

"Don't rush me, and I haven't the slightest shred of evidence...yet, but I think our investigation just took an unexpected turn."

"All right Mr Stokes, let's get on with it and we'll see if we're interested in anything that you have to say." Marks sat down opposite the fugitive, who was accompanied, at this stage, by a minor official from the Foreign and Commonwealth Office.

"I thought we already had a deal." Stokes was not the first to try the patience of DCI Marks, and many had failed.

"Look, Stokes." Marks was already becoming irritable. "You're still technically guilty of a crime under Sharia law, and I can soon have you shipped back over to Saudi and let them deal with you. Is that what you want?"

"You're kidding me!"

"No. I've never been more serious. If there really *is* something that you can tell us about Robert Grafton, now is the time to spit it out. I'm a very busy man, and have four unsolved murders on my hands. The deal, if there is one, is that you tell me what you know, and I see if it fits with anything that I currently have under investigation – that's all."

Marks stared across the table, and Stokes shifted uncomfortably in his chair. It was not until the DCI made a move that he finally caved in. He was half out of his chair, gathering up his papers, when Stokes stretched out a hand.

"Okay. I know Tony Williams; we were both members of the BDP, and Grafton had us follow this guy out of one of the party meetings. He'd been causing some trouble, and Robert wanted him out of the way."

"Go on." Marks resumed his seat, but gave nothing away.

"He made it pretty clear that getting this guy out of the way was meant to be on a permanent basis, and we waited until he'd left the pub where three of them had gone."

"You killed him." The statement shook Stokes with its flat quality.

"Yes." He sighed and his shoulders fell. "Tied him up and dumped him in the Thames near Richmond Lock."

This was what Marks had been waiting for, and pushing Stokes further revealed that the dead man was Mike Summers. The DCI wanted more, and pressed on with the questioning.

"That's one murder then – what about the others?"

"Others? I thought you only wanted Grafton."

"The more we have, the less likely it'll be that you serve a life sentence. There were other killings; how many of them were down to you?"

"There was this woman as well... Bev something."

"Beverley Drake."

"That's her. Came around asking questions about Summers, and Grafton was starting to get nervous. Me and Williams did her as well – why don't you ask him?"

"Well, that's where this thing gets a little bit complicated." Marks leaned back in his chair. "It's going to be very hard to corroborate anything that you say, since Mr Williams is, in fact, dead."

"Do what?" Stokes sat bolt upright, seeing his story starting to fade away. "It was Williams who killed Summers, and he did for the Drake woman as well. I just helped get rid of the bodies."

Marks stared out of the window whilst he considered this latest revelation from his captive. Stokes would have everything to gain from passing on all of the blame for the killings now that he knew Williams was dead, and there really was nothing that the DCI could do to counter any of his assertions. On the other hand, a signed statement from the only witness to the murders would certainly go a long way to securing a conviction against the BDP leader for, at the very least, conspiracy. He decided to cut Stokes a break.

"No promises, Stokes, but if your testimony succeeds in getting a conviction against Robert Grafton, I could make a recommendation to the CPS for more lenient treatment than the life sentence you would have got under normal circumstances."

"How long?" Williams' interest was suddenly aroused.

"Not sure." Marks scratched the back of his head. "Maybe five years, but I'm only guessing."

"Five years?!" Stokes fumed. "That's ages in exchange for what I've given you!"

"Warren, you ungrateful little toe rag, I could have left you to rot in that Saudi jail until they chopped your head off." Marks thumped the table. "Don't you understand how many strings have been pulled just to get you over here? If you want to turn the offer down go ahead; there are flights back to Riyadh every day. You do know that they carry out their executions in public, don't you? Wonder how your family would enjoy seeing that."

"All right." Stokes capitulated. "I'll take it; what about Grafton's heavies? I'll need witness protection if I help you out."

"We're not talking about the Mafia, Stokes. Grafton's mob don't carry much weight on the inside – you'll be perfectly safe. I'll get some paper and a pen – it's time for you to start writing."

36

Murmured conversation came to a halt as Robert Grafton walked out onto the stage and into the spotlights trained on the podium at its centre. The capacity at Nottingham's National Ice Centre was ten thousand, and there was not a spare seat to be had in the entire place. He stood for a few moments, glancing around the vast room, nodding his head almost imperceptibly and smiling in self-satisfaction – his time had come.

The clapping began towards the back, but gathered momentum as more hands joined in. It was rhythmical, steady and slow, but not the kind given out for a poor performance. This was a salute, and suddenly there were people on their feet as the volume increased. It was almost, but not quite, reminiscent of the *'Sieg Heil'* salute given to Hitler at the Nuremberg rallies. Grafton picked up on the significance, and with a single raised hand, stopped the act in its tracks. Everyone resumed their seats, and waited.

He made them wait; standing at the podium, he reached down and filled a glass from the carafe of water placed just beneath it. Raising it to his lips, he took a sip and walked away from the centre of the stage briefly, taking in the atmosphere, judging the acoustics, before returning to his place at the microphone. He looked up at the audience and smiled again.

"Friends and colleagues, thank you for coming here this evening. You are witnesses to the most radical change in British politics since the founding of the Labour party in 1906. What we will all see in the coming weeks is a significant shift in the awareness of the electorate of the tired old policies of the past sixty years."

A round of applause greeted the statement. It was clear that a number of plants in the audience were leading the acclaim, but it was highly satisfying to Grafton that the momentum was sustained enough to drown out what would have been his next words. A raised finger from the stage was enough to kill the noise stone dead. He had them transfixed.

"Our ratings at the opinion polls increase with each week, and today…" he paused, reaching behind himself for the only paper which he had brought along, "…comes the announcement that we have all been waiting for. There is to be a vote of 'No Confidence' in the House and, according to my reckoning, that may give us a shade over one month to mobilise the country and instil some old-fashioned British values into our society."

At no time had Grafton's voice risen above that for normal conversation, and every single person in the room truly believed that he was talking to them and them alone. A cheer, the first of the evening, suddenly split the air and he let it ride, basking in the adulation which he was sure would carry him all the way into Downing Street. Once more a raised finger was sufficient to silence the crowd, and allow those political commentators present to catch up on their note-taking.

"Our policies will be quite simple, and have already enjoyed considerable airing up and down the UK, but it's worthwhile spending a little time here reiterating some of the main proposals – proposals which will instil once more a sense of what it used to be like to be truly British. Let no-one tell you we are racist, or that we are a party hell-bent on some kind of ethnic cleansing. None of that features in the manifesto, and any of the tabloids printing such lies do so at their own peril."

Grafton's sideways glance at the press box had all eyes following his gaze, and activity amongst the scribes halted momentarily as they digested his last words.

He talked for an hour and a half, completely unscripted and without notes of any kind. The final session of twenty minutes was given over to questions from the audience, and the BDP leader's skills in rhetoric were tested as they had never been tested before. There was a thirst for information, a drive, a pull which he had never seen before in the journey north from London. It was as if a wave was moving before him and the party, picking up support with every mile that they travelled. There were, of course, those who had come along not to applaud but to heckle, and one particular individual in the centre of the crowd took exception to part of the party's line, and became vociferous. Stewards were quick to intervene, but Grafton halted their progress with another wave of the hand.

"We are not a party immune from criticism, and in a country which prides itself on the concept of freedom of speech, I for one will not seek to suppress anyone who doesn't share our views."

A round of applause followed what was becoming a series of conciliatory pronouncements from Grafton, as the now exposed speaker was led from the safety and darkness of the crowd and into the gaze of all those in the hall. Now on the stage at the side of the BDP leader, and under the glare of the spotlights, he was starting to feel considerably less confident than before.

"Perhaps the gentleman at my side would like to repeat the question issued from the middle of the room?" Grafton stepped away, and waved the newcomer towards the podium and microphone.

The incident had clearly not gone according to plan, and the speed of Grafton's reaction had stalled support from any of the man's confederates in the rest of the audience. He looked around nervously, now under the harsh lights of the stage, and his mouth dried. The words just would not come, and any script which had been prepared for him was forgotten. Glancing to his left, he saw the smiling face of the man whom he had come to barrack; Grafton raised his eyebrows in a questioning manner, and the man's nerve broke. Making a hasty and undignified exit from the stage, he was jeered and booed all the way to the exit.

"Ladies and gentlemen; tolerance, please." The mock reproof was enough to still the crowd again, and Grafton resumed his position at the podium. "This is how we in the party deal with those who oppose us – not with violence or intimidation, but tolerance and understanding. There are no threats in the rhetoric, just plain and simple patriotism – something all too sadly lacking these days. We will succeed where others have failed, and the electorate will look back on this moment when the people of Britain took back their country. Thank you, and good night."

The final soliloquy was enough to bring the audience to its feet, and this time there was no attempt by Grafton to dampen their ardour. His return for a curtain call was beyond doubt, and a further fifteen minutes elapsed before he was finally allowed to leave.

"This is without doubt his best performance yet." The heavily accented German voice was hushed as the visitor spoke to the man seated on his right.

"Indeed," replied Lawson. "I haven't come across anyone quite as charismatic. He had them eating out of his hands, and based on this I can't see the opposition offering much to stem the support that seems to be rushing to the party."

"Our friends in Bavaria were impressed with my last report, and if the BDP succeeds at the forthcoming elections we may yet fulfil the dreams that my father and those like him held dear in 1946. However, it would not seem appropriate for me to linger too long here – you really do not know who may be listening."

In a turbulent day at Westminster, the day after Grafton made his address in Nottingham, the Coalition Government fell. In a show of grassroots strength, back bench MPs, along with the entire BDP contingent, voted to remove Mark Barrowman and his coalition from power. Robert Grafton now saw his future mapped out exactly as he had imagined. The scene was set for the British public to reject the parties and policies which, according to BDP rhetoric, had hung around the country's neck like an albatross since the 1960s.

"Where did this come from?" Grafton's earlier composure had started to melt at the sight of the front page.

"It's an early sight of one of tomorrow's red tops. I have a friend at Canary Wharf who thought we might like to see it." John Farrington had been Grafton's press officer for the past twelve months, and his skill with the media had been a significant factor in the BDP leader's meteoric rise.

"What are these Nazi documents that they're on about?" He scrutinised the story for some clue.

"He doesn't know. The details are sketchy at best, but it seems that they've been around for some time. No names are mentioned at present, but there's a hint of more to come in the next few days. Is this something to do with our benefactor?"

Farrington was amongst a small number who had been made aware of the source of the new funding, part of which had ensured the continuation of his employment with the party. His suspicions about Lawson had been strictly private and, until now, unvoiced. Grafton was not one to be second-guessed.

"I don't know, but I'm certainly going to find out. This is something that we don't need just when we're on the verge of a breakthrough. If the British public are led to believe that we're tied in with it we'll be finished, whether it's true or not."

Grafton suddenly recalled a conversation with DCI Marks. What had the copper said?

"Adrian Lawson."

"Who?"

"Lawson, your backer. The man who conveniently appeared from nowhere to step into Steve Marshall's shoes – odd that, wasn't it?"

"What's all this got to do with him?"

"Ask him for yourself."

Marks had hinted at a connection with some pretty unsavoury characters in Germany. Could that all be tied up with the newspaper headline? For the second time since Marshall's disappearance, Grafton got the distinct feeling that he was somehow being used, and that events were beginning to slip out of his control. He had to meet Lawson face to face again, and it would have to be sooner rather than later.

"All right, where exactly are we?" Watkinson stood with his back to the large ornate fireplace in the lounge of his Surrey home.

He had called the meeting away from the surroundings of New Scotland Yard and Thames House, and those present had been involved in the investigations from the outset. Although significant progress had been made in respect of both Grafton and Lawson, there had been nothing either the Met or MI5 could use to raise charges against either.

"Grafton's involved in the murders, I'm certain of it, but with Tony Williams dead we're short of actual testimony." Marks turned back from the windows looking out onto the rear garden.

"What about this Stokes chap?"

"Uncorroborated statements don't go down too well with the CPS, and they've told me that there isn't enough, on his evidence alone, to make any charges stick. It's a good start but we need more,"

"Sadly, it's the same with Lawson." Watkinson poured himself a coffee and waved a hand to the rest of his guests. "We know that he's linked to the

BDP, but there's no hard evidence of anything moving between them. Even the funds that I'm certain he's providing have been perfectly legitimate. If we arrested everyone sponsoring political organisations, half of the captains of industry would be behind bars. You showed Grafton the pictures from the Czech village, didn't you?"

"Yes, but apart from an initial shock which I would have expected from anyone, he remained unflappable." Marks said. "He's now surrounded himself with a team of legal experts, so getting close to him at all is going to be fraught with problems."

"If we could just establish some criminal act against either of them, it might be enough to bring both crashing to the ground. Those files are still missing, and all we have is a small segment which Wiseman says came from the corner of a piece of his stock of paper."

"Excuse me, sir." Barry Newman was sitting away from the group at a table, staring at his laptop. "I may have found just what you're looking for. May I use the phone?"

"Of course, Barry. What is it?" Watkinson replied.

"I'll let you know when I've made the call. Don't want to waste your time."

"Does that thing go everywhere with him?" Marks nodded towards the Dell computer where Newman was typing away.

"Surgically attached, I should think," Watkinson laughed. "But, in all seriousness, he's a real find. He has talents that I'm not sure I want to know about, and with you being a policeman I'm not certain that I should even be talking to you about them."

"Thank you, that's very helpful." Newman put down the telephone with a smile on his face, and looked at the group now staring at him.

"All right, Barry. Wipe that smile off your face and let us in on the secret."

"Did you know that Steve Marshall still owns his parents' house in Derbyshire?"

"No." Marks, having sat in an armchair, now leaned forwards. "Why should that matter, though?"

"It's been marketed as a rental property by a local agent in Highridge since their deaths, and apparently he checked in with them when he was up there a while back. The really interesting thing is that he also called in at the same time he disappeared up in Yorkshire – now why would that be?"

209

"Presumably to cash in on some of the rent which the agent had been holding for him." Watkinson shook his head, uncertain of where his young IT expert was going.

"Maybe, but wasn't that about the same time those things in your safe went missing, sir?" Newman's eyebrows rose, teasingly.

"What are you suggesting, Barry?" Marks joined in.

"Well, if I were looking for somewhere out of the way to stash some stolen property, I might just hide them in the last place which you would think of looking. Would it also interest you to know that the property is currently vacant?"

"For how long?" Watkinson sensed the urgency of the situation.

"The next five days. New tenants are due to move in next Monday. It would be a good opportunity to take a look around the place. I've already made a reservation to view the house, and we can have the keys tomorrow if you wish. That was the agent I was talking to earlier."

"Good lad, isn't he?" Watkinson looked at Marks. "Fancy a trip up to the Midlands?"

37

The house belonging to Steve Marshall is a three bedroom semi-detached on Greenfields, one of the winding streets on an ex-council estate in the Longlea suburb of Aldersford. His parents had bought the property when the Thatcher government brought in its 'Right to Buy' scheme, which poured millions into the exchequer and reduced the national stock of rental accommodation.

George Watkinson and his entourage had arrived in Highridge, the location of the offices of Radley and Partners, at around 9.00am of the following day, and Dennis Marks' display of his warrant card had them falling over themselves to help. Radley's had been the estate agents dealing with the initial purchase of the house, and gave a full history to the DCI. His car pulled up outside the front gate some fifteen minutes later.

"Right, we'll do this in an organised fashion. Peter, you take the upstairs with Warner, and Mr Watkinson and I will deal with the ground floor. Shout out if you find anything at all – remember, gloves at all times."

"Yes, guv." They disappeared up the stairs and around the first turn on the landing.

"Looks like we're in for a good stay." Watkinson walked through the narrow hallway and into the kitchen/dining area.

Throughout the course of the next hour, every drawer and cupboard received a thorough examination, although Marks considered it highly unlikely that documents of the type described by Watkinson would be hidden in so obvious a place. Spencer and Warner had a similar lack of success in any of the upstairs rooms, and it wasn't until they all reconvened in the lounge that other options were discussed.

"Guv." Warner chipped in. "There's a loft area, but no means of getting up there by ladder. If someone gave me a lift, I could get through the false floor and take a flashlight with me. My mother, Rose, keeps all of her spare stuff in places like that."

"Good idea, Chloe." Marks turned to Spencer. "Peter, looks like a job for you."

They made their way back along the hallway and up the narrow stairs. Marks was the last in the line, and as he passed over one of the treads after the left hand turn which took them to the landing area, he stopped. The others had made their way to the top, and looked back down the final set to where he remained standing.

"Anything wrong, Detective Chief Inspector?" Watkinson was puzzled as Marks was staring downwards at one of the risers.

"Not sure." He replied. He turned to his DI. "Peter, come back down here and go up this final flight again."

Spencer looked at his boss, shrugged and went back down to the landing platform. He turned and made his way back to his starting position.

"Again. Do that again, and take it more slowly this time."

Spencer was accustomed to the occasional flights of fancy that his boss was apt to make, and did the bidding without question. The other two remained nonplussed at the entire performance. As Spencer recommenced his ascent, Marks squatted down and cocked his head to one side.

"Stop. Stop there and come back down one step, Peter. Now, go again and press down with one foot on that tread." He tapped the riser just in front of his DI. There was a quiet, almost imperceptible, squeak as Spencer's foot came down on the carpet.

Spencer stopped, backtracked, looked down at the same spot, and pressed his foot down again. The squeak was there all right, and the three of them going first had not noticed it. Marks' keen sense of hearing had picked it up as he was the last in line.

"There's a loose board under that carpet." Watkinson was now on the same wavelength as Marks.

"We need a screwdriver, and I think I saw one in a drawer in the kitchen. I'll be right back." Marks disappeared back along the hallway, returning with the long-handled tool.

"The carpet's been cut as well, guv." Warner had come back down and had pulled a section of the covering away from the wood beneath. "It's been done very well, and you can only just make it out. "I wonder what possible reason anyone would have for doing that." She smiled.

"One way to find out." Spencer took the screwdriver and inserted the blade between the now exposed tread and its kicking board. The upright came away easily to reveal a compartment.

"Flashlight, Peter." Marks handed the torch to his DI, who peered into the cavity, and came up smiling with a parcel in his hand.

"Would you look at that?" Watkinson took it and shook his head in wonder. "If I'm correct, this is the same wrapping which Madeline Colson used to hide the papers in the Cheltenham library in 1992. Look, there's her writing on the edge which told me that this was the batch which she'd hidden. There were just the two of us who would have recognised it."

"What's inside, sir?" Chloe Warner came forward to look at the parcel as Watkinson, now in the kitchen, undid the cord which held it together.

"In here, young lady, is information for which certain individuals were prepared to fight and die."

The unwrapping of the files was completed in almost reverential style, and when the first few pages had been turned, Spencer and Warner looked at each other in stunned silence.

"Are they really…?"

"Documents from the Third Reich? No, merely expertly-prepared copies, but they reveal a network of fascists ready and able, in 1992, to take this country to the brink of a military style dictatorship. Steve Marshall was operating as a double agent within MI5, and almost succeeded in the aims of what was referred to as the 'Organisation'."

"The question now is," said Marks, "what are they doing here, in Derbyshire, almost two hundred miles from the place where they were being kept?"

"Marshall would have planted them once he became aware of my suspicions. He used that Hahn chap to steal them, and then brought them here on his way up to North Yorkshire. That's when he faked his own death, hoping then to return and pick them up."

No-one had noticed Chloe Warner slip out of the house, but she was back a few moments later with an elderly lady in tow.

"This is Gladys Ottewell. She lives next door but one, and I think you might be interested in what she has to say." She turned to the old lady and smiled. "Tell them what you said to me outside, Gladys."

"Well, it's like I said," the old lady began, "I saw you all turn up, and you seemed to be so out of place that I couldn't help looking to see what it was that you were doing."

"Out of place, my dear?" Watkinson stepped forwards and beckoned Gladys to a chair – his charm worked wonders; she smiled at him sweetly and continued.

"Yes, well, like I said to the young lady. We don't get many smart looking people up here on the old council estate, and I used to know Mr and Mrs Marshall very well. Stephen left the area a long time ago to work in London and I hadn't seen him for ages when he turned up out of the blue a while back. Such a good boy."

"I see, Mrs Ottewell, but what is it that's so strange?" Marks sat down at her side.

"Well, like I say, he came up here some time ago, and there's been a few tenants in and out over the years, and when I heard about him getting killed in that crash, I didn't think the house would be kept on any longer, and when the other man turned up it just seemed a little bit odd."

"Other man? What other man? If I showed you some pictures would you be able to recognise him?" Marks edged forwards.

"Oh yes! Especially now that I have my new glasses. Got them a few weeks back, and I saw him as clear as I'm seeing you now."

Marks' eyes lit up - he turned to Spencer and told him to fetch a file from the car. He was back a few moments later, and the DCI pulled out a single snap and placed it onto the table.

"No, that's Stephen." She picked it up and smiled. "Such a mischievous boy, but he grew up into a really good lad. Have you got any more?"

Marks began laying out all of the other photographs from the folder, including those of Hahn, Stokes, Williams and the rest of the players in the drama. She stopped him abruptly.

"There! That's him! That's the chap who was up here not so long ago. I know that because he was so rude." She sat back with an irritated look on her face.

"Rude?" Watkinson asked, gently. "How so?"

"Well, all I did was say 'good morning' to him, and he looked at me as if I was the dirt from underneath his shoes. Then when I asked him if I could help at all, he calls me a nosey old bitch and goes inside the house. Some people should have had a regular smacking when they were toddlers, if you ask me."

"And you're absolutely certain that this was the man?" Marks leaned forwards again and smiled. "I mean, you couldn't be mistaken, could you?"

"Oh no, dear." She smiled back. "I remember him because of the rudeness; he wasn't nice like you people."

The files open on the table had been repacked prior to the chat with Gladys Ottewell, and with Warner now escorting the old lady back to her own house, Watkinson opened them once more. In the relative privacy of the empty house, the group of four leafed through the pages with an increasing sense of impending doom. Marks broke the silence.

"Marshall clearly intended to return for these at some time, but why would Lawson now get involved if, as we now know, Marshall himself didn't die in the car crash? Why not just come back under cover of darkness, pick them up when no-one was about and disappear again?" Spencer shook his head, oblivious to the knowledge shared by the two senior members of the party.

"Because, Peter, there are things going on which have only just come to the attention of the Metropolitan Police and MI5."

Fifteen minutes later, Spencer and Warner, now fully briefed, sat in bewilderment in the lounge as Marks ended the explanation of the facts he had revealed to George Watkinson a day or so earlier.

"If that's true it means that…"

"Precisely, Peter, and that must not go beyond these four walls until we are ready to act upon it. Groves knows, because it was he who first put the germ of the idea into my mind. I didn't realise the full consequences until much later – that was when I informed MI5, and when Barry Newman dug out the information relating to this house, the pieces of the puzzle began to fall into place."

"There's nothing else to be gained here." Watkinson picked up the house keys. "I suggest we get back to London without delay."

38

Charles Radley had watched Dennis Marks leave the shop, making his way back across Highridge market place to the spot where the car was parked. He noticed other figures in the vehicle but could not make out any further details, and the sight of the DCI's warrant card had set alarm bells ringing. He went to the door and looked up and down the High Street; it had not been one of his busiest days and, turning the door sign from 'open' to 'closed', he went through into the private office where he kept all of his files. Taking a small black book from the inside pocket of his jacket, he looked up a mobile number and dialled.

"Lawson." The voice was clipped and abrupt.

"It's Radley at Highridge. I've had a visit from a high-ranking officer from the Metropolitan Police – that's strange, isn't it?"

"Dennis Marks?"

"You know him?" Radley was astounded.

"Getting there. What did he want?"

"He was asking about the house on Greenfields. I thought he was a prospective tenant and told him that it wasn't available. That's when the warrant card came out; he asked for the keys and I handed them over. What do I do now?"

"Was he alone?" Lawson's voice had not changed its tone.

"I saw him go back across the market place to the car parking area, and there appeared to be a number of other people in the car, but I couldn't see whether they were men or women."

"Nothing you could do about the keys; refusing to hand them over would have just raised suspicion, and he's a devious git anyway. Just wait until he brings them back – try to get some information out of him but don't push it; you'll just make things worse."

"Worse?" Radley was becoming edgy. "How much worse?"

"Calm down, there may be nothing in it. He knows that Marshall passed your way on the journey he made up north, but I have no idea what it is that he's up to."

"I'll call you again when he returns, then."

"No, when they've handed the keys back I want you down at the house, and take a screwdriver with you."

"A screwdriver? Why?"

"Radley! No questions!" Lawson snapped, and the estate agent jumped. "Just do what I say. Go up the stairs and ease up the tread on the fourth one from the top. The carpet's been slit, and whatever is underneath I want you to bring away for me to collect. Got that?"

"Yes." Radley was afraid. He had only met Lawson once before, and the man was not one to play games with.

"And Radley..." The voice dropped almost to a whisper, and the menace came across clearly.

"Yes?"

"Under no circumstance are you to open the package – clear?"

"As crystal."

Radley had been a sleeper for over thirty years. He was the head of the cell which encompassed Highridge and Longlea plus a number of smaller towns in the area. His line of report would normally have taken him to a contact in Derby, but a specific instruction to by-pass the chain of command had been given personally by Lawson at their last meeting; he shivered, though the temperature in the office was not cold – this had all the hallmarks of a difficult situation, and none of his training had geared him up towards dealing with anything like it. Having taken back the house keys from DCI Marks, he smiled and waited until the detective's car had left the market place. Taking a deep breath, he put on a coat, and left the office.

At the other end of the call, Lawson sat in his own office musing at the information revealed to him by Radley. The estate agent was not one of the Organisation's hardier operatives, but it suited their needs to have him as a lookout in the area. That Marks, and presumably Watkinson, had chosen this moment to go poking around the house which had belonged to Tom and Mavis Marshall was a matter of serious concern. The theft of the Nazi files from Watkinson's Surrey home had been hard enough to organise, and Lawson was aware that the German burglar, Hahn, had been interrogated at MI5. He had, initially, considered taking some action to intercept and eliminate the man, but the idea of stirring up a greater level of interest had prevented him from putting out a contract. The package was well concealed in the Derbyshire property, and he could not envisage a situation where even the likes of Dennis Marks would be able to find it. He was still pondering the situation at midday when his mobile rang.

"Yes?"

"Radley. There was nothing under the stair tread."

"Nothing?" Lawson sat forwards at the desk. "You're certain that you got the correct tread?"

"Absolutely sure. Just as you said, the carpet was cut along the edge under the nosing, and the tread came up quite easily. There's a compartment there, but there was nothing in it."

"Lawson cursed, thumped the desk, and Radley jumped once more. The line went dead, and the estate agent decided that now was a good time to shut up shop for the day.

The journey back south had been one of intense conversation for Marks and the rest of his passengers, and the discovery of the files finally gave them the link they were looking for to bring Adrian Lawson in for questioning. Notwithstanding the disappearance of Steve Marshall, Gladys Ottewell's statement may have suggested that he might have placed the bundle under the stairs at Greenfields, and that Lawson's subsequent presence would probably have been to check that they were still secure. Things were about to get a whole lot better for the DCI when he stepped back into his office at New Scotland Yard. He was greeted by a uniform WPC with a message.

"Sir, a woman by the name of Polly Harris called whilst you were in Derbyshire. She wouldn't leave any other details than her telephone number, but did say that it was very important that she speak to you."

"Thank you, Smith." Marks frowned – he didn't like mystery calls at the best of times, and in the middle of a murder enquiry it pleased him even less. His feelings changed dramatically once he had made the call.

"Polly Harris? This is DCI Marks – I believe you left a message for me."

"Yes!" The voice sounded tense and somewhat frightened. "I must see you right away. It's about a case that I believe you may be working on."

"If you're a reporter trying to get an inside track, forget it. I've seen off more in my time that you've had hot dinners." Marks' naturally suspicious manner set Polly Harris back, and her voice began to shake.

"I can give you what you need on Robert Grafton. Does that interest you?"

"Grafton?" Marks suddenly sat forwards, and Peter Spencer stopped at the threshold as he was about to enter the office. Marks waved him silently to a chair. "What about Grafton?"

"I'm not telling you over the telephone, and you'll understand when we meet. Can you pick me up?"

"Why can't you come here? The Metropolitan Police isn't a charity."

"I'm sure I'm being watched, and if I set foot outside my house this may be the last chance that we have to sort things out. Please."

"Very well." He signalled to Spencer to get a squad car. "Give me your address and we'll leave immediately."

Polly Harris opened the door to her Finchley flat with the security chain in place, and Marks pushed his warrant card through the narrow gap. She took it and looked through the fish-eye spy hole in its surface before letting him and Spencer into the room. Picking up a coat and her bag, she was escorted back out into the street and the waiting car, glancing nervously around her all the way. Only when they were back at New Scotland Yard did she begin to relax, and after brief details had been noted by Spencer, she began her story.

"Robert Grafton is a murderer, and he will have me killed if he finds out what I am about to tell you."

"Ms Harris, you will have full police protection if what you tell us is enough to put him away." Marks sat back and crossed his legs.

"Beverley Drake. Does that name mean anything to you?"

"Yes." He said. "She is one of a number of people who have died in suspicious circumstances."

"Grafton organised her murder. I know the men responsible because he told me to get them on the telephone just after she'd left the office. I overheard part of their conversation from outside his door – she came looking for a man by the name of Mike Summers."

"That's very interesting." Marks was now all ears. "Go on."

"Grafton wasn't very pleased when she'd gone, and when the two men arrived later, all three were in his office for quite some time. I overheard enough of their conversation to realise what was happening."

"Do you remember their names?" Spencer looked up from the notes he had been taking.

"I do. Tony Williams and Warren Stokes, and they both scared the living daylights out of me. I got my coat at the end of that day and decided that I wouldn't be going back."

"Are these the two men?" Marks slid two photographs across the table.

"Yes! I'd recognise them anywhere." Polly Harris shivered noticeably.

"I think we need to get all of this down on paper, Ms Harris. Would you mind making an official statement? If we're going to put Grafton away, we'll also need your testimony in a court of law. Do you think you are up to that?"

"I believe so." She still sounded a little shaky.

"Has anyone from the BDP tried to contact you since you walked out?" Marks continued.

"No, I was only a temp, and the agency would never release personal details to a client."

"I'll take a statement from Ms Harris, guv, and then we'll get her to a secure location." Spencer turned to Polly. "We'll need to escort you back to your flat first, for whatever you'll need for a week or so."

With a statement and a positive ID from a reliable source, Marks was now certain that the CPS would agree to proceed against Grafton with the evidence supplied, in corroboration, by Warren Stokes. With little time remaining before the General Election following the No Confidence vote, there would be no time to lose if they were to effect a spectacular arrest and prevent a political coup.

Marks was not the only one to make significant progress following the return of the group to the capital. Barry Newman had not been amongst the search party in the suburbs of Longlea – Watkinson had him using his IT talents scouring Steve Marshall's PC and his networked files for clues to any covert actions. Initially he had come up blank, but a second pass through the registry with an amended spyware program unveiled a set of encrypted and hidden folders.

One of those carried a list of scrambled Word documents in a style which he had never come across, and all he could do was print out the names and properties. Unless another PC could be found with the same identifying characteristics, he would not be able to decipher the contents. Watkinson was at his side the minute he arrived back at Thames House.

"Any luck, Barry?"

"Yes and no, sir. These data files on Marshall's computer are on his hard drive and not the network. I cracked the passwords easily enough, but the rest of the contents are a mystery without the key sequences for decoding them."

"You mean to say that you've come across something which has actually stumped you?" Watkinson stared in mock astonishment.

"Temporarily, sir, only temporarily. If we can find where the codes are, I *will* be able to access them, I can assure you of that."

"Well, you might just get the chance, my lad. We have enough to move against Adrian Lawson now - if, that is, we can find him." Watkinson narrowed his eyes. "I think I might have a good idea where to start. Get your coat; we're off to Birmingham – and bring that laptop of yours along with you."

It was later in the day when they pulled up at the gates of FM Engineering on the outskirts of West Bromwich, and the security guard looked long and hard at the ID cards presented by the two men. He made a telephone call and returned to the gate, where he reluctantly raised the barrier to allow the vehicle inside.

"I'll have to accompany you. I don't care who you say you are, it's more than my job's worth to allow even government folks in here alone. This way."

Watkinson and Newman were led across a large car park to the same administration building which the head of MI5 had stormed years earlier in the chase for Gerald Montgomery. The security guard was momentarily caught off balance by an outsider's familiarity with the layout, and had to run to retain his position at the head of the line.

"Why have we stopped?" Watkinson frowned at his way being blocked at the main doors.

"We have to wait here for Mr Hales, the general manager. I called him when you arrived and he said to keep you here. *He* doesn't care who you say you are, either."

Robert Hales roared past the open security barrier fifteen minutes later, and the guard returned to his post, closing the premises once more. He was about the same age as Watkinson, but the spymaster did not recall him from the earlier foray in 1992.

"Right! What's this all about? I was in the middle of dinner with friends when I got a call about a pair of government spies trying to get into the plant."

His manner was confrontational, and Watkinson saw no point in beating about the bush. He met fire with fire.

"This, Mr Hales, is a matter of national security, and I'll have you detained at Her Majesty's pleasure if I don't get a little more co-operation. Would you like to see the inside of the Tower of London?" A jabbing finger helped to get the point across, and the force of Watkinson's ire found the general manager backtracking rapidly.

"What exactly do you want? I haven't got all day." Hales' tone was still belligerent, but the hard edge had gone.

"Access to all of your computer records for Mr Newman here." Watkinson waved a hand in Barry's direction. "In particular, those relating to Adrian Lawson."

"Our CEO? What's he got to do with it?"

"That, Mr Hales, is where the issue of national security comes in, and the less you know the better. Where *is* Mr Lawson, by the way?" Watkinson asked.

"We haven't seen him around here for a few weeks now; he went down south on a business trip and hasn't returned yet." Hales was beginning to feel that events were overtaking him, and that he was rapidly getting out of his depth.

222

"Well, we'll be here for a good few hours, and whilst I'm perfectly happy for you to remain and answer any questions that we might have, there'll be no objection from me were you to ask your security guard to remain on watch while we work. After all, it would be highly irregular for anything to disappear without your knowledge, now wouldn't it?"

The sarcasm was not lost on Robert Hales, but the dual pull of an interrupted dinner and a keen wish to be out of Watkinson's company had him heading for the door, muttering away to himself. Once clear of the premises however, he was immediately on his mobile to the number given by Lawson to all of his senior staff. They were not members of the Organisation, but it served his purpose to have all eyes and ears on the alert, irrespective of the quarter from which they were operating.

"Yes, Bob, what is it?" The caller display told Lawson all that he needed to know.

"Sorry to interrupt, Mr Lawson, but you remember when you told me that if anything unusual happened at the factory I was to tell you right away?"

"Yes, so what's happened?" Lawson's voice bore a tetchy edge. Hales was a good manager, but his ability to irritate by skirting the issue was infuriating at times.

"We have two MI5 guys poking around at the plant, and they want to know where you are. What do I do?"

"Who's with them now?"

"Bradshaw, sir. I gave him instructions, and he'll carry them out to the letter – he's ex-army; mindless but entirely reliable."

"All right. Go back to whatever it was that you were doing before they arrived and try to keep out of their way. Just let me know when they've gone; got that?"

"Yes, sir." Hales was becoming increasingly agitated and Watkinson's assured manner had set him on edge.

Back at the plant, Barry Newman was busy hooking his laptop up to the main FM Engineering servers. They used an industry standard Windows Server platform with Office XP as the application operating system. It did not take the young man long to navigate to all of Lawson's directories and files, but there was nothing on any of the databases referring remotely to the activities of the Organisation. At the end of his search, it was with a sense of intense disappointment that he reported the negative results to George Watkinson.

"Never mind, Barry. Perhaps it was too much to hope for. Let's pack up and go."

"There is one other possibility, sir."

"I'm listening."

"Well, I suppose if *I* wanted to maintain a set of highly confidential files, the only place that they would be safe from someone like me, is if they were kept on a standalone PC or laptop. A PC would be too cumbersome to carry around, but if Lawson had one of the new Notebooks, he wouldn't have that problem, would he?"

Watkinson had not considered this possibility, but with enough evidence against the man to put out a general alert he was not too concerned. Marks was the man for the job – MI5 getting involved in a police operation of that kind would raise a few eyebrows, and that he could well do without right now. He pulled out his mobile phone.

"DCI Marks? George Watkinson; be so good as to put out a general alert for Adrian Lawson, would you? I think we have enough to link him to the burglary at my home and also the deaths of your four individuals."

39

Adrian Lawson wasted no time after ending the call to Robert Hales, and the only option now available to him was the escape route which had been put in place shortly before the accident involving Marshall's car up in North Yorkshire. He punched another number into his mobile.

"Barker?"

"Yes, Mr Lawson."

"Is the plane ready and fuelled?"

"Yes, and I can file a flight plan immediately. Where are we going?"

"Shannon – I'll be with you first thing in the morning. Be ready.

"Of course."

Gary Barker was one of a number of Organisation chauffeurs who were on call at all times of the day or night. It was their job to transport people and assets anywhere and at any time. They were paid very well for the no-questions-asked service, and all knew the penalties for failure. It took Lawson an hour to pack up what belongings he would need immediately following his flight from Britain, and his departure at 6.30am the following day, from the Organisation's safe house on Candle Meadow close to Nottingham's Colwick racecourse, allowed him a further thirty minutes to make the short trip to Tollerton Airport where the Cessna was housed.

Gary Barker was in the plane's cockpit, and taxiing to the end of the runway when he arrived. They were cleared for take-off moments later and, to Lawson's relief, left the airfield without a hint of a problem. He smiled for the first time that day - it was not to last too long.

"Gone? What do you mean 'gone'?" Marks was up on his feet as the news came to him of Lawson's flight from the Midlands, earlier in the morning.

The recipient of the rebuke was a DC with the Nottingham CID, and took the full fury of the DCI's anger at the failure to intercept their quarry once details of the Organisation safe house had been obtained. He slammed down the phone and shouted for Peter Spencer.

"Peter! Get that estate agent from Highridge picked up – I want him down here ASAP!"

"On it now, guv." Spencer had anticipated not only his boss's fury, but also the likely source of the leaked information. The call to the Derbyshire constabulary at Ripley would have their target in custody within the hour.

"Warner." Marks' instructions were about to come thick and fast. "Put out a nationwide alert for Lawson. Release a description and photograph, and alert all ports and airports – I want the man prevented from leaving the UK."

"Yes, guv." She too had learned very quickly to read the DCI's body language as well as his tone.

She was back half an hour later with a report from the Tollerton air traffic control of a last minute flight from the Nottingham airport to the Irish Republic. There was one passenger, and the description matched that of Lawson. Marks' call to Thames House had Watkinson calling Downing Street.

"Get me the Prime Minister, this is important."

"PM's office – Bradbury speaking."

"George Watkinson, MI5, get me the Prime Minister immediately."

"He's in a cabinet meeting – there's an election coming up, you know."

"Listen, you little pencil pusher! If you don't get the PM to this phone right now he won't *have* a government after the election! Got that?" He bellowed down the line, and the reaction at the other end was immediate - it was accepted in government circles that Watkinson was not a man to be stalled.

"George? What's the emergency?" The accent carried a soft Scottish burr.

"Sir, I need you to contact the Air Chief Marshall and have two fighters scrambled on an intercept course right away."

The details relayed by the head of MI5 over the following five minutes set in motion wheels which demolished the normal levels of bureaucracy prevalent in Whitehall. The two Typhoons left RAF Coningsby in Lincolnshire and were heading for the North West moments later.

Dennis Marks, in the meantime, had headed for the place which was beginning to feel like a second home – Thames House. He and Peter Spencer were ensconced with George Watkinson and his staff, as a live feed was being relayed to them from the Air Chief Marshall's office.

"Where are they now, Sir John?" Watkinson was immersed in conversation as they entered, and he waved them to a pair of chairs at the conference table.

"The flight path they logged will take them over Snowdonia and close to the Ogwen valley. The two Typhoons that we scrambled have instructions to shepherd them that way, and try to force a landing close to the Nant Ffrancon on an isolated stretch of water. There's a small corrie called Llyn Idwal, and that's where the Cessna will be grounded."

"I've got the detectives from the Yard here with me now. Can we patch into the live feed from the fighter radios?"

"Yes, but it will be listening only."

The transmission fell briefly silent before a new voice came over the radio waves, and the live feed began. Marks and Spencer leaned forwards in fascination.

'Blue Leader, what is your position, over?'

'Blue Leader here. We are forty miles south-east of the target area. Intercept course is established, and we should have sight of the Cessna soon, over.'

'Last radar contact placed it ten miles ahead of you and heading for the Irish Sea, over.'

'Target located. We are moving to intercept. What is his identification? Over.'

'Golf, Papa, Bravo, Oscar, Tango. Over.'

'Roger that, moving in. Over and out.'

The radio transmission went silent once more as the two Typhoons altered course to match that of the Cessna, and pulled in, one on either side of the light aircraft. All those present held their collective breath as the mission moved into its final phase. Marks broke the silence with a sudden question.

"What have we got on the ground if this comes off?"

"Territorial units in the area have been mobilised." Watkinson responded. "We're trying to keep the local police out of the matter, and the place they're heading for will only have a few walkers at most. The commander has instructions to hold Lawson and the pilot, and await instructions."

"That's good, but they need to be aware that he's probably carrying a laptop which is vital to our investigations."

"Way ahead of you. The plane won't go down right away, and the territorials have been equipped with inflatables to rescue anything that floats. It'll be fine."

The radio crackled into life once more as the commander issued his first instruction.

'Golf, Papa, Bravo, Oscar, Tango. State your course and destination.'

The message received no reply, and the pilot issued the same request on two more occasions. There was silence on the frequency, and the next phase of the operation came into play.

'Golf, Papa, Bravo, Oscar, Tango – you are instructed to change course and heading. Do you copy?'

Again, the silence in reply was followed by two more identical commands. The three planes were now fast approaching the target area, and the Cessna made a sudden course change in an attempt to shake off the Typhoons. His speed and manoeuvrability were no match for fighters, which quickly repositioned themselves to either side, and closed to within twenty feet. Gary Barker looked to his right to see the Blue Leader pointing downward with a gloved finger. He turned to the figure in the passenger seat.

"What now, Mr Lawson?"

"Can you put down anywhere here? They'll have less of a chance in following if you can."

"In Snowdonia? I don't think so. If I try to land this plane in a glaciated area like this, we'll break up and you can kiss goodbye to the rest of your life." He brightened. "Hang on, they're pushing us up the Ogwen valley, probably towards the Nant Ffrancon –I know that area; I was born around there."

Lawson sighed. He was running short of options, and the Cessna's range was a mere 700 miles. Shannon was well within it, but a race against two super fast fighter jets was simply out of the question.

"All right. Contact the lead plane and ask for instructions."

'This is Golf, Papa, Bravo, Oscar, Tango – what are your instructions?'

"That's more like it." Watkinson smiled, back in the office at Thames House.

They listened in to the rest of the conversation as the Cessna was herded towards the small glacial lake of Llyn Idwal, and the awe-inspiring sheer rock wall at its southern tip which was The Devil's Kitchen. Back in the Cessna, Lawson was not yet done with his escape.

"Gary, try to land at this end of the lake and as close to the shoreline as you can. Once we're down I'm going to make a run for it. You stay here and wait for the welcoming party to arrive." Thinking on his feet had become second nature to Lawson since the crash involving Marshall's vehicle, and so far it had stood him in good stead.

"Very well, Mr Lawson. Hold on tight – here we go."

The Cessna banked sharply right as they approached the junction of Llyn Ogwen and its smaller neighbour. Barker cut the throttle as they made their approach and the light aircraft headed steeply down towards the small lake. It was a bumpy ride, and caught the two typhoon pilots unawares. They overshot the landing site and banked up left and right for another approach. That gave Lawson the time which he needed. They hit the water with a jolt and came to rest some hundred feet from the shoreline. He was out of his harness in an instant, and produced a small hand gun from his coat pocket. Gary Barker stared in disbelief as he considered his final moments alive.

"No need to worry, I'm not going to shoot you but I can't have you telling anyone where I went. Get out – we'll wade to the shore."

The lake was shallow at the northern edge, and Lawson laboured to the shore, carrying the laptop across his shoulder and with his pilot walking ahead. Once clear of the water, Barker turned to face his captor, now fearing the worst.

"Turn around and get down on your knees." The instruction was given calmly and, despite what Lawson had said, Barker now prepared himself for execution. "Can't have you telling anyone where I went."

It was the last thing that he heard, as the butt of the hand gun came down on the back of his head and he crumpled unconscious to the ground. Lawson looked around – the road ahead was the A5, and he set himself for the one mile walk. Once there, he would flag down a passing motorist and make good his escape.

'This is Blue Leader. Target has left the plane and is now proceeding on foot, north-east towards the A5. One casualty remains at the crash site – condition is unknown. Over.'

'Roger that, Blue Leader. Return to base. Over and out.'

Marks and Watkinson had been sitting in silence throughout the exercise, but now sprang into action. The territorial units mobilised were within five miles of the area and closing in. Road blocks were set up at either end of the A5 with orders to stop Lawson at all costs, and a helicopter was despatched to the scene to monitor the situation from the air.

On the ground, and approaching the main road, all was quiet, and Lawson was beginning to sense that he was pulling free of the net which had been closing around him. The green Land-Rover approaching from the north-west slowed to a halt as he stuck out a thumb in the time-honoured manner. The driver, a park ranger, smiled but suddenly stared in fear as the gun was once more produced from the fugitive's pocket.

"No tricks – just drive!" Lawson snapped out the command and slammed the passenger door behind him. "I'll use this if I have to."

The route took them east along the shore of Llyn Ogwen and in the direction of Capel Curig. The road block was already in place just outside of the town, and was manned by a detachment of the territorial units which had been mobilised. The second section had been stationed at the opposite end of the A5 south of Bethesda. Lawson spotted the army vehicles half a mile away and called a halt to the four by four.

"Get out! I'm taking over from here." The driver followed the command, relieved to be out of immediate danger. Lawson pulled the door shut, eased over into the driver's seat, and gunned the engine. He was up to sixty within ten seconds and roaring directly towards the blockage.

"Let's take out the tyres, sergeant." Major Bradshaw gave the calm command. "Try not to hit the driver – he's wanted alive."

"Sir."

The sergeant took up a kneeling position and steadied the SA80, staring down the telescopic sight. The Land-Rover was now only two hundred yards away and well within the gun's range. It was clear that the driver had no intention of stopping, and Bradshaw had only one option.

"Take the shot, Sergeant."

Two shorts bursts, one to either front tyre, shredded the rubber and had the vehicle careering off the road and into a stand of trees to the left. Lawson fought to regain control, but impacted with the first obstacle and was rendered temporarily unconscious by a collision with the windscreen. By the time his senses had returned, he was surrounded by a platoon of well-armed recruits and the chase was over.

40

George Watkinson replaced the receiver with a smile the size of Cheddar Gorge across his features. Adrian Lawson would be in London by early evening, and the process of debriefing could begin. Barry Newman had been right about the Notebook which had been found undamaged. MI5 would very soon be in possession of whatever secrets had been hidden amongst its files. He turned to DCI Marks.

"Over to you now - just Grafton to pick up. Any plans in that direction?"

"According to the latest opinion polls, he's the best thing since sliced bread. Looks like he's currently significantly ahead of both the PM and the leader of the Opposition." Marks did not carry the same level of enthusiasm as Watkinson – he still had his target on the loose. It was Peter Spencer who lightened the mood.

"Guv, take a look at this." The TV in Watkinson's office had remained on during the pursuit of Lawson, but with the sound off. Now that the episode was over, the DI had reactivated the commentary, which was coming from the front of St Stephens Porch, and the BBC's chief political reporter was on the scene.

'With an election now a certainty, we will be interviewing all of the main party leaders in turn. Today it will be the turn of the Right Honourable Robert Grafton MP, leader of the British Democratic Party, and I will be speaking to him outside the Palace of Westminster at six-fifteen.'

"That's it!" Marks Exclaimed. "What better time and place to arrest him? Quarter past six, on the main early evening news, and in front of millions of the viewing and voting British public."

"Do you have enough?" Watkinson asked.

"The CPS reckon so. He's implicated by two parties now, one of whom is a reputable source, and another who can nail him right down. His lawyers can huff and puff all they like, but the case looks pretty solid to me."

"With his rating as high as it is, this could well be the death knell for the BDP. I can tie them in to Adrian Lawson and the Organisation as well. Now that we have the Nazi files back they'll have nothing to rebut any of our claims at MI5. This will be the biggest exposure since the days of Burgess, Philby and McLean. It'll have made the Krogers look like a couple of Sunday school teachers."

Watkinson could hardly contain his delight. He had been waiting for this moment for fifteen long years, looking over his shoulder and always aware that there could well remain at least one renegade within his staff. Losing Steve Marshall had been the hardest blow – the young man had been earmarked as his replacement, but now appeared to have been lured over to the other side by God only knows what promises. He took a deep breath, shook Marks by the hand and reached for the Glenmorangie.

Robert Grafton was preparing for his entrance onto the big political stage. The invitation to a live interview outside the Palace of Westminster on College Green had come as something of a surprise, but there was very little which fazed him these days. His personal rating was sky high, and with any luck at all the BDP would, at the very least, be in a position to negotiate a power-sharing agreement in the new parliament. From that point on, full proportional representation, demanded as part of any deal, would then see his party assume full control of the British political system. He had never been as ready as he was now.

"Robert, have you seen this?" Mark Crawley, the BDP political spin doctor, handed Grafton an early copy of the London Evening Standard.

'Spymaster captured in North Wales'

Grafton read about the pursuit and capture of Adrian Lawson with a knot of unease slowly forming in the pit of his stomach. The story had come from a reputable source at Westminster, and gave details of the involvement of MI5 and the Royal Air Force. More information, it continued, would be forthcoming in later editions. Grafton gathered himself and smiled – the surprise had been a minor setback.

"Don't worry, Mark, our funding is all in place. We had no further need of him anyway. There's still enough in the bank after the election to carry forward with what we've started. Let's get this interview out of the way – the British public have been waiting for us for too long."

It was a few minutes after six when the two of them made their way out of the Houses of Parliament and onto the small grassed area of College Green which the TV political commentators had chosen for their sound bites, and the final preparations for the ten minute slot were well under way. Grafton smiled and raised a hand to the well-known BBC journalist, straightened his tie and stepped forward into the full glare of the arc lights which were used to artificially brighten the set. There was the usual wait for the outside broadcast links to tie in with the six o'clock studio news team, and a general level of chit-chat ensued as the minutes passed. Then, suddenly, the countdown began.

"And, five... four... three... two... one." The director pointed at the group.

"I have with me this evening Robert Grafton MP, leader of the BDP. Mr Grafton, you've taken the country by storm. What are your plans for the remainder of the run-up to polling day?"

Grafton opened his mouth to speak, just as DCI Marks appeared through a group of newspaper hacks – a smile beaming widely across his features. The BDP leader's throat dried and the words, so well-rehearsed, suddenly would not come. The cameras continued to roll as Grafton stood transfixed.

"Mr Grafton?"

Robert Grafton never heard the whispered prompt from behind the lens as Marks appeared in the shot. He was not concerned with the media, and stood directly before the BDP leader and his interviewer.

"Robert Grafton, I am arresting you for the murders of Michael Summers and Beverley Drake. You have the right to remain silent; but it may harm your defence if you do not mention, when questioned, something that you later rely on in court. Anything you do say may be given in evidence. Do you understand?"

The effect was electric as the group was suddenly besieged by reporters and cameramen alike. Grafton was handcuffed and led away by uniformed police as DCI Marks fought off all attempts to elicit comment from him.

Back at New Scotland Yard, Robert Grafton was charged with conspiracy to murder, perverting the course of justice, and embezzlement. The latter charge had come to light after a detailed investigation into the BDP funds revealed some unexplained withdrawals from the party bank accounts.

Once faced with the mountain of evidence, and the corroborating statements of a number of witnesses, he knew that his time in the political limelight was over. With only a matter of weeks to go until election day, support for the party was already beginning to slip away – opinion polls were hourly showing a falling away of popular support, and mounting public disquiet was beginning to polarise around the MPs who had crossed the house to join the swelling ranks of the BDP. Grafton, however, was not beyond one final throw of the dice.

"You have no evidence to link me to the deaths of Summers and Drake."

"On the contrary, Mr Grafton." Marks opened the case files. "We have a number of witness statements which not only give evidence of motive, but also, on one occasion, provide actual testimony of a conversation which you had with two of your assassins."

"Williams is dead and as for Stokes…" The statement was cut short by pressure on his arm from one of the party lawyers. A shake of the head was sufficient to prevent any further comment.

"Mr Stokes has given us chapter and verse on the circumstances surrounding the abduction and murder of both, their disposal in the Thames at Richmond Lock, and the fee which you paid for the service." Marks looked across the table for a response.

"Detective Chief Inspector," William Pilkington, the party lawyer, sighed, "Mr Stokes is a known violent criminal who is looking for a way out of a death penalty on the other side of the world. I hardly think that his testimony would be given much credence under cross examination."

"That may be so, Mr Pilkington, but he is a known associate of Tony Williams, a man found at Heathrow with a bag full of money, which we were able to trace back to Mr Grafton's personal bank account." Marks smiled; Grafton's tight corner was getting even tighter.

"That is circumstantial at best, and does not prove that the money was in payment for any service which may or may not have been performed. Nor does it prove, as has been suggested in part of your documentation, that it was given to Mr Williams as some sort of blackmail payment."

"Perhaps," Marks persisted. "But there is also the matter of BDP funds which appear to have been misplaced, and Mr Grafton's bank accounts do seem to have benefited from a series of large deposits over the past six months – we checked. You see, all of this is beginning to mount up, and a jury may well be inclined to make a judgement on Mr Grafton's character when faced with it."

"You still have nothing which absolutely places my client in a position of commissioning these killings." He sat back, a smug, self-satisfied look on his face.

"Polly Harris." Marks opened another file and looked down at it, deliberately avoiding the eyes of either man.

Peter Spencer, also in the room, missed nothing, and the wide-eyed panic on the face of Robert Grafton had him nudging the DCI covertly. The BDP leader stared at his lawyer, who shrugged and shook his head.

"Polly who?" Grafton cleared his throat.

"Harris. A temp employed by your party. A woman who heard your conversations with Stokes and Williams. The conversation which had you agreeing to pay them both for eliminating Beverley Drake." Marks looked up from his papers.

"She's lying."

"Lying? Now why would she do that? What would she possibly have to gain by making false allegations? According to her statement here, you asked her to 'get them here'. She followed them to your office and stood outside the door. Apparently she heard the entire conversation, and we have it down word for word. She's a credible witness, no criminal record, and is currently under police protection. Your counsel will, of course, have the opportunity to challenge her testimony at trial, but let me assure you that her appearance alone will sway any jury if there is an attempt to bully her in court."

Marks sat back in his chair and stared at the crestfallen figure that was Robert Grafton. The smile on his face was that of the cat with the bowl of cream all to itself.

"What's the deal?" William Pilkington asked, clear now that there was nothing more that he could do to save his client from jail. "Robert can give you all he knows on Adrian Lawson; I'm sure that must be worth something."

"Adrian Lawson." Marks frowned in mock concern. "Ah yes, the spy whom MI5 now have in their hands. Well," he sighed, "I'd say that the security services will have all that they need on Mr Lawson to ensure that he spends the better part of some considerable time at Her Majesty's pleasure. There's nothing that Mr Grafton can add to that particular mix which could possibly be of benefit to him. I think we're done here – we'll see you in court."

"Good job all round, then." Peter Spencer remarked when they were back in their office.

"Time for a celebration, and I might just stay up on election night this time. Come on, get your coat and find Warner. We're eating out, and I'm paying."

41

In a similar interview room across London, George Watkinson and Sandra Wallace sat facing Adrian Lawson. He was alone – there were no lawyers in attendance at Thames House to help him. The room was bare apart from a table and three chairs, and was lit by a single blue/white fluorescent tube. It was a tactic designed to intimidate, but the figure before them seemed to have no fear of the surroundings.

"Finally." Watkinson opened the proceedings. "We have the entire Organisation at our fingertips. By the time Barry Newman has worked his way through the files on your laptop, we will have the name and address of every single one of your members."

"I have absolutely no idea what you're talking about." Lawson sighed; he yawned, stretched and smiled. "That laptop belongs to Steve Marshall, and I have no idea where you will be able to find him."

"I see." Watkinson smiled – he was the master at this game, and Lawson's apparent nonchalance had no effect at all. "Then please enlighten me as to the circumstances whereby it came into your possession, and why you took such care to rescue it from the Cessna."

"Merely safeguarding it until it could be collected. I haven't a clue what's on it."

"Then why run? Why club Gary Barker when you were both safe? What was the reasoning for that unless you were intent on escaping with the computer?"

"Barker pulled a gun on me and we struggled once clear of the plane. He thought he could get rid of me, take the laptop and disappear." There was a slight shift in Lawson's manner and Watkinson was on it in a flash.

"So *he* is the spy, then. Ah, now I see. So *you're* the innocent in all of this. Is that right, Steve?"

"Yes, you see I'm…" The voice trailed off and Sandra Wallace stared at Watkinson in utter disbelief.

The scene stood frozen in time as those last words started to sink in. Watkinson had called Lawson 'Steve', and the response, far from being quizzical, had been as if it were second nature. Watkinson turned to Wallace and waved his arm across the table.

"Sandra, excuse my manners, let me introduce you to your predecessor… Steve Marshall."

"You mean…?"

"Indeed. Somewhat changed in appearance, I'll grant you, but Steve Marshall nonetheless. Oh, he's put on fifty pounds, dyed his hair and is probably wearing tinted contact lenses. It took me a while to figure out what was going on, but once the pieces started to come together there was really only one credible answer." He looked across the table. "I assume you were wearing a body suit until the weight gain became apparent."

"Very clever, George. I ought to have known that you'd get there in the end. What was it, the house on Greenfields?"

"Eventually, yes, that was the clincher. We did, however, get a rather fortuitous break when your aunt turned up at the funeral." He looked at the quizzical expression on Marshall's face. "Amanda Pietersen, your mother's sister. Bit of bad luck for you, that. George Groves, the Home Office pathologist, matched her DNA to that of the records held at the City Hospital in Derbyshire for your mother. Once we had that reference sample, the fact that it didn't tally to the records on your file here set the wheels in motion."

"Silly cow!" He shook his head and scowled. "Why did *she* have to turn up?"

"It would seem that you were, or rather still are, her favourite nephew. Oh, she told us quite a lot about your early adult life and its political leanings. I must say you kept those very well hidden at MI5. You even had me fooled in Nottingham when Montgomery died – was he about to spill the beans?"

"We couldn't take that risk." Marshall shook his head. "Once he lost it, there was only one solution, and I was the man on site."

"You took a real risk with the car crash though. Mind you, if that Derbyshire gas fitter hadn't been halfway up Sutton Bank at the time you might have got away with it even then. There are one or two things that still puzzle me, though."

"Oh, yes?" Marshall eyed his former boss suspiciously.

"Off the record of course, but why did you leave the mobile at the crash site? Such an obvious clue."

"Ah, that." Marshall smiled, ruefully. "Almost got caught in the explosion there, and I dropped it in the dark. Didn't find that it was missing until much later, and going back for it was out of the question."

"You were down at the tree?"

"No, but close by. I couldn't be sure that the car would explode, so we took a can of petrol along... just in case, you know. When the thing went up I must have dropped the mobile, and it was more important to leave the scene quickly in case anyone passed by."

"You said 'we'; who is 'we'?" Marshall's slip of the tongue had not gone unnoticed. "We had a witness who heard the sound of running feet, and it stands to reason that you would have needed another car to make a getaway."

"That's something that you're going to have to figure out for yourself. As far as MI5 is concerned I acted alone." Marshall kicked himself for the gaffe, and sat back in the chair.

"All right, but what about Pearson, the body in the Audi?" A change of expression on Steve's face had Watkinson smiling. "Oh, we know who he was; George Groves figured that one out - but why him?"

"Single bloke, lots of money problems, and we offered him a way out. The trouble was that he didn't realise how permanent that way out would be. You're not going to be able to tie his death back to me, though. He was just kept nice and cool until he was needed. I suppose your boffin found that piece of wood that I used to wedge the accelerator down as well."

"He did." Watkinson said. "They're cleverer at the Met than you think. I shouldn't be surprised if we haven't heard the last of that one."

"So, I suppose it's the high jump, is it?" Marshall's demeanour had remained quite calm throughout, and his service with the department had prepared him for all of the consequences which were now about to materialise.

"Yes, there will be a trial. Treason will be the charge I would imagine, but you can rest assured that it will be a long time before you see the outside of a maximum security establishment." Watkinson paused, and Marshall sensed that there was something else. He continued. "Unless, that is, you could be persuaded to reveal your contacts abroad."

"What?" Marshall laughed. "You must think I'm mad."

"No, not at all, but it stands to reason that there must be others. The files which are now back in my possession do strongly suggest the existence of other branches operating on the continent, and I'm certain that the DCRI in France or the BND in Germany would be more than a little interested in anything that you would care to reveal. A deal could still be arranged for you, even at this late stage."

"Not a hope; this has taken far too long to set in motion." Marshall's face had become suddenly very serious. "I'll take my chances in jail first. The people I've been dealing with are not averse to shooting first and then not bothering with asking the questions. Their fingers can reach just about anywhere."

The trial of Steve Marshall was one of the sensations of the decade, and by the time Barry Newman had exhausted his search amongst the files on the laptop, three hundred other individuals had been rounded up and charged. The Organisation was, this time, finished as a force in the UK, and George Watkinson took particular care to be present at all pre-trial briefings with government lawyers. There would be no loopholes for Marshall or his confederates to crawl through, and documents from all across Britain were collated and examined before being passed across to the security services of the UK's European partners.

In the first cottage in the row on St Mary's Lane in Tewkesbury, Julie and Doug Martin, now both in their fifties, followed the trial with a sense of increasing amazement. The activity along the far end of the lane had been sudden and frenetic, with a fleet of unmarked black saloon cars arriving in the early hours of one morning during the week of the hearing.

"All this from one little train ticket," Julie reminded her husband. "Who would ever have thought that about Roger and Madeline."

"You know Roger thought he might have been the last person to see Martin Bormann alive, don't you?" Doug folded away his newspaper.

"Really? Did they ever find his body? There have been all sorts of stories about sightings around the world."

"I think so. I remember reading somewhere about a couple of skeletons being unearthed in Berlin when some work was being done to the Lehrter station. They matched the dental records, and there was other stuff, like old injuries, and even shards of glass in the jawbone suggesting suicide by cyanide."

"So it's conclusive, then."

"Not back then." Doug added. "That was in the early seventies, but when DNA profiling came on the scene in the late eighties, that provided the conclusive proof. They took samples from the skull and matched them to some relative. It wasn't until 1998, though. He's dead all right, and it's been a real blow for all the conspiracy theorists."

"Would the defendant please rise?" Mr Justice Webb glanced across the courtroom at Robert Grafton.

The former BDP leader rose slowly to his feet and gripped the handrail at the front edge of the dock. His face was pale, and his eyes displayed a clear lack of sleep.

"Ladies and gentlemen of the jury." The clerk to the court at the Royal Courts of Justice looked up from the indictment before him. "Have you reached a verdict upon which you are all agreed?"

There was a hush around Number One Court as the foreman stood to her feet. Robert Grafton's head snapped sharply to the right, as she prepared to address her reply to the judge.

"We have."

"With regard to Michael Summers, on the charge of conspiracy to murder, do you find the defendant guilty or not guilty?"

"Guilty."

The hushed room was suddenly a cacophony of noise, and it took the stentorian voice of Mr Justice Webb to silence the interruption and restore order.

"With regard to Beverley Drake, on the charge of conspiracy to murder, do you find the defendant guilty or not guilty?"

"Guilty."

A glance around the courtroom from the bench was enough to stifle a repeat performance, and the judge directed his remaining remarks to the dock.

"Robert Grafton, you have been found guilty on both of the charges on the indictment, and it now falls to me to pronounce sentence. I shall dispense with the customary remarks as to the seriousness of the crimes in question, and pass on directly to the penalty. You will go to jail for a term not exceeding fifteen years on each count." There was an expectant air, almost as if those present sensed that the drama still had one more line to play. "The terms of each sentence shall run consecutively, with a recommendation that a total of no less than thirty years be served. This court is adjourned."

Grafton collapsed in the dock; the sentence was indeed a savage one, and its like had not been seen in a British courtroom since the 1963 trial of the Great Train Robbers. His lawyers gave immediate notice of appeal, but with the links to the Organisation still to come to the attention of the public, they already knew that it was an almost hopeless cause.

42

On 9th August 2007, the voters of Britain went to the polls and elected a new government. The Coalition under Mark Barrowman was unceremoniously ousted from office. What it will fail to reveal is the knife-edge upon which the entire democratic system had teetered during the earlier part of that year.

The British Democratic Party's popularity peaked at 45% of those interviewed by a range of opinion pollsters, and had that been carried forward to the day itself, Robert Grafton may well have been waving to the press from the threshold of Number Ten Downing Street. His government, committed to a regime of full proportional representation, would have used its mandate to change the British voting system to match those of its European counterparts. This sop to democracy would not have lasted long, and other, more contentious, policies could then have been brought to the fore.

George Watkinson knew this and, now in possession of the full set of files from the laptop so carefully guarded by Steve Marshall, was staggered at the ease with which Grafton was suckered into the Organisation's plan. There was no doubt in his mind that, once established via the new BDP government, Marshall's people would have turned Britain into the same totalitarian dictatorship which beset Germany in the thirties and forties.

"A close call then." Marks' comment over the top of his single malt was one of the understatements of the century.

"Indeed, and had we in the service been a little more vigilant back in 1992, it may not have come to this."

"Looks like support for the BDP has all but evaporated now."

"So it would seem." Watkinson drained his glass and poured them both another. "I would imagine that there are a considerable number of voters presently kicking themselves, and thanking their lucky stars that you and I stepped in at the last minute."

"I believe they lost their deposit in every seat contested," remarked the DCI, "and at five hundred pounds each, that cost them over three hundred and twenty-five thousand. What about the Organisation? Did you manage to track down all of their cash?"

"Unfortunately not. We were able to freeze all of the assets which we identified in this country, and the new government is going to need every single penny the way things are going. Still, it's over now, and we can relax somewhat."

"Yes, but going back to the humdrum routine of normal police work will feel a little strange after all of this cloak and dagger stuff. I haven't forgotten what I went through with all that business over Michael Roberts."

"Don't knock it, Dennis; you did a good job there. Are you certain that you and your staff wouldn't like a change of career?" Watkinson smiled, and downed a mouthful of the amber liquid.

"Absolutely. Far too dangerous, and you never know who is on which side. At least I have the satisfaction of knowing the faces of the villains that I'm chasing. Thanks, but no thanks."

"Such a pity. You do know that Chloe Warner has passed her Inspector's examinations, don't you?"

"Yes I do, she told me yesterd..." Marks frowned at the smug figure before him. "Just a minute, what on earth has that got to do with MI5?"

"Oh dear, how embarrassing. I see she hasn't yet had the time to inform you of my little suggestion."

"You've done it again, haven't you?" Marks shook his head resignedly. "First Wallace, and now Warner. Something wrong with your recruiting, George?"

"Wallace was never yours, and you know it. I've made young Chloe an offer she simply cannot refuse, and her pedigree *is* impeccable. I gather she's running the idea past that brother of hers before giving me her answer. She'll replace Wallace - I need a number two as Steve's replacement, and she's already accepted the promotion."

Marks had no way out of the cul-de-sac into which Watkinson had manoeuvred him, and with one more resigned smile, he drained his glass, picked up his coat and took his leave, he hoped for the last time, of the head of MI5.

Epilogue

In the Bierkeller at the Hofbräuhaus on Munich's Bräuhausstraße, two men sat at the large oak table at the end of the ground floor beer hall. It is customary in the Hofbräuhaus that only locals occupy that particular table and receive service – any 'Fremder' being singularly ignored. Markus Koh and Gunther Bachmeier were both sons of the fathers whose backsides had occupied those very seats years before. Those men had served in Hitler's Sturmabteilung and had ridden on the crest of the wave which had seen the man become Reichskanzler in January 1933.

"So, it is over, Ja?" Bachmeier finished the last of his Halbe, and banged the glass noisily on the table to signal a refill.

"For sure." replied Koh, his gaze fixed at the bottom of his own glass. "All of our members over in Britain have been rounded up and imprisoned awaiting trial."

"Are we doomed to failure? Do the British not see what it is that we can offer them? First Moseley, their unions in the seventies, and now Marshall. We gave him everything in 1992 and still he was not successful. This time I did think for certain that we would win them over. So close, and yet so far." Bachmeier shook his greying head sadly.

"There is nothing left from where we can start over again. The British security services have seized all of our property and cash, and the leader of the British Democratic Party will be eliminated by one of our contacts over in their prison system. We have failed."

"What about the Irish?" Bachmeier asked. "Their distaste for the British is well known. Maybe there is yet a way. Our U-Boot fleet was given shelter in their waters during the last war, and that was a fact to which the British took great offence."

"Nein." Koh shook his head. "The IRA taste for blood has died since the Good Friday Agreement, and what remains of the paramilitary arm is very small and ill-equipped. They now wear suits instead of fatigues. I'm afraid, my friend, that it is truly over."

"So, we must begin again somewhere else. Somewhere where the true ideals of the Reich will take seed and flower once more." He pointed at the now empty glass. "Noch Eine?"

"Zu Befehl!"

As the two fifty year-olds made their unsteady ways home at the end of an evening replete with the drowning of sorrows, Dieter Hahn watched from the shadows on Münzstraße. The deal which they had offered him at the beginning of the adventure had been far outweighed by their treachery in allowing him to be captured from his own doorstep and taken to London for interrogation. This was not how it was supposed to have been, and he was thirsty for revenge. Members of the Organisation did not betray each other, and these two would pay this night with their lives. Stubbing out the remains of the Marlboro beneath his army boot, he unsheathed the commando knife which would be their silent assassin.

Books by Neal James

A Ticket To Tewkesbury

Julie Martin is the most unlikely of heroines in a struggle for supremacy which reaches to the very pinnacles of power within modern Britain. The letter, found amongst her recently deceased aunt's belongings, sets in motion a chain of events which had their roots in the death throes of Nazi Germany in 1945.

Roger Fretwell and Madeline Colson, two young lovers at the end of hostilities, are in possession of a set of files which fleeing survivors of the Third Reich would rather had lain buried. Now exposed once more, the secrets which they hold put their very lives in peril, and set in motion a chain of events from which there could only be one winner.

Set against the idyllic backdrop of the West Country, Roger and Madeline's love story weaves its way into the dark and troubled waters of espionage, as competing forces will stop at nothing to gain control of a situation so vital for the future of democracy in modern Britain. The breathless pace of the storyline is unrelenting, as the chase over the length and breadth of the country comes to a shattering climax on the platform of Nottingham's Midland Station. The final solution to the drama leaves a surprise ending for the reader to ponder.

Short Stories Volume One

How would you write to God for clarification on matters of the utmost urgency? Find out how Moses might have done it.

Dry your eyes after a heart-rending tale of Aunty Rose, and the tragic story of Liz when she finds the father she never knew. Shake your head at Mike's naiveté in dealing with a stranger in black, and share with Dave his hidden guilt when Tommy Watkinson returns to talk to his son, Paul.

Fly into the realms of fantasy with James Taylor as he gets lost in a place that he knows only too well, and try to sympathise with Ray when the old couple ask him to save humanity.

Follow Dennis Marks in a trilogy which brings the book to its close as he searches for the truth about his grandfather. This collection of little gems will expose every emotion on the rollercoaster which you are about to ride.

Two Little Dicky Birds

On Saturday 8th April 1975, in a fit of rage, Paul Townley took the life of his father, Harold. The significance of that single event was to affect the rest of his life, as he resolved to make it his mission to rid society of the kind of person that the man had become.

The first killing took place six months later, and over the following fifteen years seventeen more were to follow, as the trail of devastation left by a serial killer covered the length and breadth of England.

Detective Chief Inspector Colin Barnes looked down at the letter which lay on the desk before him. An icy hand gripped his heart as he read once more the details of the eighteen murders. Murders which had come back to haunt him from his past as he realised that he would, once more, be faced with the serial killer who had called himself... Petey.

Follow the chase for Petey, two and a half decades after his first appearance, as its climax takes you across the Atlantic to New York's JFK airport and into the arms of Detective Tom Casey of the 113th Precinct, in a plot so intricate it will leave you breathless.

Threads of Deceit

George Carter is a man with problems – big ones, and of the financial kind. Accustomed to getting his own way, he rules his roost at Brodsworth Textiles with an iron fist.

James Poynter is a young man out for revenge. Set up for a crime which he did not commit, and by someone whom he believed he could trust implicitly, his sole focus becomes one of retribution against his former boss and the firm which he is defrauding.

His future at Brodsworth Textiles disintegrates one Friday evening prior to his wedding, when conscientiousness overtakes him and he returns to the factory after work to rectify an administrative error.

What he learns in that moment sets off a chain of events which sends him spiralling downwards, and out of a job which had promised to propel him to senior managerial level.

Murder, deception, drug trafficking and embezzlement combine to derail the futures of everyone connected to the company, and set off a Europe-wide chase for the man at the centre of a plot so intricate that the forces of law and order in several countries are thwarted at every turn leading to a stunning climax at Bristol Airport.

Full Marks

Dennis Marks thought he had seen it all. That was before Solomon Goldblum crossed his path – after that, things were never the same again. The trauma which the old Jew had inflicted upon him had brought about a near psychological collapse. That the DCI had been able to conceal the fragility of his mental state from the shrink whom the Met had forced him to see had been down to his sheer determination.

Now, all of that effort was about to be challenged by one of the most daunting figures at New Scotland Yard – Superintendent Eric Staines. The Independent Police Complaints Commission were about to take Marks' life apart, professionally and personally, and Staines, as one of its fiercest inquisitors, was not a man inclined to show mercy.

A month was all that the DCI had to prove his innocence of a range of charges dating back to his days as a detective sergeant. A career spent putting away the dregs of London's criminal world was to hang in the balance, and he was, he believed, for the first time...alone.

About Neal James

Neal James began writing in 2007 when a series of short stories found favour on a number of international writing sites. Since then, he has released five novels and one anthology. He has appeared in both the national and local press, and has also been a regular at branches of Waterstones and local reading groups and libraries in his home counties of Derbyshire and Nottinghamshire.

'Day of the Phoenix', the sequel to 'A Ticket to Tewkesbury' has taken him into the realms of politics and the murky waters of espionage, and takes his 2008 novel to its logical conclusion.

An accountant for over 30 years, that training has given him an insight into much of the background required in the production of his writing so far. He lives in Derbyshire with his wife and family.

Find out more about Neal James and all of his writing on his website: www.nealjames.webs.com

Connect with Neal James

http://www.nealjames.webs.com/
http://www.goodreads.com/user/show/6864216-neal-james
http://www.facebook.com/neal.james.125
http://www.linkedin.com/profile/view?id=116462215&trk=tab_pro

Lightning Source UK Ltd.
Milton Keynes UK
UKOW02f0852060215

245811UK00001B/28/P